THE GIRL WHO RAN AWAY

THE GIRL WHO RAN TRILOGY: BOOK ONE

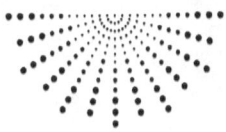

SUSAN LUND

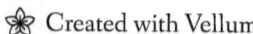 Created with Vellum

CHAPTER ONE

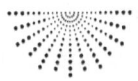

No one rented cabins at that time of year, so it wasn't really his fault...

When Matt Logan, security guard for SecureTek, got a call that a driver passing through the area saw light coming from the cabin farthest from the main highway, he knew it meant his usually slack Sunday night was going to be different for a change.

His job was pretty sweet, all things considered. Most of his patrols included the businesses in the small towns between Bellingham and the border with Canada. Every night, his route took him along the road circling the lake, checking on the cabins to ensure they were secure, and none had been broken into. Occasionally, some vagrants or teenagers would jimmy a lock and spend the night, eating whatever food they could find before moving on, so he always had his gun in his hand when he saw any sign that the cabin was occupied.

He was supposed to drive by each cabin and check to see if things looked secure, but for the past few days, it had rained hard and the weather was cooler than normal for that time of year. He didn't check all the cabins as a result. Instead, for the past three nights, he sat in his truck on a side road and drank hot coffee from a thermos, listening to a metal station on the satellite radio. In fact, he hadn't driven by the cabin in question for six full days.

Now Matt knew he better check every cabin, just in case. The caller hadn't left his name, just said he was on his way through the area and had noticed the lights and thought someone should know. Matt thought that was suspicious, but it had been almost a week since his last check, and he felt a sinking feeling in his gut. If there was any damage to the cabin, he'd get the blame for not checking every night the way he was supposed to. Anyone could have come and broken in during those days.

He parked his truck on the side of the road and walked the path to the cabin, the wet ground squishing under his boots. Heavy spring rains had hit the region and the ground was soaked. He stared up at the night sky as he trudged along the path to the cabin, the tall pines reaching up around him. The sky was clear after the storms had passed, and dozens of stars sparkled above him. Soon, he'd be able to head back into town and get a fresh thermos of coffee, but for the next half hour, he had to finish that part of his route.

When he got closer to the cabin, two things looked unnatural.

First, the side door was open, which put him immediately on his guard. Light shone from the interior, out the door and onto the small yard. He could see into the house from where he stood at the edge of the property line, but he didn't see anyone inside nor were there any cars in the driveway. Whoever broke in was long gone.

He removed his cell and called dispatch.

"I think you better send police out here. I'm at the last cabin on Silver Lake Road."

Travis, the night dispatcher, responded, his voice sounding interested. Usually, nights were pretty quiet.

"Stay on the line and I'll let you know when I've talked to them."

"I will."

Matt wanted to be a cop one day, so instead of going back and waiting in his vehicle the way his book on procedure suggested, he decided to go in and see what was up. There were no vehicles in the driveway, so whoever had been there was likely gone. They'd left the lights on, however, and the door open.

When he got closer, he scanned the yard and noticed the outhouse door was open as well. He shone his flashlight inside as he stepped closer.

He stopped up short at the sight and stood a dozen feet from the outhouse. Were those feet? The beam of his flashlight passed over the two pale limbs, stained with what looked like blood.

Yes, those were two feet sticking out of the receptacle.

"Looks like a body in the outhouse," he said into his cell. "Head-first into the hole."

"Holy *shit*, so to speak," Travis replied on the end of the line.

"You got that right."

Whoever it was, he'd been murdered and stuffed inside.

You didn't just fall into an outhouse head first unless you were really *really* unlucky. Matt wracked his brain trying to think of a way it could happen and not be foul play, but he couldn't. The man – and it looked like a man because of the hair on the legs – was also naked. You just didn't go out to an outhouse naked in this weather, open the lid to the receptacle and fall inside.

"Jesus," he said to Travis, trying to make light over the rapid beating of his heart. "Of all the ways to die, this is the shittiest."

"*Christ,*" Travis replied. "You should go back to your vehicle and wait for the police."

"'Yeah, I will, but I wanted to make sure the guy wasn't alive in case I could help him, but he's dead."

"Holy *Jeez,*" Travis said, whistling low. "You sure there's no one else around? It might not be safe."

"Nah, there's no car in the driveway. I'm going inside, but don't report me, okay? I just want to make sure no one's inside who needs help. I'll be fine. I won't touch anything."

Matt went to the cabin, and peeked inside the entry, his weapon drawn. There was a single light on in the place -- a table lamp beside an old brown sofa. On the floor beside the sofa, another body. Face down, also naked with what looked like at least a dozen stab wounds in his back, blood soaked into the beige rug beneath him.

"I got another one," he said into his cell. "White male. Looks like this one was stabbed to death. We got us a double homicide."

"Ho-lee *shitshow,*" Travis said. "Police are on their way. You go back to your vehicle. Do not disturb the crime scene. Repeat. Do *not* disturb the crime scene."

"I won't."

Matt finished searching the small cabin, which was

nothing more than one big living room and kitchen area with two bedrooms off the back.

What he thought was strange was that there were several tripods with cameras mounted, like whoever used the cabin was filming something. He stepped closer to the body and saw a set of plastic zip ties that looked like they were cut with a knife or something sharp. There was an assortment of sex toys on the coffee table, some lube. Thin rope. Knives.

Whoever these men were, it looked like they'd been filming pornography. Given they were both naked, he wondered if it wasn't gay porn, but he didn't know for sure. It set him to thinking about the case down in Paradise Hill he'd read about in the papers -- couple of local creeps had been filming child porn for years right under everyone's noses. He glanced around and saw a couple of children's toys on the dining table -- dolls. God, he hoped they weren't making child porn. He had two little girls himself and stories of the child porn ring and serial child killer from Kittitas County in central Washington made him sick.

He grimaced at the smell. The man on the floor had been dead for a while and even though he wasn't trained in forensic science, he knew enough from watching Law and Order to see lividity along the man's lower body. He had no idea how long the guy had been dead, but probably much more than twenty-four hours. He'd shit himself and the smell was awful.

It was at that point that he decided to leave and wait for the police in his vehicle. Maybe he wasn't cut out for being a cop if he had to deal with dead bodies on a regular basis, although it was pretty quiet in the county most of the time.

He left the cabin and walked down the lane to his truck, glad to be alive. He took out his pack of cigarettes and lit one, needing the familiar habit of a smoke to help him process the scene he'd just witnessed. His hands shook as he lit the cigarette, and he smoked it with relish, glad to be alive.

When a police car drove up about five minutes later, lights flashing, he was happy to finally have someone else at the scene.

The cop jumped out of his vehicle and shone a light on Matt's face.

"You called this in?"

"I did," he said and dropped his smoke onto the ground, stubbing it out with his work boot. "Two bodies. One in the outhouse, the other in the cabin stabbed to death, far as I could see."

"Jesus," the cop said, his hand on his sidearm. "We'll take over now. Thanks for your help."

"You're welcome," he said. "Do you want me to stay and give a statement?"

"Yes, but please remain in your vehicle. We'll take your statement once we've secured the scene. Detectives from Bellingham are on their way."

Matt nodded and got into his light-duty truck, turning it on so he could get warmed up while he waited.

What. A. Night.

He'd have a great story to tell the other security guards when he got back to the office. There'd be an investigation and if they caught the suspect or suspects, there'd be a trial, likely in Bellingham. He'd have to testify as one of the first witnesses on the scene.

Hell.

This story would be good for months.

CHAPTER TWO

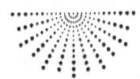

Tess woke with a start, sitting up straight, her heart racing, a cold sweat covering her body. It was still pitch black out, and Michael was asleep beside her.

She covered her mouth with a hand to stifle her sob. Beside her, Michael woke and sat up, turning on the light on the bedside table.

"Hey," he said and took her in his arms. "It's okay. You're okay."

She lay back down with his arms around her.

"More nightmares?" he asked and stroked her shoulder.

Tess nodded, not speaking, trying to catch her breath.

Michael pulled her closer into his embrace. "What was it this time?"

Tess couldn't reply. Her mouth was dry and the image of Eugene with the goggles was still vivid in her mind's eye. Finally, she cleared her throat.

"The same ones, over and over."

He squeezed her. "You should get counseling. What you

did was so brave, but anything traumatic like that will leave a mark on you."

Tess knew he was right. Of all people, he would understand. "I will," she replied and gave Michael a faint smile. "How's your therapy going? He actually hurt you."

"He hurt you, Tess," Michael said. "Don't deny it."

She nodded, remembering him hitting her from behind, then biting her mouth when he stood over her. The memories made her shudder. But it wasn't the physical wounds he caused that haunted her. It was the dark threat she felt being in that pit with Elena, waiting for him to return. By then, she knew exactly what he was and what he did. What he'd most likely do to her, too. The physical wounds were already healed, just faint scars on her lip, on her wrists and ankles, and on the back of her head.

The emotional wounds would take much longer to heal.

"As for me," Michael said and held up his left fist, pumping it in the air. "I'm great. On one side of my body, that is. Besides, not all wounds are visible." He raised his eyebrows meaningfully.

"You have PTSD, too," Tess said softly. "You had to quit."

"We're a pair," Michael said and kissed her gently. "I can still work, but just not as a special agent. I won't do any work that might require I defend myself. Just investigations. While I can shoot with my left hand, that's about all I can do. And not very well, either."

"It's good that you're getting to work cases," she said and finally smiled. "Even if it is freelance and contract work. I'll have to get over this if I want to work with the FBI."

"You will," Michael said and pulled her more tightly against him with his good arm. "You're strong. The nightmares will stop, eventually. Besides, it'll be a year before you even know for sure whether you get into the FBI. You have time."

"Will the memories ever stop just popping into my head?" Tess asked, feeling exhausted.

"They will. I saw Colin's little body for months afterwards. I still do, but now, I'm able to distract myself before it gets too bad. You'll learn how, too."

"I hope so."

Michael reached over and turned off the light, casting the room back into darkness.

Tess sighed, snuggling beside him for an extra moment or two. It was Monday, and soon, she needed to get up and go to work. But for now, she found comfort in his arms.

The next time Tess woke up, it was to the scent of coffee brewing in the kitchen. Usually, she needed the blazing noise of an alarm clock to wake her in the mornings, but when she glanced over to it, she saw it was well past her usual time to wake. Michael was already up and had gone for a run without her. He'd showered and was now in the kitchen, making coffee. She felt lazy in comparison, the bad night of interrupted sleep making her still groggy.

She had a quick shower and dressed, wishing she was more ambitious and had woken early enough to get in a run like Michael. If she wanted to join the FBI, she'd have to get into better shape. She and Michael had been running together every morning in an effort to build up her endurance, and for Michael to fully recover from his own ordeal, but he'd let her sleep in, no doubt because of her nightmares the previous night.

"You should have woken me," she said when she got to the kitchen and took the thermos of coffee that he'd fixed for her.

"You needed your sleep," he replied and leaned against the kitchen island. "You're handing in your latest article today, right?"

Tess nodded, her mind leaving the nightmare and turning to the real-life horror she covered for the *Sentinel*. The serial killer from Paradise Hill. Eugene Hammond aka Eugene Kincaid. That's how she thought of Eugene -- not really a Hammond, although he had been raised by Joe and his wife. Eugene was more like his sick depraved biological father than his adoptive father or his biological mother. Poor Allison. She never had a chance. Even now, people were suggesting that the police re-examine the ME's report, wondering if Daryl Kincaid had been responsible for her death after all.

Pornographers, drug dealers, abductors, rapists and murderers. That was the Kincaid family. Tess's research had turned over a lot of stones and all the creepy crawlies had scrambled around in search of more darkness.

"I have a few more edits to do but yes. I'm meeting with Kate this afternoon and will turn in the latest installment."

"Good," Michael said. "I think it's very well-written and compelling. You really nailed Eugene. You've got good insight. Have you considered writing a true crime book based on the case?"

Tess shrugged. "Maybe. Once I'm done with the series."

She wanted to get the articles finished and published in the *Sentinel*, fulfilling her end of the bargain she'd struck with Kate when she went home to Paradise Hill the previous fall. It would be a while before the series of articles were completed. She planned on covering the trials but applying for the FBI might interfere with that. Maybe she'd receive the offer to join the FBI. Maybe she'd stay working as a crime reporter. At that point in her life, Tess was uncertain.

Sure, she had been able to shoot Eugene and prevent him from killing them all. It had been a lucky break that Michael had arrived when he did and shone the light in the forest where they were. It was lucky that she was close enough to kick the gun out of Eugene's hand and then take it, shooting him in both shoulders. It could have gone the other way.

She knew that.

"Well, I'm off," she said and grabbed the bagel Michael handed her. "Early meeting."

"Have a good day," he said and pulled her against him for a quick kiss. "Text me if you want to go out for supper and celebrate."

"I will." She grabbed her coat and bag, waving to him as she closed the door to their apartment.

Tess sat at her desk in the newsroom and worked on her article.

She'd been deep into the story, her mind focused, but was dragged away by a news report that appeared on one of the screens across from her desk and by one image in particular. She recognized the man in the photo next to a caption which read, *Local Man Questioned in Missing Persons Case.*

Craig Lang, a work friend of hers, and a freelance photographer who often worked for the *Sentinel.*

On the screen was a video of a small car with both its doors open, parked off a dirt road in the middle of the forest. Tess went over to the screen and took hold of the remote, turning up the volume.

Craig had a lot of contracts with the paper and was a regular face at staff parties. One of Tess's closer friends at the paper, they had worked on a number of stories together. She met his girlfriend and interviewed her for her article on missing and murdered women and girls.

Craig was what Tess's mother would call an 'odd duck' but Tess suspected he had Asperger's Syndrome. He didn't make eye contact when he spoke with people and averted his eyes, looking at the floor or strangely, the ceiling when he spoke with you. Only occasionally would he actually meet your gaze and only when asking a direct question. Behind the camera, however, he seemed unafraid and unselfconscious. Perhaps it provided a distance between him and the other person that he needed to feel comfortable.

The other writers and staff stopped what they were doing and crowded around Tess, watching the news report.

"Hey, that's Craig," Jenna, an admin said. She turned and glanced at Tess as if waiting for some explanation. Tess tried to ignore the expression of gloating on the woman's face.

Jenna turned to the other workers. "It's Craig. The photographer. You know -- weird Craig."

Tess frowned and turned up the volume, wishing the other staff would keep quiet while the news report was on. According to the reporter, Craig's girlfriend Rachel Martin and her young daughter Sadie had gone on vacation more than a week earlier. Craig hadn't told anyone, but the previous night her car had been found abandoned in the mountains near Mt. Baker, the door still open, the keys in the ignition. Police had no suspect, but it didn't look good for Craig. Next of kin and intimate partners were often guilty in these kinds of disappearances, and so he would be a prime suspect.

"Do you think he did it?" Jenna asked, her eyes wide. "I always thought he was strange. Never looked you in the eye."

"He has Asperger's," Tess said defensively. "They have problems making eye contact and small talk."

"The report said he was a person of interest in the investigation," Jenna replied, her tone sounding like she was pleased. Tess knew that from now on, Craig's guilt or innocence would be the only topic of conversation at work, around the water cooler, and in the staff room. It irritated her. She just couldn't believe Craig was a killer. He seemed sweet to her. Harmless.

Of course, she hadn't suspected Eugene, either.

Tall and lanky with fair hair and green eyes, Craig seemed awkward in any social situation, but he disappeared behind the lens. His photos were good. Really intimate. Maybe, taking pictures was a way for him to connect with people without actually having to interact with them.

Whatever the case, Tess hadn't spoken with Craig since she returned from Paradise Hill. The last time they'd seen each other was when they'd gone to interview some witnesses to a shooting in Seattle's red-light district. Craig had tagged along, camera in hand, and photographed a few of the street people Tess spoke with. They'd been together a lot on the Missing Women and Girls project, and he had been the main photographer since she'd started working at the *Sentinel*.

Tess liked Craig. She even felt affection for him and Rachel. A wisp of a woman, Rachel was short, fair and frail-looking. Sweet. She'd had a hard childhood, had run away from an abusive home, and had a child at thirteen.

Father's identity unknown.

Tess listened to the reporter go over the details of the

missing persons case. Rachel was just twenty-one to Craig's twenty-eight years old. Her daughter Sadie was eight.

Rachel had lived in a Catholic shelter for a while, had been an addict at one time and lived on the streets, but she had been lucky to have a good foster family who raised Sadie while she got clean. The reporter spoke with the foster mother, an older woman with short steel-gray hair, who shook her head sadly.

"I don't know why he didn't tell any of us she was gone. She was obviously abducted and taken to the forest. Who knows where they are now?"

Tess turned the volume down once the news report was finished and went back to her desk, frowning. Had Craig killed the woman and her daughter and hid the bodies somewhere in the forest?

Tess couldn't believe it, but many people were capable of much more than she imagined. She didn't suspect Eugene until the end.

Killers seemed like everyone else, which made her shiver. It meant that pretty much anyone could be a killer...

Later that afternoon, Tess sat in Kate's office while the older woman read over the article Tess had written about the missing persons case.

"We're all still pretty shocked," Kate said, examining the copy she held in her hand. "Craig's such a quiet man. So pleasant. You'd never suspect him of, well, anything. But everyone's insinuating that he did it. I know that a lot of women are harmed by their significant others, but Craig? He's harmless."

Tess shrugged. "Unfortunately, most murders are

committed by ordinary people in the heat of the moment. There are no red flags until it happens. Then, people go back over a person's life to find clues, but honestly, many of us have those clues in our lives and we don't go on to kill anyone."

"Most of us could kill, if we were in the right circumstances. If we felt our lives were threatened."

"Only a very few people do so in cold blood. They're fundamentally different from you or me. They're sociopaths and luckily, there aren't many of them around but there's enough. They cause all the mayhem in society."

"That's for sure. My sister in law is a bona-fide sociopath and she drives us all crazy with her lies and manipulation. A serious bullshit artist. I wish someone would have committed her years ago, but I guess there's no law against being downright nasty."

"No, there isn't," Tess said, putting down the article. "Have you spoken with Craig?"

"Not yet," Kate said and made a face. "He called in to Keith and asked for some time off to deal with things. I feel so bad but I'm kind of trying to avoid talking to him. I sent him an email and said we'd be sending a reporter around to talk to him about the case. This is a good start," Kate said and handed the story back to Tess. "See what else you can dig up. Talk to Craig, talk to Rachel's boss, her foster family. Give me a picture of her and her daughter."

"I will," Tess replied, eager to dive back into her work. "I'll ask him for some background. See how he's doing."

"Ask that handsome boyfriend of yours for tips on the case, if you can."

Tess laughed. "He's pretty tight-lipped when it comes to

his work, due to privacy considerations, but I'm sure he'd offer me advice on how to think about the case."

"Every little bit helps," Kate said and closed the file. "Let me know when you have anything else you want me to read."

"I will," Tess said and stood up to leave. "How did you like my latest piece on Paradise Hill?"

"It's good," Karen said and waved her hand. "Of course, it's good. You're part of the story. It's really gripping as a result."

Tess nodded. "I know that journalists aren't supposed to become part of the story, but in my case, I couldn't exactly help it."

"It makes it more compelling to know your personal connection to one of the victims and to the serial killer. You guys had no idea that he was a psychopath?"

"None," Tess replied, sighing heavily. "I never really knew him because he was so much older than us when I lived in Paradise Hill, and then when he married my best friend, I was living in Seattle. I only met him a few times. He seemed really nice."

"He was a lot older than your friend, though. No one thought that was weird?"

"I think once Kirsten got pregnant, all anyone cared about was her getting married and becoming more respectable."

"Typical small-town thinking. If she was my child, she would have had an abortion and the guy would have been charged with statutory rape."

"Well, she had two really great kids with him. So, there's that. She was happy for a while."

"But still. Won't her kids inherit his bad genes? Isn't psychopathy hereditary? How on earth will those poor children feel, growing up knowing their father was a serial killer? What would that do to a growing child? They'll be scarred for life."

Tess felt a wave of sadness at the prospect of Kirsten's boys facing the truth about their father. Eugene always seemed like such a devoted father from what she'd heard, but of course, it was all just show. Eugene knew how to act to make people think he was just an ordinary Joe, but he didn't feel any of it.

"There are some genes that are linked to anti-social personality disorder but usually, you need a history of abuse to see psychopathy develop. In this case, Eugene was abused and neglected right from birth. Probably was exposed prenatally to drugs and alcohol. His mother was young when she conceived him and died of a drug overdose when he was just a little boy. He was used in a pedophile porn ring for years without his adoptive parents knowing. Whenever they let him visit his uncle John Hammond, he was abused."

"*God*," Kate said and shook her head in disgust. "It makes me sick."

"Me, too," Tess said. "But he still had a choice. He chose to kill all those girls. He planned it out and carried through with those plans. Some of them were months in the making, so he knew exactly what he was doing and had self-control. He even killed Elena's father in order to provide an excuse for Elena going missing. Who knows how many others he killed?"

"Your final articles will cover the trial, once it happens. If you're still with the *Sentinel*."

Tess nodded. "I'll look forward to attending the trial, but it may be a long way off."

"Of course, you may be with the FBI by the time his trial date comes around. I hate to lose you, but I understand your desire to join the Bureau. How exciting!"

Tess smiled, a surge of adrenaline in her gut at the thought she might become an FBI Special Agent. "I have to get in a lot better shape before I'll get in. Michael and I started running together every morning. I need to practice doing pull-ups and get in shape generally. Sitting at a desk isn't the most conducive to fitness."

"You'll do fine. If you really want this, you'll put in the time."

"I will," Tess said and picked up her file. "I'll leave you to your meeting."

"Thanks for dropping by. Keep me up to date with any developments in Craig's case. Let's hope his girlfriend and her daughter turn up safe but given the dried blood on the steering column near the ignition, I doubt it."

Tess stood and went to the door. "I hope so, but I suspect you're right."

She left Kate's office and went back to the main newsroom, sitting back at her desk, staring at the article in front of her about Craig and the missing persons cases. Rachel Martin and her daughter Sadie.

God, she hoped he wasn't guilty...

CHAPTER THREE

Michael ran around the park, needing the exercise to drive away the demons.

He'd been awake with Tess in the middle of the night, trying to calm her down after her latest nightmare. It was normal to have problems dealing with a trauma like Tess had experienced. She'd have to learn to deal with it if she was going to make it as an FBI Special Agent involved in cases like those in Paradise Hill. He'd thought she was a natural, but she had to develop an emotional distance from cases in order to deal with them without lasting trauma.

He figured that it was his own personal issues that made him vulnerable to PTSD when he worked on the Lawson serial case involving little Colin Murphy. He had been going through the separation from Julia and the boys and had been unable to let it go. For an FBI Special Agent, it helped to have a completely solid home life. Special Agents were as human as anyone else. They divorced and had family problems, but it sure helped if they didn't.

If he and Tess stayed together, and he hoped they did, he intended to give her that stability. He was glad to be working for the DA, even if he wasn't able to be involved in any direct law enforcement work that might involve him using his weapon. He'd applied to go back to school to get a PhD and become a profiler once he was done. That would give him the ability to continue to work serial cases, but he wouldn't be involved directly in any aspect that required him to defend himself or anyone else. Instead, he'd be a consultant. He could freelance if he wanted more freedom, working with FBI field offices and police departments as a consultant wherever Tess was posted to help with difficult cases. He'd wait and see how things developed between them and with his PhD.

He was already thinking long-term with Tess, because his marriage to Julia was over and all that was left was signing the divorce papers and dividing the spoils. He still felt a small amount of resentment towards Julia for leaving, but he had to admit he'd been neglectful, absorbed as he had been with work, overwhelmed with the Lawson case. Then, he'd been too traumatized to be able to care for anyone else besides himself.

In truth, he didn't blame Julia.

He wouldn't make the same mistake again with Tess.

He spent the morning at the field office, sitting with his former supervisor, Dan St. James, discussing his plans and getting caught up on developments in the case in Paradise Hills.

"Glad to hear you'll be working with Nick. I hate to see your skills wasted," Dan said, when he took the signed document from Michael and glanced over it. "I'd have loved to put you back in play if you were able to work in the field."

"I can't lift my right arm up to shoot, but I can do investigations. Doctor says I might never be able to shoot with my right arm again. I've been practicing at the shooting range with my left hand, but there's no way I'll ever be as proficient. Besides, I can't do a single push-up. Can't risk it for fear I hurt myself even more. I have to do more mental work."

"Nick will get good use out of you until you go back to college. If you ask me, profiling is just what the doctor ordered," Dan said and tucked the piece of paper into a file on his desk. "I know the Assistant Director was pleased to be able to provide a glowing letter of support, considering what happened in Paradise Hill."

"I'm just happy to be able to keep working law enforcement in some capacity."

Dan leaned back in his chair and ran a hand over his bald head. "I'm glad you're still involved. I know the DA's office is backloaded with cases and so I'm sure they'll be glad to see you walk through the door. They likely need an admin person for filing and mail, whatnot."

Michael frowned momentarily, but then caught the gleam in Dan's eyes.

"Oh, sure," Michael said, realizing the man was joking. "I'll get to shuffle paper instead of finding bad guys."

Dan laughed at that. "Nah, you have to do something using your mind. I always said you had a good instinct for suspects. You never did like your brother-in-law. I seem to recall you checking up on him over the years."

"No, I never liked him. He gave me a bad feeling and of course, I hated that he was dating my sister when she was so young."

"You have a good sense of when someone isn't trustworthy.

You also have a good eye for details and can connect the dots when other people fail. That will make you a good profiler, once you've finished your degree."

"Thanks. I'm excited to go into profiling."

"You'll still get to see all the evidence in cases but won't have to actually go out and chase down bad guys." Dan nodded. "It will be perfect. Given your experience with the Lawson and Hammond cases, you're a shoo-in."

"I'll start classes in January, if I get accepted somewhere. I'm still waiting for letters of offer. Then, I'll have to move, depending on where I end up."

"Not in Washington State?"

Michael shrugged. "Like I say, depends on where I get accepted and what happens with Tess."

"Oh, yeah... Tess McClintock. The girl from Paradise Hill. Or should I say, the hopeful-FBI recruit from Paradise Hill. She has grit."

"You can say that again," Michael said, a surge of pride in him about Tess. "She's been interested in crime since her friend was abducted as a child. Actually, we share that in common, since I was the babysitter that night."

"Quite the story," Dan said and leaned back in his chair, his hands behind his head. "Quiet towns are never really all that quiet under the surface."

Michael nodded. "I always thought Paradise Hill was a sleepy little town tucked into the valley between mountains. Underneath that facade was a child porn ring and a serial killer."

"Who would have thought, am I right?" Dan replied and shuffled some papers on his desk. Michael took that to mean it was time to leave. Dan must have had another appointment.

Michael glanced at his watch. "Well, I should go. I'm meeting with some of the guys for coffee. Then, I've got to get to the DA's office and shuffle some papers this afternoon. It's my first week and I don't want to leave a bad impression."

"Keep working on your left-handed shooting," Dan said and stood when Michael did. "You never know when you might need to defend yourself." Dan came around the desk and shook Michael's left hand warmly. "I'm sorry to see you leave the Bureau, but I'm glad you're working for the DA until you go back to school. I think you'll be happy once you start profiling cases or whatever you end up doing."

"Hope so," Michael replied turned to leave. "I hate to leave the FBI, but that's life."

"Call me if you need anything," Dan said and sat back down behind his desk. "And I mean anything."

"Thanks. I will. See you."

"Take care," Dan said.

Michael closed the door behind him and left the wing of the building, glad that was out of the way but sad that signing that paper meant the end of his career as a field agent with the FBI.

He could be depressed about it, but he wouldn't let himself be. That was life. He was lucky to be alive. Four inches difference would have meant he died instead of losing the use of his arm.

Besides, he would still work on cases and he had Tess. He had the boys on one weekend a month and every other holiday. He was going back to school to get a PhD and become a profiler.

Life was good, all things considered.

. . .

Later that afternoon, he finished meeting with his new boss, Nick Hampton, the lead investigator on the Homicide Investigation and Tracking System unit, who hired Michael to help with background on various cases they were working.

Nick pointed to a wall filled with news clippings and images relating to a new missing persons case. "We got a call late last night about an abandoned car found up near Deming in Whatcom County. ID found at the scene is from a woman from Seattle, whose boyfriend didn't report her missing although she's been gone for a week. Go and have a look. Let me know what police find."

Michael was eager to get back out working a case again. "I'll be glad to get back in the saddle, so to speak."

"You okay driving?" Nick asked, motioning to Michael's arm, which was no longer in a sling.

"I can shift the gear okay, and work the turn signal, but I can't do anything that requires lifting anything heavier than a pen. I'll manage."

"Good," Nick said. "Good to have you on board. We have a lot of cases and it's nice to have someone with some experience to act as backup."

"Glad to be of help."

Michael left the office and made his way down to his vehicle. Abandoned cars weren't quite the same as the cases Michael used to work for the FBI's Task Force, but at that point, Michael was up for anything involving police work.

Besides, if the abandoned car was part of the new missing persons case, it would get him right back into the game.

CHAPTER FOUR

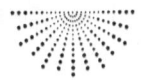

MONSTERS WERE REAL.

They weren't under her bed. They weren't in the closet, either.

Instead, they were all around her.

They were in her father's office late at night when everyone else was sleeping and he made her go there.

They were in the warehouse on weekends, while her mom worked late, and he took her there to meet his friends.

Most of all, the monster was inside him.

She could see the monster in his eyes when he told her not to cry out, not to scream, not to fight or he'd kill her mother. He'd kill everyone she knew, and no one would know the truth.

He killed Sadie and got away with it.

He even bragged about it to her when she resisted. She knew he would kill her mother, like he threatened. Once, when she fought back, he'd put his hands around her neck and squeezed until she fainted. When she came to, he was leaning over her, his ugly face inches from hers, smiling that evil smile.

"*I'll do it again, but the next time,*" he said, panting, his hot breath on her face. "*I'll do it until you die, and you'll go straight to hell. If you die disobeying me, you'll burn in eternal hellfire. Do you want that?*"

There were times she almost fought back just so he'd kill her and end all the pain, but she didn't. She was too afraid. She wanted to live. She wanted to tell her mother what he did, but his words would come back to scare her into silence those few times she was close to confessing.

He promised he'd kill her mother if she ever told.

He *killed* Sadie...

When Sadie didn't come out to play in the yard anymore, or at the playground, no one asked where she was. No one even wondered why Sadie was no longer around because no one knew who she was or even where she lived. Worst of all, no one cared.

The girl was haunted by that fact. One day Sadie was there. The next, she was gone, and no one asked where she was.

It was then the girl knew she had no hope of escaping the same fate. Nothing would change. Her father would kill her one day and no one would even know she was gone -- just like Sadie.

The girl, and that was how she thought of herself -- *the girl* -- because that was what they called her. Not her real name. Just '*Tell the girl to come over here. Tell the girl to bring more beer. Tell the girl to bend over.*'

She didn't want to run away, because she'd be alone. She longed to tell her mother. She just wanted it to stop.

"Honey, what's wrong?" her mother asked. "Tell me. Why are you crying?"

She wiped her eyes. Could she tell her mother? Would she believe it? Would she say she was a liar, like he told her?

She was so tired of everything...

So, she told her mother, and like he said he would, her father killed her.

One day, she told her mother what was happening at night and on the weekends. The next day, her mother was gone. When the girl asked him where her mother was, he said that she was gone and was never coming back. It was then, she knew he'd killed her mother, too. Burying her body somewhere in the forest just like he did with Sadie.

Just like he'd do to her if she ever disobeyed him again.

"Now, it's just you and me," he said. "Just you and me."

That was when the girl started planning to run away.

She remembered what her mother had said. There was a place in Seattle where they didn't turn you away. A shelter run by the Sisters of Mercy. They would feed you and bathe you and clothe you.

That's where the girl would go.

Her mother had lived there for a while. Then, she lived on the streets and that was when her mother met her father and got pregnant. The girl would go and live there. She wouldn't tell them that her own mother was once one of theirs because then they'd know who she was. No one could ever know that.

If they did, *he* would find her.

And then she'd die.

So, one day when the girl got enough courage, when it got too much to bear, she decided to run away.

. . .

It turned out that she was right -- when she went missing, there were no search parties. No missing persons reports. No posters tacked to telephone poles with pictures of her face.

MISSING: HAVE YOU SEEN...

For the first few nights, she stayed in an old garage she found when wandering alone in the small village the few afternoons she was free in the summer.

In the mansion near the edge of town lived an old woman who never went out except to collect rainwater from a cistern at the side of her old two-story house with the wrap-around porch. The old woman used it to water her plants.

This, the girl knew because she'd watched from their yard, which was across the street. The girl knew she would have to sleep somewhere if she was going to make it to the highway and hitchhike to safety. The garage would do until she had enough courage to go and stick out her thumb, hoping for a ride to civilization.

The garage was dusty, with cobwebs in every corner. On one side of the garage sat an ancient car rusting to pieces -- a remnant from when the old woman was younger and actually drove. Now, the old woman was too old and never went anywhere. The small grocery store in town delivered whatever food she needed.

The girl admired the old woman. She was able to live by herself and care for the huge old mansion alone. No one made her do anything she didn't want. There were no monsters in her life. No father forcing her down on her knees to make him happy. No men in long black robes judging her performance. No handcuffs and gags to keep her quiet and trapped, in the correct position for inspection.

The girl envied the old woman and wanted to be just like her when she was old.

Free. Completely and wonderfully free. Rich enough to pay men to mow her lawn and deliver her food.

The girl made the plan to run away after a particularly tiring night when she'd been introduced to a new form of torture by her father. She'd decided it was too much. She was used to bruises. They were an inevitable consequence of what happened to her. But this new form of torture was too much to bear.

Already, the stitches were starting to itch. She had to be careful not to do anything requiring too much exertion or her stitches would pop, and she could bleed to death.

That's what her father said.

She knew she had to get out because if she didn't, she'd die one of the next times they played the game.

So, she hid in the garage for a few days, eating food from the old woman's garden, drinking at night from the hose, pulling a few carrots from the soil, some snap peas, even a zucchini. If the old woman noticed her vegetable garden had been raided, she didn't think to check the garage for the culprit.

The girl had taken some crackers and some beef jerky she found in the pantry at home. They'd kept her stomach from rumbling too loudly the first night but by the third day, she was ravenous, and she felt her wounds were healed enough to make it to the highway and hopefully, to freedom.

Whatever lay in store for her on the road couldn't be worse that what she faced at home.

CHAPTER FIVE

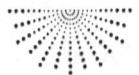

DEMING WAS a tiny town in Whatcom County, population just over 343 according to the Wikipedia entry. The trip there took longer than Michael expected, due to construction along the route. To reach the logging road where the abandoned vehicle was located, he had to take a small secondary road east and then went north on the logging road, about three miles out of town. Michael couldn't believe anything happened there, but he'd been wrong before about small towns and big crimes.

The vehicle had been abandoned on a side road in the middle of the forest. The area had been clear-cut a decade earlier and now the trees had grown back so that the new-growth forest offered a lot of cover. The Whatcom County Sheriff's office had control of the site and the crime scene investigators from Bellingham were combing the area around the vehicle, checking for signs that the driver and any passengers had fled the vehicle and were in the surrounding forest. Michael parked away from the side road where the vehicle had been abandoned, to avoid adding even more tire tracks to complicate the scene. The area had been marked off with yellow tape, not that there were any observers that far into the mountain. Michael got out of his Jeep, grabbed a pair of latex gloves from a box in his glove compartment and tucked them into his pocket so he could examine any contents of the abandoned car without leaving prints.

He scanned the scene to find the common approach. The old logging road extended farther up the side of Mt. Baker but the side road where the vehicle had been abandoned was barely wide enough for a car, let alone a truck. There were footprints leading off into the forest, and several different sets of tire tracks leading to the vehicle and away.

Michael suspected that whoever was driving the abandoned vehicle had been followed and had tried to escape. They'd either find a body in the forest, or they'd find evidence that the driver had been abducted.

Michael presented his credentials to the detective who was in charge of the scene.

"What have we got?" he asked when he arrived at the vehicle, a late model Ford Escape, the driver side door open.

Detective Palmer from Bellingham's major crimes unit, replied. "2014 Ford Escape. In the glove compartment, we found registration to Craig Lang, twenty-eight, from Seattle. There's a handbag in the vehicle as well, and a wallet with ID for a Rachel Martin. Twenty-five dollars and some change, so whatever this was, it wasn't a robbery. We popped the trunk and found a couple of suitcases. One with women's clothes and personal items, and one with girl's clothes and some dolls. A name on the smaller suitcase read Sadie Martin."

Michael nodded. Rachel Martin and her daughter Sadie appear to have been going somewhere with a plan to stay for a while, based on the amount of clothing and personal items they had taken with them. Palmer had searched through the contents of the handbag, looking for a cell phone. He found one, an Android, and luckily, there was no lock screen.

One call was to a Craig Lang, made the previous week.

Craig Lang.

He'd most likely be prime suspect number one.

Michael could almost write the case from past experience. Woman wanted to leave the relationship. Told the boyfriend they were leaving, and there was a confrontation. Woman left with the child, boyfriend followed, abducted them both, killed them, buried the bodies, reported them missing. Cried on camera, begging for them to come home.

He hoped that wasn't the case, but he expected the worst.

"We got local officers searching the area for any evidence they escaped on foot, but it looks like whoever did this, took them," Palmer said. "There are multiple tire tracks leading to the spot. One of our crime scene analysts is taking impressions now."

Michael nodded and glanced around. "Why would she be taking this road in the first place? She must have become lost. If she and her daughter aren't in the forest, it looks like whoever abducted her and her daughter followed her up here."

Palmer shrugged, his hand on his belt, his jacket collar pulled up against the cold. "Can't say there'd be any reason for her to be up here. This area looks like it hasn't been used for a long time."

Michael heard a shout from deeper in the forest.

"This way. Found something."

Michael and Palmer glanced at each other and then went into the forest towards the sound of the officer's voice. Michael hoped it was just some evidence and not a body or bodies, but he had to be prepared for anything.

They climbed over fallen trees and pushed through the thick undergrowth until they came to where two police officers stood, glancing down at something in the brush.

"What've you got?" Palmer asked when he arrived at the officer's side.

Michael glanced down and saw what looked like freshly-turned earth and below it, a bone.

"Looks like a body," the officer said, pointing to the rib bone sticking out from under some dirt and decaying leaves. Michael could just make out the base of a skull, a long bone that appeared to be from an arm. The body had been placed on its side in a fetal position.

"The ground is freshly disturbed," Palmer said. He bent down and pointed the dirt around the rib bone. "Someone was digging here recently. It's still wet."

"We'll have to call in a forensic team," Michael said. "That looks like an arm bone, and from the size of it, it's a child. But it can't be one of our missing persons, because there's no way a body would decompose that quickly in a week. This has been buried for much longer."

Palmer nodded in agreement. "You're right. This body's been here for more than a year."

"We'll have to get the ME from Seattle out here to check it out," Michael said. "Luckily, she doubles as a forensic anthropologist."

It wasn't the missing woman and her daughter, but it was a child who died and was buried out there in the middle of nowhere. Now, they had a new case. Another missing child, Jane or John Doe.

It felt good to be back working a crime scene, but there was a sinking feeling in Michael's gut that they'd likely found the skeletal remains of another murdered child.

"Seems like a huge coincidence that we have a missing persons case turn up here and the skeletal remains of a child within twenty feet of each other, the ground recently disturbed."

"Yep," Palmer said, his hands on his hips as he surveyed the bones. "Too big of a coincidence. It looks like someone came here specifically to dig up this grave, but only partially. Why?"

Michael shrugged. "Can't say until we learn who it is."

They spent another half-hour at the site, walking around the perimeter of the shallow gravesite, checking for evidence and waiting for the Medical Examiner to arrive. There wasn't much to find, other than a few cigarette butts and an old paper cup that had clearly been there for a long time. The technician bagged both and collected them in a larger garbage bag. Michael waited while the forensic tech placed a set of perimeter markers in the ground around the gravesite to protect it from contamination.

Michael shivered. It was cold out, that early in April, and the police officers rubbed their hands together while they waited for the ME to arrive. Once the forensic team was satisfied that they'd collected all the evidence, the tow truck operator loaded up the Ford Escape onto its truck bed and drove away, leaving Michael and Palmer to watch as it disappeared around the curve in the road.

"There's really nothing else for us to do except wait for the ME to arrive and process the scene. Are you going to head out?"

"I think I'll stay," Michael replied. "Wait to hear what the

ME says. I'd like some idea of how long the body's been buried so I can start checking through missing persons cases, see what turns up that might be a match."

"Okay," Palmer said. "You're welcome to stay."

Michael nodded and stuffed his hands into his pockets.

It was a two hour drive up to the site, so it was going to be a long day.

The ME arrived a little over two hours later. A middle-aged woman with greying hair pulled up into a bun, dark rimmed glasses and a fur-trimmed parka, she had a pleasant smile for him when he walked up to her vehicle to introduce himself.

"Grace Keller," she said and extended her hand to Michael.

"Michael Carter, investigator with the DA's office in Seattle," Michael said and shook her hand. Palmer came over and introduced himself as the lead detective on the case, then gave her the quick rundown about the scene while she put on her protective clothing, the white coveralls, hood, mask and gloves. She covered her boots with blue booties and then stood up straight. Michael and Palmer followed her over to the shallow grave, taking care to keep on the common path.

Keller bent down and examined the bones closer. "Looks like it's been here for quite a while."

"How long do you think?" Michael asked.

Keller stood up and shrugged, then began removing tools from a black bag she carried with her. She removed a camera and snapped some photos. "Given the state of the body, it could be a year, could be a decade, could be longer. Until I get a better look at it, I won't know for certain."

Michael nodded.

"One thing I can tell, which you already know, is that the scene was recently disturbed. Someone dug this up and within the last week, given the rain. The dirt's been removed around the shoulders and neck, and the rain has washed even more away. You can see the side of the skull here," Keller said and pointed with her gloved hand to the skull. Michael had noticed earlier that it was exposed.

"Do you think it was an animal who dug it up?" Michael asked.

"No. An animal would have taken the bones and we'd find more scattered around. The remains look intact. If I had to guess, I'd say that someone wanted to retrieve something from the site. Maybe something that could immediately identify it."

"Like jewelry or something else buried with the body?" Michael offered.

"Exactly." Keller smiled at Michael. Rain started to fall, the drops fine. Keller glanced up at the sky through the tall pines surrounding the site. "You gentlemen game to help me set up a tent to protect the scene?"

"I'm always glad to help," Michael offered. "But I have limited mobility of my right arm."

"I knew you'd come in handy," Palmer said jokingly and clapped Michael on the back.

"Suit up and be my assistants," Keller said.

Michael and Palmer followed Keller to her vehicle. Once there, they slipped on white coveralls that Dr. Keller handed them, then wrapped their wrists and ankles with duct tape to prevent contamination of the scene while they worked. After suiting up, Michael slipped on his hood, mask and goggles. Together, they removed the tent materials from the back of her SUV and set up the tent at the site. Michael wasn't very much help because of his arm, but he was able to contribute, and more than that, he was curious about how Keller worked. He'd been trained in the general processing of crime scenes, of course, but the way a forensic anthropologist worked was new to him.

He settled in and watched as she carefully marked out the gravesite and took photographs, before proceeding to unearth the bones. Seeing the final skeletal remains uncovered, lying in a fetal position with the hands held in front of the face made him think that the child, whoever she or he was, had been placed in that position after death, hands folded in prayer. If that was the case, it suggested that the one who buried the body had a relationship to the child. A stranger didn't pose their victims in postures implying piety and innocence.

There was a story to tell behind the death of this child, whether it was murder, accidental or even due to natural causes.

Michael was determined to tell that story so the parents and family could have closure and the killer, if any, would be brought to justice.

CHAPTER SIX

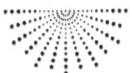

JUST BEFORE DAWN, the girl gathered up some extra carrots and snap peas, and left the garage, walking the ten miles along the back road behind the town to the main highway. When she got there, she stuck out her thumb and waited for someone to pull over and offer her a ride.

A trucker pulled off to the shoulder and opened the passenger door for her.

"What's a young thing like you doing out on this road so early in the morning?" he asked.

"I'm going to visit my cousin in Seattle."

"I'm going to Seattle, but I have to stop in Bellingham and won't get there until tomorrow night. If you want, you're welcome to catch a ride there with me." He looked her over. "Hop in," he said and pointed to the back of his cab. "There's a bed back there if you need to sleep."

"Thanks," she said and jumped up, climbing to the back where there was a single bench bed. The space smelled slightly of sweat and that man smell that she knew only too well, but she was tired, and it was a real bed instead of the cold hard ground.

"How long have you been walking?"

"A couple of hours."

"Are you hungry?" the trucker asked.

"Yes," she said, for her stomach was growling.

"When was the last time you ate a real meal?"

"Three days ago."

She heard him click his tongue in disapproval. "There's some chips and sodas on the floor. I'll go to the next truck stop and get you some food."

"I don't have any money."

"I do," he said.

The truck drove off into the darkness. After a while, he spoke.

"What's your name?"

She hesitated. She didn't want to use her real name. She didn't want anyone to take her back to the family. She thought about the old woman in the mansion. She liked the name.

"Rachel," she said simply.

"Call me John."

"Thank you, John," she said.

"You're welcome. Just being a good Samaritan, I guess. Maybe earning some good Karma points."

They drove for a while and she ate some chips and drank a soda.

"What's your cousin's name?" John asked. "Maybe I can call her and tell her where to meet you."

She hesitated. She didn't have a name in mind because she didn't have a cousin waiting for her in Seattle.

"Sadie," she said, using the only other name that meant

anything to her. "I don't know if Sadie has a cellphone. She's homeless."

"You were just going to meet her on the streets?"

"Yes," Rachel said and it was then that her plan to run away to Seattle seemed like a really bad idea. She started to cry, her eyes welling up, a sob escaping her lips. She covered her mouth and squeezed her eyes shut, not wanting him to hear her, for she was not allowed to cry. She got a beating when she cried. "I'm sorry, I'm sorry," she said between sobs.

"It's okay," John said. "Don't cry. I'll take you to her."

When she got control over herself, she wiped her eyes and nose on her sleeve.

"Thank you, John."

In a while, he spoke softly. "You know you can get into foster care if you need to. You don't have to live on the streets."

"No, I don't want a foster family," she said a little too firmly. She cringed, used to being slapped for such insolence. "I'd rather live with Sadie," she said in a soft voice.

"Okay," he said. "That's your choice, I guess. How old are you, anyway? Maybe I should call the police and let them know you're a runaway."

"No, please, don't. They'll just send me back."

There was a long silence and Rachel -- as she now thought of herself -- Rachel knew he was deciding whether to turn her in.

Finally, he sighed audibly.

"Okay. I'll take you to Seattle. You can go to meet your cousin. Like I said, I have to stop in Bellingham, but you're welcome to stay in the back and sleep while I load up. If you change your mind, I can call the authorities, and someone will find you a home. A foster family if your own family is bad."

"I'll be fine," she said, but she was afraid that was a lie. "Please don't send me back."

"I won't. We'll be in Bellingham soon. You should sleep."

"I will."

They drove down the long winding road, the radio tuned to a country and western station. After she'd eaten half a bag of potato chips and drank down a diet soda, she slept, the motion of the truck lulling her to sleep.

When she woke, she was alone in the cab, and John was inside the truck stop. It was starting to get light, and there was a faint sliver of light in the east. Dawn was coming but the lights of the truck stop were still bright. A dozen trucks lined up side by side, the drivers in the restaurant or shop, eating a meal or getting supplies or gas.

John returned to the cab and saw that she was up.

"There you are. You fell asleep and I didn't want to wake you up."

She nodded and gave him a smile. "The bed is soft."

"It's hard as hell," he said with a laugh. "But it's good for my back. Here's some bacon and eggs. I bought you an apple. You should eat something healthy."

She took the food happily and settled back, eating the bacon with relish. "This is so good. Thank you. I haven't eaten a meal for ages."

"How long have you been gone?" he asked, sipping a milkshake. He was in the driver's seat but had craned his neck around to speak with her.

"Four days," she said.

"Four days? Isn't anyone looking for you? I haven't heard any Amber alerts or any reports on the news of any runaways."

"No one would report me missing," she said with a shrug. "No one cares if I live or die."

He frowned at that. "What about your parents?"

She raised a shoulder, feeling sad all of a sudden at how alone she really was. "They're both dead," she lied. She didn't want to tell him the truth -- that her father was alive but a monster. He might as well be dead.

"I'm sorry," he said softly. She heard him sigh heavily. "It must be hard for someone as young as you to lose her parents. This world's a fucked-up place, pardon my French."

She nodded without speaking.

"When you're done eating, you should use the bathroom if you have to. We won't get to Seattle until later tonight because I have to load the rig and then make a couple of stops along the way to do my drops."

"Okay," she said and took her backpack, climbing out and jumping down from the passenger side. She found the bathroom inside the service station, feeling the eyes of the truckers and the clerk on her. She used the bathroom, washing her face and brushing her teeth with her old toothbrush. She stared at her reflection in the mirror. Her pale hair was thin and greasy after four days without a shower. She ran her brush through her hair and sighed.

There was nothing to be done about it. When she got to the Sisters, she'd be safe.

She went back to the line of trucks, half expecting John to have left her alone, but he was still there.

"Aren't you tired?" she asked when she sat in the passenger seat.

"I slept before I left last night. You should sleep more if you want. We'll be in Seattle sometime this evening."

She yawned. "Maybe I will."

She climbed back into the bed and laid on the rumpled blankets. She hadn't felt this safe for as long as she could remember.

Things had turned out better than she expected. She was fed, she had washed up, and she had slept.

Now, all she had to do was get to the Sisters of Mercy and she'd be fine.

They arrived in Seattle just after sunset.

"Can you take me to the Sisters of Mercy Shelter? My friend hangs out around there."

"Sure thing," he said. "You should definitely stay there. I heard good things about them."

Rachel watched the streets while John drove to the Sisters of Mercy shelter for homeless youth, located in north Seattle.

"This is it," John said when they pulled up to a curb. Rachel glanced out at the street and saw dozens of people standing on the corner or walking along the sidewalk. Young people, boys and girls her age and older.

"Thanks," she said and grabbed her backpack. "Thanks for the food and the ride."

"My pleasure," he said. Then he reached into his pocket and pulled out a business card. He handed it to her. "Call me if you get into trouble and need a place to stay. You can always come with me if you need to get off the street."

"Thanks," she said and took the card. It had a picture of a semi-truck and the name Henderson Freight Ltd. Beneath the title was an address and a phone and fax. A cell phone # was written by hand.

"Call the cell if you want to get in touch with me."

"I will," she said and gave him a smile. "You were really nice to help me."

He tipped his baseball cap to her. "You take care. Watch out for yourself. These are some mean streets. You're so young. Too young and innocent to be on the street."

"I will," she said. "The only thing worse that can be done to me is to kill me," she said, and she meant it. "I'll survive."

He shook his head as if he was sad to hear what she said, but it was the truth.

CHAPTER SEVEN

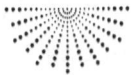

TESS THOUGHT about Craig and felt uncertain whether he was capable of being a killer. Having gone through the experience in Paradise Hill with Eugene, a man she thought was a perfect gentleman and good father, she had to suspect everyone. But while Craig was awkward at times, and avoided eye contact like it actually pained him, he was really nice -- actually sweet -- once you got him to talk to you.

He definitely had some form of Autism, probably with Asperger's Syndrome, with high intelligence but very poor social skills. He stuttered as well, and Tess had always tried to be patient, letting him struggle to get the words out instead of finishing his sentences. It meant conversations took longer than normal, but the reward was a smiling Craig, who seemed to appreciate that she took the time to hear him out.

She remembered the first time she worked with Craig on a story about missing women in Seattle's seedier districts where the homeless spent their days and where drug addicts did their hits in back alleys and dark doorways. She and Craig had traveled to Aurora Avenue where the prostitutes hung out. Tess had just started to work the story after the murder of a street prostitute, whose body turned up in a dumpster at the edge of the city.

While Tess interviewed a few of the women, Craig took photos and together, they had worked on the piece. The final article was filled with haunting black and white images of women dressed in scanty clothes, scanning the streets for potential Johns. Dark alleys and doorways loomed large in the images, making it seem like some unnamed evil lurked just around the corner.

According to Jenna, who served as the newsroom's grapevine, Craig met Rachel a few years earlier on one of those excursions into Seattle's red-light district for a story. She was working at one of the seedy bars that serviced the local population. A former runaway, who had lived on the streets for a while, Rachel had gone to rehab and gotten cleaned up. Her daughter Sadie lived with Rachel's foster family during the time she spent in rehab and she had straightened out, working two jobs while her daughter went to school and daycare. Rachel seemed to finally be doing well for herself, having escaped the streets, living with her daughter in a slightly better part of the city.

"They moved in together less than two months after they met," Jenna said and raised her eyebrows suggestively. "He moved fast -- or she did. She probably saw him as a father figure for her daughter."

"Did you ever meet her?" Tess asked, for Jenna seemed to know quite a bit about the young woman and her daughter.

"Yes," Jenna said. "Several times. I used to meet them at the local market on Saturdays. They seemed happy enough. The last time I saw them was only a month before she disappeared, so if there were strains in their relationship, I didn't see it, but often, people hide the truth, don't they? They put up a good front."

Tess nodded. That was the truth. People fought to keep up a good public image, all the while screaming in their own heads for someone to help them. Behind closed doors, all kinds of private hell existed. The case stories Tess had read during her research for articles made her despair at times. That may have been why she hesitated to get too close to anyone, whether it was female friends or lovers, which were few and far between.

Working the crime beat had tarnished her view of relationships. Growing up without a strong father figure in her household didn't help. She felt lucky to have met Michael once more in Paradise Hill. They both seemed to share so much and had their eyes open to the darkness in the world. Tess didn't have to explain how she felt about things, because Michael shared her vision and sentiments. They were comfort to each other.

Tess felt she could face the darkness in the world that she explored in her articles because Michael was there, waiting at home or on the phone if she needed to talk or ask a procedural question. Most of all, she felt safe with Michael. He was a good guy, a good man, who wanted to fight the darkness.

She was lucky, and she knew it.

She called Craig's cell but her call went right to voice mail.

He was probably not up to taking calls and was trying to avoid talking to people. She pulled up to the apartment block where Craig lived and parked on the street, glad there was a free parking meter. She plugged it full of quarters and went to the front entry, searching the keypad for his name. She pressed the buzzer and waited. In a moment, she heard a tired male voice, garbled by static.

"Yes?"

Tess cleared her throat, feeling awkward now about stopping by. "It's Tess. Kate asked me to come by and do the interview. Get some background on Rachel."

"I wondered who they'd send," Craig replied. "I'm glad it's you. Come on up."

The buzzer sounded and Tess pulled the door open, entering the small foyer with a bank of mailboxes on the wall. Beneath it on a bench was a collection of shopping flyers and a stack of free community newspapers. The building was well-kept and clean, smelling of fresh laundry. Tess could hear dryers from down the hallway when she entered the main floor and walked along the hallway to Craig's first floor apartment.

She arrived at Apartment 112 and knocked on the door. She could tell Craig looked through the door's peephole for the light from behind it was cut off momentarily. A chain lock was removed, and a deadbolt turned before the door opened wide to admit her. In the entry stood Craig and he looked a real mess, his hair standing on end like he just got out of bed, his eyes bloodshot, an old bathrobe thrown over a pair of jeans and bare feet.

"Hi, Tess," he said, sniffing. He wiped his nose with the back of his hand. Had he been crying when she arrived?

She glanced at his face but as usual, he avoided her eyes and stared off to the left.

"Hey," she said and came inside. He closed the door behind

THE GIRL WHO RAN AWAY

her and stood there, like he didn't know what to do next. "How are you? You must be sick about all this."

He nodded without speaking. "Come in. I was sleeping. Sorry."

"That's okay," she said and removed her boots and coat. "Thanks for agreeing to the interview."

"I'm glad it's you," he said.

"I'm glad it's me, too," she replied. He took her coat and hung it up in the front closet and then led her deeper into the apartment. She followed him to a small living room with a pair of sliding doors opening out onto a green space at the rear of the building. The furnishings were old but comfortable. The place looked like a woman lived there, with a lace cloth on the coffee table, knickknacks on the dark wood mantle over the fireplace, throw pillows that brightened up the room. Black and white photos of the city covered one entire wall. They were Craig's photos, and showed the darker side of Seattle. The back alleys, the abandoned buildings, the old waterfront with rotting wood pillars sticking out of a grey Elliott Bay, the water rippled by wind, the sky overcast.

She turned and looked at Craig, who stood by an overstuffed chair like a zombie, his eyes staring off into space. He looked a mess, bleary-eyed, exhausted. Defeated.

Was he also a killer?

All her instincts told her he wasn't guilty. This was a man who feared for a missing loved one. This wasn't a man who was trying to hide his guilt.

But her instincts had been wrong before, so she exhaled, sat down on the sofa and pulled out her recorder. She held it up.

"Do you mind if I record our session? It ensures I get things correct. For the record."

He shrugged and glanced out the window. "Whatever."

"Please have a seat," Tess said. "Relax. I'm a friend, Craig."

He sighed heavily and then sat across from her.

"Tell me about Rachel," Tess said, hoping to give him the chance to talk about her without any restrictions.

"Rachel is," he said and shook his head. He glanced out the window. "Rachel is my life." Then, he cradled his head in his hands and wept.

Tess felt terrible, seeing Craig like that, crying so openly.

"I'm sorry," she said in a soft voice. "This must all be so upsetting to you."

He appeared to get a hold of his emotions and wiped his eyes but stared at the floor. "It's my fault."

Tess frowned. "What's your fault?"

"We had a fight," Craig said and held his head again. "She wanted to move away, and I wanted to stay in Seattle. It's where my work is. I can't just move to somewhere new at the drop of a hat, but she said I could get a job doing anything. Janitor. Construction worker. I can't just go somewhere and get a job. This is all I know. You can't just move away and get work as a photographer and that's all I'm really good at."

"She wanted to move away? Why?"

"I don't know," he said and shook his head. "She said her past was catching up with her and she needed to move. But it's the middle of the school year and Sadie was really happy with her teacher and friends."

"So, you fought about moving away from Seattle," Tess repeated. "Then she left? Packed up and left with Sadie?"

Craig nodded. "She said she was going south to Oregon.

She had some money saved and was going to drive until she found a nice little town in the mountains with a good school and find a place to live."

"You were going to stay in Seattle?"

"What can I do in a small town in the middle of Oregon? I can't get work there. I work for the *Sentinel*. Sometimes, I sell my photos to stock companies, and I can do industrial photography, but I can't really do portraits or weddings or anything like that. It's not my thing."

Tess nodded, knowing that it would be hard for Craig to deal with people in general. He could photograph subjects of a news article as long as it wasn't posed and was natural, like he was in the background capturing a scene. Dealing with the public would be too hard for him.

"So, she left on what night?"

"I was at work on Friday at a crash site, taking photos for the paper. I got home early and she came home after being out somewhere. She didn't say where. She packed up and wanted to leave then and there, but I couldn't. I just couldn't." He shook his head. "It's all my fault."

His head went back into his hands again and he cried silently. Tess went over to where he sat and placed her hand on his shoulder.

"I'm so sorry about this," she said. "You must be afraid for her."

"The police called me. They found my car up near Mt. Baker and wanted me to give a DNA sample. One of the cops who interviewed me swabbed the inside of my cheek. What was she doing up there? She said she was going south, to Oregon."

"Did she have friends or family up there?"

"Not that I know of," he said and shook his head. He wiped his eyes again. "We used to drive up there to see the mountains. She liked to see the volcanoes, but she *said* she was going south. She always told me her family was from Montana. They're a bunch of survivalist nuts. You know, one of those sovereign citizen groups that keep to themselves. They're waiting for the second coming or world war three."

"Do you know where she's from exactly?" Tess asked, jotting a question down on her notepad.

"She just said Montana. She said they were all crazy and that she was lucky to escape when she did. I don't know. They're survivalists who expect a civil war in America to announce the rapture or something nuts like that."

Tess frowned and wrote down *survivalists. Montana.* She needed to do some reading on survivalist groups in Montana for background.

Craig told Tess about meeting Rachel while they were working a story on missing and murdered girls and women in Seattle. When he spoke, Tess could hear emotion in his voice. How Rachel had made it easy for him to talk to her. How it was nice to have a little ready-made family to look after. How Sadie wanted a father-figure so badly and had sat with him for hours reading books and doing her homework.

What Tess got from the interview was a man living in fear for his girlfriend and her daughter's safety. She didn't get a man putting on an act. With Eugene, he was always so relaxed and friendly. Easy to talk to. He was charming, always saying the right thing in any situation. Except when he was alone, at home with Kirsten. Then, Kirsten said, it was like Eugene was empty. Hollow.

It just didn't feel like Craig was performing.

"Someone must have abducted her. Maybe someone from her past, like she said. She said her past was catching up with her. I asked her to explain what that meant, but she didn't want to talk about it. I should have gone with her. I should have," he said and finally looked up and into Tess's eyes. "It's my fault. I have a bad feeling about this. A bad feeling."

Tess shook her head. "It's not your fault. You couldn't be expected to just pack up and leave with no notice."

"If I agreed to go with her, she and Sadie would be safe and sound. Now, who knows where they are?"

Tess gave Craig a look of compassion, but there was nothing she could really say.

Craig glanced at his watch. "I have a shoot," he said. "Down by the docks. I have to get ready."

Tess stood, gathering up her things. Craig looked like he was glad to have an excuse to stop talking about it and she didn't blame him. He was torn up inside about it -- or he was a very good actor.

"Can I come back and talk some more?" she asked. "I want to ask more about Rachel. What she said about her past. Where she worked. Her foster family."

He nodded. "Sure. I get off work late tonight because I'm taking photos of the game, and I'll be working all day tomorrow. I'm off in the morning day after tomorrow. We could meet somewhere else or come here."

"It's up to you. Whatever you prefer."

"Maybe we could do it here? I've been staying in the apartment, waiting for her to call or come back home. Now, I don't think she will be." Then, he covered his eyes once more and fought his emotions.

"I'll go," she said and stood by his side, squeezing his arm.

"Thanks, Tess," he managed. "Call me when you want to come by."

"I will."

She saw herself out of the apartment and went back to her car, a knot in her gut at the pain she'd heard in his voice and seen on his face. He couldn't be responsible, could he?

CHAPTER EIGHT

THEY FINISHED PROCESSING the crime scene after dark. Michael could have returned to Seattle much earlier, but he wanted to stay and help Dr. Keller do her work.

"What's your best guess as to the cause of death?" Michael asked.

Dr. Keller shrugged. "Too soon to know. While it could have been a natural death, I see evidence that could be interpreted as abuse. There are healed fractures on the bones of the forearms and evidence of a broken rib."

Michael shook his head, sick at the prospect. Despite his years of experience with crime scenes and child murders, when faced with the reality, it was still hard, and he thought about his own boys.

"You think the child was murdered?"

"These injuries could be the result of an accident or abuse. Until we know the identity of the child, we can't say conclusively. I suspect there was child abuse involved based on the multiple broken bones that healed over time. As to the cause of death, there are no ligatures around the feet or wrists, or around the neck. There are no obvious wounds to the skull or recent broken bones. Cause of death will have to be inconclusive as a result."

"What about the sex? How long has the body has been buried?" Michael asked as they finished up processing the scene.

"I can't be entirely sure about the postmortem interval or sex," she replied. "It's a prepubescent child based on the length of the humerus bone and condition of the growth plates, but I can't tell which sex conclusively as a result. There aren't enough differences at that age to be sure, but I suspect it's a girl based on how fine the bones are. Maybe seven or eight years old. As to how long the bones have been here, the body was buried so it was protected from the elements and from scavengers. There's no evidence of any recent decomposition, so I'd say two to three years and possibly up to a decade. Based on the condition of the soil surrounding the body, I'd say closer to a decade. Look for children aged between seven and nine who went missing up to ten years ago. Could be longer."

"I'll go through our records and see what I can come up with."

They finished packing up and he walked to Dr. Keller's vehicle. When they got there, Detective Palmer got a call and took it a few feet away. While Michael removed his protective clothing, he tried to listen in but only caught one side of the conversation.

When Palmer finished the call, he came back to where Michael and Dr. Keller stood.

"What's up? Michael asked.

"Ran a check on the ID found in the handbag. Looks like it

was fake. There are no records of a Rachel Martin or Sadie Martin in any state registry."

"Oh, that's strange. Nothing came back on either of the names on the ID?"

Palmer shook his head. "Nothing for their names or dates of birth."

Michael frowned and turned to Dr. Keller. "I'd appreciate it if you could keep me informed on anything you find about the remains," he said.

"I will. Thanks for your help," she said, and they shook hands before leaving. "It was nice to have some company for a change. Usually, I work a scene alone unless I bring along a student."

"No, thank you for indulging me and explaining everything. I'm returning to do a PhD in the fall or winter semester and so I need to get back into the learning mode. You're a great teacher. How long before you have more of an idea how long the body has been buried?"

"I'll run some tests on the soil, look at various concentrations to see how long and let you know. We'll do a DNA test and see if we find any matches in the database. I'll be sure to keep you in the loop."

They parted ways and Michael turned back to Palmer. "That's quite the development. We'll have to speak to her family, see what they know," he said.

Palmer nodded. "I expect the Seattle PD will take this over, given it's a Jane Doe and looks like a murdered child."

"FBI and Seattle will work together on it," Michael said. "If I was still with the FBI, I might work this case."

"Funny how fate works," Palmer said and they shook hands before getting into their respective vehicles.

Before he drove off, Michael sent Tess a text to let her know he'd be late and to go to bed without him. Then, he started his Jeep, his mind full of the information he'd gathered while watching Dr. Keller process the scene. Keller thought the child had experienced abuse. That could mean the parent killed the child during an abusive situation and buried the body.

Hopefully, the child would be in the missing persons database and they could work from there. He went back over his memory to see if there was a missing child reported that stuck out in his mind but drew a blank. Most of the children close to that age had been linked to Eugene Hammond/Kincaid. He'd speak with Tess and together, they'd search for likely victims.

He thought about the cases he'd investigated -- most of them young women under the age of eighteen, right down to children. Too many women, too many girls, were victim to a man's anger and resentment or perversion. Children were always vulnerable, helpless and at the mercy of parents or guardians.

It was almost impossible to prevent, and so those with a burning need to protect children were left with prosecuting those who hurt them. He wasn't sure what could be done except to make it more acceptable for the public to intervene when they suspected child abuse, but it was something most people did not want to do.

Before he left, he got a call from Nick Hampton in Seattle.

After he filled his new boss in on what they'd found at the scene, Nick gave him a surprise.

"Get this. We just got a call from police in Whatcom County up near your location. Security company responsible for the cabins around Silver Lake responded to a call about a cabin being broken into. When they got there, they found a body inside, and get this -- another one in the outhouse shitter. Went head-first into the chute. Both of them dead for over a week."

"Wow," Michael said, the thought making him grimace. "I hope he was dead before he fell inside."

"Looks like he was stabbed and then shoved through the hole. Medical examiner thinks he was still alive when he went in."

"So, you got a double murder up in Whatcom County and an abandoned vehicle all at once?"

"Yep," Nick said. "Body inside the cabin was naked, stabbed and the other was as well. Naked, stabbed then shoved down the hole. From the report on the scene, it appears there was some kind of filming taking place in the cabin. There was lighting and camera equipment set up in the living room."

"Porn?"

"There were no memory chips in the cameras and no hard drives in the computer they recovered so who knows? Doesn't seem to be any other reason for having all that equipment inside a cabin than homemade porn."

"Have they identified the bodies?"

"Nope," Nick said. "There was absolutely no ID on either of the men. No wallets, no papers. Just the two bodies and empty cameras. There's a forensic team there now taking prints and we hope to be able to ID them soon."

"Pornographers, huh?" Michael replied, thinking of Eugene and the pornography ring in Paradise Hill. He didn't want to assume there were any links between the cases, but of course, he couldn't help but make the connection. "You got any details you can share?"

"When you come in, you can read the case file we got via fax as information from Bellingham PD. I'm going to want you on this case as well."

"Sounds good." He ended the call, energized despite the long day at the scene.

The double murder would be a real meaty case. He wanted to drive up north and check out the scene himself, but he'd wait until Nick sent him there.

He arrived home much later and drove up to the parking lot where he kept his Jeep. Tess would be in bed, likely asleep, so he tried not to wake her when he entered the apartment. To his surprise, she was still up, sitting in her nightgown and robe on the sofa, her laptop on her lap.

"Hey," he said and after he finished hanging up his coat and shucking his boots, he went over to where she sat. "You should be asleep."

She shook her head and kissed him. "Couldn't sleep. My mind's obsessed with a case.

"I understand the problem, unfortunately," he said and sat beside her on the sofa. He stretched and placed his feet on the coffee table, careful not to knock over the cup of coffee there. "What did you do all day? Not that I have any doubt what, but I thought I'd ask if you want to talk about it."

"I have a new case," she said and snuggled closer to him, her head on his shoulder. "Craig Lang, the photographer I work with on some stories, is a suspect in a missing persons case. I interviewed him and spent the day wondering how someone I thought I knew pretty well could possibly be a suspect in a disappearance. But then I remembered what happened in Paradise Hill and nothing is beyond comprehension any longer."

"I'm working that case," he said. "In fact, I spent the afternoon at the scene of the abandoned vehicle she was driving."

"No," Tess said, her eyes wide.

"Yes," he replied. "I went to the location of the abandoned vehicle his girlfriend's been driving, registered to Craig, and we found the half-buried remains of a child just inside the forest."

"What?" Tess said, her voice shocked. She sat up and faced him, a hand on his arm. "You found a child's body? Was it the girl, Sadie?"

Michael shook his head. "No, this body had been buried for years. Possibly a decade. For whatever reason, a fluke or intentional, she drove up to that location and it appears someone unearthed the bones. The child's body was fully skeletal, so it had been there for years."

"Oh, my God," Tess said, a hand over her mouth. "What on Earth?"

She sat back beside him, momentarily stunned by the news. "So, Rachel -- or someone with her -- knew that the body was there and dug it up intentionally? Why?"

Michael shrugged. "Don't know for sure. The Medical Examiner thought that someone might have taken something off the body by the way the shoulder, neck and skull had been specifically unearthed."

"Could she tell what killed the child? I mean, any signs of trauma?"

"Unfortunately, no. She said she couldn't see any obvious signs that could give a cause of death, but the bones had evidence of either an accident causing broken bones or long-term abuse. There were several healed fractures on the arms and broken ribs that had healed."

"So, the child might have been abused?"

"That or she could have been in an accident. Without further study, Dr. Keller couldn't tell which. She'll have to examine the bones more closely to determine if it looks like repeated trauma or one-time. Regardless, someone dug up the body and it was recent, which suggests that either Rachel or someone else knew the bones were there and went to that location intentionally."

"Craig blamed himself," Tess said softly.

"Oh, yeah?" Michael replied, frowning. "How so?"

"He said they had a fight about moving away. She wanted to move to Oregon that Friday night and he didn't because of work. She left. He feels like if she'd stayed or if he'd gone with her, she would still be with him. She wanted to leave because she said her past was catching up with her, whatever that means."

"He didn't elaborate?"

Tess nodded. "He said he'd asked her but she wouldn't explain. I interviewed her once for background on a case, and while she didn't want me to use her name or any details, she did tell he that she'd had a hard life, ran away from home, then lived on the streets for a while when she was thirteen. She lived in foster care for a few years, after she had her baby. Then, she had problems with substance abuse but was never really a serious addict and got clean because of the baby. But she became afraid for some reason and wanted to move away."

"So, she left without him," Michael said. "He feels guilty that someone maybe abducted her, abandoned her car."

Tess nodded.

"Whoever did must have known about the burial site," Michael said. "It's too much of a coincidence for the recently-unearthed burial site to be less than two-dozen feet from the car."

Tess sat in silence for a moment, an expression of sadness in her eyes. "Now, I'll never sleep," she said with a sigh. "Do you suppose Craig did it, followed her up there, then abandoned the car? That's what Eugene did with me. It was a diversion, to get you and the police to think I was in a different part of the state than I was."

"It's possible. It's too soon in the investigation to be developing a story of the case with any confidence." Michael pulled her against him for a kiss. "You need some chamomile tea."

He got up and made them both a cup. It took a while watching a show on television that was in no way connected to crime or criminals to get their minds off the case. When they finally went to bed, they lay in each other's arms and he knew she was doing the same thing he was -- obsessing about the current case.

"I just don't know what to think," Tess said. "Craig seems so harmless. He seems like he really loved Rachel and Sadie. Really broken up by it and afraid that finding the car abandoned means someone has her. Someone from her past that she was afraid of."

"That sounds like a convenient story," Michael said doubtfully.

"I know it does, but until we know more about her, I have to keep that possibility open."

Michael exhaled and pulled her more tightly against him.

"You're right. Rachel is an unknown. Police ran her ID and it seems to be fake. We have no idea who she really is."

Beside him, Tess tensed. "What?"

"That's confidential information, so it can't go into your news story or be repeated to anyone until it's public, but yes. Her ID was fake. We have no idea who she really is."

She turned to him, her eyes wide. "How did she get fake ID and be part of the child welfare system? Wouldn't they have checked her birth records?"

"I have no idea. Until we can speak to her foster parents and find out who she really is, all we can do is speculate. Oh, and get this. There was a double murder farther north, maybe twenty minutes away near Silver Lake."

"What?"

Michael nodded. "I'm assigned to the case, so it's right back into the saddle again for me."

"Are you okay with that?" she asked, a hand on his arm.

"Absolutely," he said. "I feel useful, and that's a good thing."

"A double murder," Tess said, her voice low. "This gets more and more curious."

Michael shrugged and turned off the light on the bedside table. "That it does..."

CHAPTER NINE

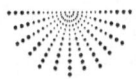

RACHEL STEPPED out onto the street and took in a deep breath, hoping that she'd be allowed to stay at the shelter, because if she wasn't, she'd have to find somewhere else to sleep. She figured she could stay awake all night until dawn, and the maybe she could sleep in some old building if she could find one. She thought that it would be safer to stay awake at night if the Sisters turned her away.

If worse came to worst, she could always sleep in the bus shelter or one of the ATM locations. She'd lie down with her head on her backpack, her hoodie pulled up over her face. Hopefully, no one would bother her, but she had a small pocket knife if she needed to defend herself.

She walked to the front entrance of Sisters of Mercy and opened the door, putting on a neutral expression, not wanting to look too hopeful. The building was warm and smelled of moldy clothing. Inside was a reception area with a desk, a couple of plastic chairs and a coffee table with a collection of magazines. No one was currently sitting behind the desk, but she could hear voices coming from another room. She sat in the chair across from the desk and saw a name plate.

Sister Jean, Night Manager

On the wall behind the desk was a large photo of a group of women in a tropical rainforest, with large floppy hats on their heads and walking sticks in their hands. Large crosses hung on chains around their necks. A couple wore wire rimmed glasses, but otherwise, they were plain looking white women. Beside the photo was a plaque with the saying:

"Suffer the little children to come unto Me." Matthew 19:14.

A large filing cabinet sat at the side of the desk, and a bookshelf to its left. A doorway led to the back of the building. Rachel assumed it led to the bedrooms where the homeless youth slept.

She hoped they had room.

From the doorway came a tall woman dressed in a long black gown, a black scarf on her head.

The sight of her wearing black robes scared Rachel and she suddenly felt panicked.

"I -- I have to go," she said, barely able to speak. She stood up and grabbed her backpack, turning towards the door.

She made it to the front entrance, the bell jingling when she opened the door. The woman called out to Rachel before she could leave.

"Don't go," she said, her voice sounding upset. "Please," the woman said. "Stay. You look like you need a place to sleep tonight. Am I right?"

Rachel stopped, her hand on the door. Did she really want to go back out onto the street? Spend the next eight hours walking, looking for a safe place to stay until she could sleep?

She turned around and faced the woman, whose smile seemed pleasant enough. She looked much older than Rachel's mother, the last time Rachel had seen her. The woman's skin was wrinkled and spotted, and her she wore eyeglasses. But she was smiling. Her expression was gentle.

"Don't run away again," the woman said. "Come and sit. Can I get you something to eat or drink? You look tired and hungry."

Rachel decided to stay, see what it was like.

"Okay," she said and went back, sitting down on the chair across from the desk. She didn't look directly at the woman. Instead, she glanced to the right, keeping the woman in her peripheral vision.

"I'm Sister Jean," the woman said. "What's your name?"

"Rachel."

Sister Jean smiled. "Your last name?"

Rachel shook her head. She hadn't thought that far ahead.

"You don't have a last name, or you don't want to tell me your last name?" Sister Jean smiled.

"Do you have to know my last name?" Rachel asked, a sinking feeling in her stomach.

"No," Sister Jean said. "We don't have to know. But maybe I could help you if I knew."

"Just Rachel. If you knew my real name, it wouldn't help me at all. It would make things worse."

"Okay. Just Rachel," Sister Jean said playfully. "I assume you need a place to sleep and something to eat. You're lucky you came in when you did. One of our usual residents found a foster home and won't be staying with us tonight. Beds here are first come, first serve. You can have her bed."

"Thank you," Rachel said, relief flooding through her.

"Where are you from?" Sister Jean asked. "Or don't you want to tell me that, either?"

Rachel shook her head. "Montana," she said, making it up on the fly. "That's all I'll say."

"Oh, that's a very long ways away, Rachel. Did you just arrive in town now? Or have you been on the streets for a while?"

Rachel nodded. "Tonight. A trucker gave me a ride."

Sister Jean smiled. "Well, you have a place to stay if you need it. Come with me and I'll take you to your room. You can have a shower if you want and wash your clothes in the laundry room. There's a kitchen area you can use. We have coffee and tea and some juice plus water. There's bread and jam in the fridge and some cookies and cereal. When you're finished showering, you can have something to eat."

"Thank you so much," Rachel said, exhaling. "I was afraid I'd have to stay up all night. My mother used to stay here long ago."

She kicked herself mentally, because she'd decided not to mention it, but the woman seemed so nice.

"She did? How long ago?"

"She was here when she was fourteen. She would have been twenty-nine."

"So, that's fifteen years ago. I wasn't here back then. In fact, I don't think anyone was who works here now. We can check our records, see if her file is in our archives if you give me her name."

"Don't bother," Rachel said. "I don't want anyone to know I'm here."

Sister Jean frowned. "Are you in danger?"

"Not now, but if anyone knew I was here, I might be. I

won't tell anyone who I am. Don't ask me. Please." She finally glanced up into Sister Jean's eyes. "Please don't ask."

"I won't," Sister Jean replied with a sigh. She stood and Rachel grabbed her backpack and followed the older woman into the back of the building. They walked down a short hallway past several offices with desks and filing cabinets to a series of rooms in the back of the building, their doors all closed. The room Sister Jean showed her was tiny, with a single bed, a desk and a chest of drawers, but it was far bigger than the closet she used to sleep in. The room had a small window at the end with a heavy curtain. There was a painting of Jesus over the head of the bed, his hands folded in prayer, and on the other wall, a wooden crucifix.

"This is where you'll stay," Sister Jean said. "It's yours for as long as you need it. Since you're so young, you can be a long-term resident if you want. All you have to do is abide by our rules. No visitors. No drugs or alcohol. No fights with the other residents. We have a medical doctor who comes by to check on new residents and we have a psychiatrist who can do an evaluation. They can help you if you need medication. Other than that, there are activities in the common room -- a pool table, ping pong, chess, checkers, cards. We have a flatscreen and cable and a computer with internet. There's WiFi in the building if you have a cell phone."

Rachel shrugged. "I don't have one."

"We have a payphone in the common room, and if you don't have money, we have a house phone, if you want to call home."

Rachel shook her head. "I won't be calling home."

"If you want to call relatives or friends, you could use it."

"I don't have friends. I don't have any relatives I want to call."

Sister Jean sighed. "Okay. Here's the bathroom," she said and took Rachel across the hall to a small white bathroom with a bathtub, shower, toilet and sink. There was a small cabinet with towels and tiny bars of soap and shampoo bottles. "Make sure you put your dirty towels in the laundry basket. Keep your own soap and shampoo. If you need a toothbrush and toothpaste, we usually have a small welcome package we give to new residents, but I haven't had the time to make one up for you. If you need tampons or sanitary napkins, we have those as well."

Rachel went back to her room. "I need a shower first. Then, maybe some toast and tea."

"You can come and talk to me if you need anything else. I'll be out front all night."

"Thank you so much," Rachel said, and she meant it. "You've saved my life."

"Oh, Rachel," Sister Jean said and laid her hand on Rachel's arm. "I'm so sorry that you feel your life was in danger."

Rachel glanced down at the hand on her arm, not liking to be touched. Sister Jean must have sensed Rachel's discomfort for she quickly removed her hand, but her smile remained. "Are you Catholic?"

Rachel shook her head, feeling like she wanted to rub the spot where Sister Jean touched her, but she didn't.

"No. I'm nothing. I don't believe in God. Not anymore."

"I'm sorry that bad things happened to you, Rachel," Sister Jean said, her tone sad. "If you want to talk about anything that happened to you, I'm here to listen."

"I'll be fine." Rachel forced a smile to be polite. What she really wanted was to be left alone and have a shower, wash her clothes and eat toast and tea.

When Sister Jean turned to go, Rachel spoke. "Thank you again for saving my life."

Sister Jean stopped and turned to Rachel. She smiled. "That's why we're here."

Then she left Rachel alone.

CHAPTER TEN

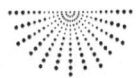

TESS WENT into work the next morning and sat in Kate's office, waiting while she finished a call so they could talk about Craig's case.

When Kate was finally finished, she ended the call and turned to Tess, her hands folded expectantly.

"Well?" she asked, her eyebrows raised. She stared at Tess from over her reading glasses, which were perched on the end of her nose. "What do you think? Is he a killer? I just got a report that police found a body buried near the site where the car was abandoned."

"Yes, Michael told me. He was there and helped the forensic anthropologist at the scene." Tess exhaled. "I don't know about Craig. He seems so broken up..."

"I thought you'd be an expert by now," Kate said, humor in her voice. "After Paradise Hill, sniffing out that Hammond guy."

"Craig seems truly upset about it," Tess said, remembering Craig with his head in his hands. "Seriously destroyed when he learned they found the car abandoned in the mountains. I don't know what he'll do when he learns there was a dead body nearby."

"Could it be an act? I've seen husbands and boyfriends begging on camera for their victims to come home. Frankly I don't believe any of them anymore."

Tess nodded. She had the same thought. Often, killers felt really upset -- that they'd been caught. Not that they'd killed their wife or girlfriend or child. They cried tears for themselves, not their supposed loved ones, whom they so callously murdered and then dumped their bodies in vats of acid or buried in shallow graves or stuffed into huge duffle bags.

Could Craig be one of them?

"Was Craig friends with anyone here at work?" Kate asked. "Was he becoming involved with anyone else? Maybe he wanted Rachel and Sadie out of his life."

"I'm surprised he even ended up with Rachel," Tess said. "He has such a hard time making eye contact. I can't imagine he was cheating on her and wanted to get rid of her and Sadie."

"None of us know what goes on in other people's minds," Kate said with a sigh. "So, you don't think Craig's guilty?"

"No." Tess shook her head. "I don't."

Then, Tess filled Kate in on the contents of her discussion with Craig.

When she was finished, Kate shrugged and leaned back in her chair. "Well, that suggests that someone took Rachel and Sadie. Her comment about her past catching up with her suggests a previous boyfriend or someone she knew before she met Craig. Did she have any friends? Any family? And what about the body being found at the scene? I doubt that's just a coincidence."

"Me, neither. I wonder if whoever did this went there on purpose. Maybe, they wanted the body to be found."

"Like Hammond," Karen replied. "Didn't he set the cabin on fire deliberately so the police would find the body?"

Tess nodded. "Yes. He was bored and wanted to read about the case in the news and listen to people talk about it. He got a thrill knowing they had no idea it was him."

Tess thought about the skeleton of a child discovered in a shallow grave at the site. Had the killer gone there on purpose so police would find the car with the ID still there and the remains of the child? Why?

Was the killer like Eugene and wanted the body to be found so he could enjoy the ensuing publicity?

Then she thought about the fake ID Rachel -- or whomever she was -- used. She couldn't reveal that tidbit of information until the police made it public without getting Michael in trouble.

"I'll see what more I can find from Craig. He agreed to meet with me again. I'll ask him about Rachel's family and friends. She had a really hard life. That much I do know. She was on the streets for several years before meeting Craig."

"So, someone she knew from the streets might be her abductor." Kate sighed and glanced around the office as if looking for some answer. "For Craig's sake, I was hoping she just ran away to escape her past and is living somewhere new, but with the car being abandoned, I guess that's not likely. If she was okay, you'd think she'd know enough to send him a message so he wouldn't worry. Especially if she knew the police were looking for her. He looks guilty as hell, otherwise. If she cared about him, she wouldn't let that stand."

"If he didn't do it, she must be so afraid that she won't even contact them to clear his name." Tess picked up her files and stood. "That is, if she's still alive."

"What's your gut tell you?"

Tess shrugged. She considered it for a moment, searching her feelings and thoughts, trying to get a larger impression from everything she knew, but she had nothing.

"I can't tell," she said truthfully. "My instinct is to say Craig's innocent, but I don't trust myself to be able to judge. I went to the gun store with Eugene and he helped me buy a gun. I went out to the firing range with him. I went with him in his car, alone, Kate. Who the hell am I to evaluate whether someone is a killer?"

"But you eventually suspected him."

"Only after Kirsten told me that she thought he was empty inside," Tess admitted. "That she thought it was all an act -- his good husband and father routine. It was only then that I started to suspect him. Even Michael didn't suspect him. He just didn't like him, but Michael never thought he was a suspect or was the killer. We often can't see those we love or are friends clearly. Our emotions get in the way."

"And your emotions about Craig?"

Tess shrugged. "I like him. He's on the Autism spectrum, which doesn't mean he couldn't be a killer, but I can't see him having a girlfriend on the side and wanting to get rid of Rachel and Sadie. If anything, he might have wanted to stop them from leaving." Tess glanced at Kate. "Maybe that's the story. Maybe Rachel wanted to leave Craig and he couldn't face it. If he did it, that might be the reason."

"There you go," Kate said and pointed at Tess. "See if that story fits. Talk to someone who knows Rachel. See if she was unhappy with Craig and wanted to leave."

"I guess you're right. I've read too many stories of men who couldn't face their girlfriend breaking up with them and killed them in anger to not keep that option open."

"Sounds like a plan," Kate said and then turned to her laptop.

Tess went to the door and before she left, she turned back. "Did you hire Craig?"

"I did," Kate said. "He's a wonderful photographer. Can't look you in the eye, but his photographs are fantastic. I was happy to have him on staff."

Tess nodded. "He is good. I hope he's innocent."

"Me, too. Tell him if he needs time off, he can take it."

"I will," Tess said and left the office.

She went back to her own desk in the newsroom and sat down, spreading her file open and reading over the notes she'd made about the case. She glanced around at her fellow reporters and writers. Craig hadn't really been overly friendly with anyone besides Tess and Jenna. He kept to himself although he did attend the Christmas party and other staff functions despite his stutter and awkwardness.

Other than Jenna, who seemed to know everything about everyone at the *Sentinel*, she'd have to talk to Craig himself if she wanted any more background on Rachel. She saw Jenna enter the newsroom from the coffee room and went right over, sitting on the chair beside Jenna's desk.

"Hey, can I talk with you about Craig?" she asked.

"Sure can," Jenna said and sat at her desk, fresh cup of

coffee in hand. "What do you want to know? I don't know him really well, but he confided in me somewhat."

Tess wasn't surprised to learn it, because Jenna was both a talker and a listener. She talked to everyone. Her eyes seemed to light up when you agreed to talk about yourself to her. Like info about her co-workers was gold. If anyone could get Craig to open up, it was Jenna.

"Yes," Jenna said. "He used me as a kind of confessor, I suppose. A sounding board. I'm a good listener I guess." Jenna smiled brightly; her apple-red cheeks dimpling.

Tess settled in, realizing she should have come to Jenna sooner, because apparently, Craig did.

"Were they happy?" Tess asked. "As a couple?"

"Craig was," Jenna replied. "That much I do know. He said he had a ready-made family with Rachel and Sadie. He liked being a foster father. He took Rachel and Sadie fishing and camping. They did a lot of hiking in the mountains. He would take along his camera and take pictures that he'd post on those stock photo sites to make money. I think he was really happy. I don't know about Rachel. She always seemed afraid of the world, when I met her. She'd stand close to Craig, like he was a big strong man, protecting her and her daughter. The girl, Sadie, was so small. Like Rachel."

"What was Rachel like? Did she tell you about her job working at the bar on Aurora?"

"Yes. Mickey's Bar and Grill. It's a real dive, but I guess Mickey helped her out when she was on the streets and she wanted to work with him once she was clean. He's a real humanitarian, according to Rachel. A former biker, who was reformed. Looks after the street kids and prostitutes. Even on weekends, he has this semi-truck with a portable shower, washing machine and dryer. He has a food truck with hot soup and bread he takes around to the homeless so they can eat and get clean. They go out every Friday and Saturday night."

"Thanks," Tess said and wrote that down in her notebook. "I'll check it out. Did you know anything else about her? You're a good listener, like you say. Did she tell you anything about her past? Her family?"

Jenna frowned. "No, she was pretty quiet, the few times we met. Believe it or not, Craig did most of the talking. He seemed to speak for her, if you can believe it, so maybe she was as quiet as him. Shy. I never went to Mickey's. It has a decidedly more street clientele, if you know what I mean."

Tess nodded, remembering seeing Mickey's when driving along Aurora Avenue, Seattle's notorious prostitution track. Tess didn't relish going there to interview the owner and workers, but Mickey sounded like a decent man. A lot of Seattle's prostitutes moved back to Aurora Avenue after most of the internet websites they used to connect with potential Johns, like *Backpage*, were shut down.

Instead of working along Pacific Highway South, a notorious part of town where the old Westside Street Mobb gang operated, the prostitutes moved back north and started walking the old streets where girls were pimped. Often, girls were lured into the sex trade on the promise of friendship or romance with some guy they met on the internet, only to be taken to a hotel room and repeatedly raped, drugged and put into service. These were girls who were already experienced in sexual abuse. In fact, up to sixty percent of all prostitutes experienced child sexual abuse in their homes or communities before entering the sex trade, and up to ninety percent had some kind of trauma arising from child abuse and neglect.

They were victims who were re-victimized once they tried to run away from their abusers.

It made Tess sick. Her friend, Lisa, had been brought into that world after she was abducted. Tess couldn't help but want to find her, see if she was still alive, and even rescue her if she could. She understood that Lisa might not want to be found, but that didn't stop Tess from wanting it.

She thanked Jenna for the information and went back to her own desk. She searched for the phone number for Mickey's and called, hoping to speak with Mickey himself. A female voice answered on the fourth ring. Tess asked to speak with Mickey and waited while the young woman went to find him and put him on the line. After Tess introduced herself, she said she knew Rachel and wanted to come there and speak with him.

"You work for the *Sentinel?*" he asked, sounding hesitant.

"Yes," Tess replied. "I work with Craig Lang, Rachel's boyfriend. I wanted to come and talk to people who know her, hoping that we might be able to get some leads on her possible whereabouts."

She heard Mickey sigh heavily. "I already spoke with the cops," he said. "I told them that Rachel said she and Sadie were going away for a short vacation and she needed time off. That's it. I don't know where they were going. I just covered her shifts."

"I understand. I'm writing a series of articles on missing and murdered women and girls in Washington State. I would appreciate some background on Rachel. I interviewed her for an article once, and know she used to live on the streets. She told me that you helped her get clean and that she worked for you as a waitress at the bar."

"She was a success story," Mickey said. "Sure. Come down tonight. I'll be bartending during happy hour, so I won't be able to talk with you until it's over and my relief bartender comes in."

"Thanks," Tess said and ended the call. "I'll see you tonight after seven."

She ended the call and sat back, glad to be able to meet with Mickey. Maybe she'd ask Michael to come along and sit in the back somewhere, so she didn't feel too alone in a very bad part of town.

CHAPTER ELEVEN

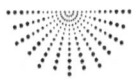

Michael stood in front of his whiteboard at the DA's offices, working on timelines.

"Tell me what you got," Nick said.

"Not much," Michael said and went over to a wall of photos and maps. He recounted the case so far. "At first, Local police thought it might be auto theft, the thief abandoning the vehicle, but it wasn't reported missing. Besides, there was a woman's purse in the front seat with all her ID and suitcases in the back. When they contacted the owner of the vehicle, he said it was his car and was used by his girlfriend. He said that she told him she was leaving, and wanted to move somewhere else, so that was why he didn't report her missing."

"Likely story," Nick said.

Michael glanced at the wall and checked out the pictures. One was of a young woman with pale hair and light blue eyes. She was tiny, thin, and looked frail. Delicate. The other was of a child who looked very similar to her. Fair hair and light eyes. Wearing a school uniform. The other pictures were of a vehicle with the door open and an arrow marking a dried blood spot on the steering column near the ignition.

"Looks like she and her kid were leaving town, and something happened. There's dried blood in the car."

"Jeez," Nick said, shaking his head. "You think the boyfriend followed her and killed her and the daughter? Was the girl his?"

"Not his. They met a few years ago and had been living together until she left. The boyfriend said she had a troubled past that she didn't like to talk about, so he didn't ask."

"Yeah right," Nick said. He shook his head. "Convenient story, if you ask me," Nick replied.

"I spoke with the detective who interviewed him. He was broken up, crying like a baby."

"Why didn't he report her missing sooner if he was so upset? Didn't they text or call each other in that entire week? If you ask me, what likely happened was that she told him to fuck off and he couldn't take it, killed her and who knows what he did with the girl."

Michael felt his gut knot at the thought that another woman and girl had been murdered.

"What's next?" Nick asked.

"Police are interviewing his family and friends. We have yet to identify the woman. Seems she used a fake ID to work her job at a local bar and was paid under the table, according to the boyfriend. She said she was from out of town and had been on the streets for a while after she gave birth to her daughter. That the father wasn't involved in their lives and never had been. The boyfriend said he knew she had a rough life and didn't want to push."

"What's your impression of the boyfriend? Do you like him

for it?" Nick asked.

Michael shrugged. "I watched the interview tape. He's a strange guy. Almost autistic, if you ask me. Doesn't look people in the eye. Stutters a lot. Cries a hell of a lot." He shook his head. "Something's not right there, but whether he killed her or not, I don't know. The woman is attractive, and the boyfriend is kind of forgettable, if you know what I mean. Tall. Skinny. Pasty-looking guy."

Nick pursed his lips as they both examined the photo of the boyfriend. Craig was forgettable. He was fair, plain and on the skinny side.

"What does he do for a living?" Nick asked.

"He's a photographer. Does freelance work and works for the *Sentinel* now and then."

"The *Sentinel*? Your lady Tess might know him, if that's the case." Nick slapped him on the good shoulder. "See? You might be more useful that we all thought."

Michael laughed. It was good to be working for the DA, even if he was going to be just a pencil pusher.

Later that morning, Tess texted him, asking him if he would go with her to Mickey's Bar and Grill on Aurora Avenue while she interviewed the owner for her article on the missing persons case.

TESS: *Mickey hired Rachel and helped her get off the street. If anyone knows her, he does. We can try to track down more people through him.*

MICHAEL: *You're a natural at this. Sure, I'd be happy to go with you. Does Mickey know I'm coming?*

TESS: *Maybe you should just sit at a table and let me meet* with him alone. He might not like it that former FBI Special Agent and current investigator for the DA's office is asking him questions.

MICHAEL: My thoughts exactly. We can drive in separate vehicles and I can go in first, get a table and then you can arrive. No one needs to know we're together.

TESS: Thanks. I'd rather not go to the bar at night alone.

MICHAEL: Don't mention it. Luckily, I'm pretty scruffy looking so I'm sure I won't set off anyone's radar as being police.

TESS: You do need a haircut. Is your new boss letting you look disreputable for a reason?

MICHAEL: He's cutting me a lot of slack. I'm happy to take it. I'll see you when you get home.

TESS: Bye.

When he finished work, he popped into Nick's office, to let him know he was going with Tess to interview Rachel's employer.

Nick sat behind his desk, an expectant expression on his face.

"The police have already spoken with Mickey, but maybe Tess can get something interesting out of him that they can't. He was pretty tight-lipped with the police, probably seeing them as the enemy. Tess may be more sympathetic."

"Hope so. I'm going as backup in case she needs me. I'll go early and sit by myself, have a beer."

"Good plan. Keep me in the loop."

Michael left the building after cleaning off his desk. He drove home, arriving in time to have a shower and change into some casual clothes. He stared into the bathroom mirror, noting how his hair had grown below his collar and fell into his eyes, his jaw a little scruffy. When he hired Michael, Nick said it was good he blended in with the ordinary people and to not look too professional. Most of all, he didn't want Michael to look like a cop. Still, it was time for a haircut and shave, but that night, his slightly disreputable appearance might help him blend in with the bar's usual clientele.

Tess arrived home a while later and sat with Michael for a while, talking over the day's events. They decided to go to Mickey's first, so Tess could speak with him about Rachel, and then go out for a late supper. Michael needed to unwind after his day, and he was certain Tess felt the same. They could talk about the interview over their meal and then come home and hit the sack.

"Let's go," Tess said and pulled on her jacket and boots.

The drive to the bar took them from their apartment in Westlake to Mickey's on Aurora. Once there, Michael parked his Jeep on the street, and watched as Tess parked her car farther up and across the street from him. They had already agreed on a signal that Tess would use when she was ready to leave. She'd tuck her hair behind one ear as a sign that she was finished with the interview and would be leaving in five minutes after using the restroom. Michael would leave the bar and go to his car, waiting for her to get into hers. That way, he'd be sure to see if anyone followed her out. He didn't expect trouble, but all the same, he didn't want Tess to take any unnecessary risks.

The neighborhood was populated by several seedy motels and side streets where the street prostitutes walked, trying to pick up customers. The bar was filled with patrons on a weekday night, watching sports on several big screen televisions. Michael took a seat at the bar and ordered a beer, intending to watch the game and keep an eye on Tess from his position. The wall behind the bar was mirrored so he could watch what was happening in the entire bar. Some noisy Country music played on the sound system, grating on Michael's nerves. It was too loud and made it hard to relax, but he tried to shut it out and focus on his beer and on what Tess was doing. She walked in about five minutes after him and went down to the far end of the bar, speaking with the bartender.

Michael tried to appear uninterested but couldn't help but watch Tess out of the corner of his eye. She gestured to the wall and the bartender left his station, heading back to the kitchen, through a swinging door. On her part, Tess took a seat at a table against the far wall and waited for Mickey to join her. She removed her jacket and settled into her seat, glancing his way for only a moment, rubbing the end of her nose as a sign she saw him, and all was okay. He smiled to himself and took a drink of his beer. She was good at this clandestine stuff.

In about five minutes, out walked a large silver-haired and bearded man with tribal tattoos covering his arms and running up the side of his neck. His hair was long and thin on top, and he sported a very rebellious and dangerous demeanor. He was wearing a blue t-shirt and a leather vest over top, a pair of jeans and cowboy boots. Michael noted that his belt had a thick silver buckle visible under a big beer gut, the buckle reminiscent of a rodeo rider. The man looked like he belonged in a biker gang.

Mickey went right over to Tess and leaned forward, extending his hand to her in welcome. They spoke for a moment and then Mickey sat down, gesturing to the nearby waitress to come and take their order. Michael wished he had a mic on Tess so he could listen in, but that was out of the question. He was there to ensure she was safe and that she left in one piece with no one tailing her. She'd fill him in on what they talked about at the restaurant.

Michael amused himself while he waited for Tess to finish the interview by watching the clientele and imagining who they were and what their lives were like. One woman sat down at the bar a few stools down from him, slightly older, maybe early forties, her blonde hair puffed up, lots of makeup, and a pretty revealing blouse that showed some cleavage. She glanced over in Michael's direction and he wondered if she was a 'working girl', hoping she didn't get the wrong idea about him. He tried to ignore her. The last thing he needed was for some prostitute to hit on him while he waited for Tess.

While he was waiting, he got a call from Nick.

"Got the blood results back from the vehicle," Nick said, his voice sounding enthusiastic. "You're never going to guess whose it is..."

Michael rubbed his forehead and frowned. "Not Craig's?"

"Bingo."

"*Crap*," Michael said, a sinking feeling in his gut. "That's too bad. He's a friend of my partner. She's not going to be happy about it when I tell her."

"Well, it's not likely that his blood would be on the steering column near the ignition for any reason, is there?"

"Not likely," Michael replied. "I can't imagine that there's a single drop of *my* blood in my Jeep and I've had it for five years."

"My thoughts exactly," Nick replied. "No blood in mine either." Nick sighed heavily. "But that's all we got. Prosecutor doesn't think it's enough to arrest him. We're going to get a search warrant for his apartment, however. Care to come along? We're going to execute it tomorrow, bright and early. Just in case he decides to delete any incriminating evidence from his computer."

"I'll be happy to come along," Michael said.

They spoke for another few moments about the skeletal remains found near the vehicle, and how Dr. Keller was still studying the bones.

"Who the hell do you expect it is?" Nick asked, sounding perplexed. "There's no way it was a coincidence that the body was buried where the car was abandoned."

"That's what Dr. Keller said. Whoever took her there knew the body was there. Either that, or she knew. If she knew, that raises all kinds of interesting possibilities."

"That it does," Nick said. "This case gets more interesting by the minute.

"I'll stop by the office on my way home," Michael replied. "We're going to have a quick meal first, but I should be there in an hour or so. We can talk then."

"Sounds good," Nick replied.

Michael ended the call and watched Tess and Mickey in the mirror, speaking at the table across from the bar. Mickey was a large man, with an ample gut and big biceps. He looked like he could be a bouncer at a club or an enforcer with a motorcycle gang. Yet, he did a lot of charity work with the homeless and street workers. He probably had a hard life himself and understood what the people who lived on the streets needed.

Michael made a mental note to check into Mickey's history. It might prove nothing more than interesting background, but you never knew where a tidbit of information could lead.

CHAPTER TWELVE

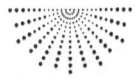

FOR THE FIRST FEW WEEKS, Rachel stayed pretty much to herself, keeping clean, bathing daily, the bathtub a luxury she never had back home. She always came late to meal time and sat alone, eating her toast and hot tea, or whatever was being served, by herself. The nuns tried to get her to socialize with the other girls, but she stayed aloof. The only other girl she'd ever really known besides her mother was Sadie, and Sadie was dead.

The first sign that she was pregnant was her missed period, two weeks after she came to stay at the Sisters, but she'd missed it before due to poor nutrition. The only good thing about her home had been the huge library her father had, which she had been able to use, and all the medical reference texts her father bought. He'd home schooled her, so she'd never had friends, and he was trained in veterinary technology, so she never saw a doctor. When she'd been cut or sick, he doctored her as best he could. He sometimes used homeopathic remedies, which she thought were just hokum, as her grandfather called it.

Not that her grandfather was any sort of advocate for her. He was old and sick, widowed years earlier, and he only came to visit occasionally.

So, she missed her period, and while she had before, this time was different. This time, her breasts hurt, and she felt sick every morning. She spent time on the shelter's computer, searching the internet for information on pregnancy and the various signs used to tell. If she'd had any money, she would have gone to the drug store and bought a pregnancy test. She knew about those, because her father had tested her before when she'd missed her period. Most of the time, the men who abused her used condoms, but sometimes, her father didn't. She figured the baby was his. That meant she was giving birth to her own brother or sister.

Rachel read up on babies born of incest, worried that there would be something wrong with it due to inbreeding, but the chance was pretty small.

She knew she was too young to have a baby, as her mother was before her, but this time, Rachel was determined not to let what happened to her and Sadie happen to this baby. Her mother had gone right back into the frying pan from the fire, moving in with her father, but Rachel wouldn't ever become dependent on some man. She was going to get a job and raise this baby right. She'd stay single the rest of her life or she'd find a good man who wouldn't abuse her and her child.

One day, when her morning sickness had been especially bad and she slept in, running to the bathroom to dry-heave, she had to finally tell Sister Jean that she was probably pregnant.

"Oh, dear," Sister Jean said and hugged Rachel. Rachel didn't cringe at the woman's touch. Over the past few weeks, she had grown used to all the nuns and their penchant for touching. Besides, she needed a hug when she realized she was pregnant. She wanted to cry, but she'd do that when she was alone. "A baby? We haven't had a baby around here for a while. Not since Heather. You need prenatal vitamins. I'll call Dr. Alvi to come and check you.

"Thank you," Rachel said.

"That's what we're here for, sweetheart," Sister Jean said, stroking Rachel's face. "We're here to help you find your way."

Rachel was grateful. She was glad the one thing of use her mother had told her was about Sisters of Mercy Shelter in Seattle. Where her mother lived when she was a girl. Where Rachel's baby would be born. But there, the curse on women in her family would end. Rachel would see to it.

She'd do everything in her power to never submit to a man again, and to see her children safe. No matter what.

Dr. Alvi was from somewhere in the Middle East. She was really nice, fine boned and beautiful in her dark skin.

"Are you Muslim?" Rachel asked, surprised that the Sisters hired a Muslim doctor to care for the girls.

"No, I'm Catholic, born in Islamabad, Pakistan, and I worked for Sister Theresa's charity in New Delhi. I trained in London, England. Now, I'm here."

Rachel smiled, amazed that she was so young.

"You've been to so many places. I've only ever been to Seattle," Rachel said in awe.

"Sister Jean said you were from Montana," Dr. Alvi said softly.

"I mean Montana and Seattle," Rachel said quickly.

"You have your entire life ahead of you," Dr. Alvi said. "Travel when you can. It's a big world."

"I will," Rachel said, dreaming of traveling to Scotland where Harry Potter took place. She'd survived the ordeal of her life by losing herself in books, imagining having magical powers and magical tools so she could become invisible, so she could stop bad men from doing their bad things to her and Sadie.

Dr. Alvi made her undress completely and put on a gown, and Rachel balked.

"Do I have to?" she asked in a whispered voice, not wanting anyone to see her scars.

"I need to examine you, make sure you're healthy," Dr. Alvi replied with a smile.

Rachel reluctantly complied, lying on the examination table in the medical treatment room. She held her breath when Dr. Alvi pulled aside the gown and saw the scars -- tiny stab wounds on her breasts and stomach that were still healing.

"Oh, my dear girl," Dr. Alvi said in a hushed voice. "Who did this to you?"

She stared into Rachel's eyes, taking her hand.

Immediately, Rachel's eyes filled with tears and she let Dr. Alvi continue to hold her hand.

"A man," she said, sobbing out loud, not wanting to admit it was her father.

"What man?"

"Just a man," Rachel replied, refusing to say who.

"You poor thing," Dr. Alvi said and stroked Rachel's hand. "Did he stitch you up as well? A few of these are infected and will need to be cleaned. Maybe redone."

Rachel nodded, and lay still, her eyes squeezed shut while

Dr. Alvi examined her from head to foot, clicking her tongue whenever she found some new bruise or old cut.

She gasped when she saw the scars from the handcuffs and ankle cuffs.

"You poor child," Dr. Alvi said while she rubbed Rachel's ankles and wrists. "You simply must tell the Sisters who did this to you, so they don't do this to anyone else."

"One day, I will," Rachel said, wiping her eyes. "Not yet. Not until I'm safe."

Dr. Alvi shook her head in disapproval. "When will that be? When will you be safe? Not until the person or persons who did this to you are behind bars."

"Not yet. One day, I will. I promise."

Dr. Alvi exhaled in frustration but continued her exam. The pelvic exam was the most uncomfortable, but Dr. Alvi was gentle.

When she was finished, Dr. Alvi also took some vials of blood from a vein in Rachel's arm and made Rachel pee into a cup.

"We'll check your blood and urine, make sure everything's okay. I'll be by once a month to do a pre-natal check. When the time comes, I'll deliver your baby, if you're still here."

"I'm not leaving," Rachel said and finished dressing. "I like it here."

"It's a good place," Dr. Alvi said and ran her hand over Rachel's hair. "The nuns will take very good care of you, body and soul."

"They do." Rachel smiled at Dr. Alvi.

Rachel went back to her room and lay on the bed, not wanting to face anyone after the examination. She switched off the light and turned to face the wall, her eyes tightly closed.

She was probably eight weeks pregnant and would deliver a baby in thirty-two weeks, based on the date of her last period.

There was only one man who could be the father. There was only one man who did not use a condom.

She would be a mother to her own half-sister or brother.

She would not cry.

She *wouldn't*.

Sister Jean knocked at her door a while later and popped her head inside the darkened room.

"Are you all right, sweetheart?"

Rachel inhaled, debating whether to tell the truth or lie.

"I'll be okay," she said finally. "Just upset is all."

Sister Jean came inside and sat on the chair beside the bed. She took Rachel's hand and stroked it. "I don't want you to worry about anything. We'll take care of you. This is what we do best. We'll make sure you get the best food. We'll make sure you get good medical care. When your child is born, we'll work with authorities to find you a good home to live in, so you can go to school and your child will be provided for."

Rachel pulled her hand out of Sister Jean's and sat up. She felt bad but she did not want to go and live with another family. "Can't I stay here? I don't want to go live with a foster family."

"You can stay here as long as you want. I just thought you'd like to live in a home, with a family who can help you raise your child."

"I should give it up for adoption," Rachel said quietly. "Maybe it will have a better chance at life than I ever did."

"If you want," Sister Jean said, but Rachel could swear she

heard a note of disapproval in the nun's voice. "Or you could keep the child and raise it the way you know it should be raised -- the way you should have been raised."

Rachel shook her head. "I don't know what that even means. How should I have been raised? I never went to school. I never had friends except..."

She shut up at that, not wanting to mention Sadie. That would raise all kinds of issues and could lead Sister Jean to finding out who Rachel really was.

Above all else, Rachel did not want that.

"Except who?" Sister Jean asked, her eyebrows raised. "Don't you have one friend in the world?"

"I did have one, but she died."

Sister Jean's face fell. "Oh, I'm so sorry. Was she a street kid, too?"

"No, she's just dead."

"You must feel very lonely," Sister Jean said. "Isn't there someone in your family we can contact? An aunt? A cousin? Surely, someone must be missing you and want to know you're all right and especially now that you're having a baby."

"No. There's no one." Rachel sighed, her breath shaking with emotion.

No one could know who she really was, or contact her family, because that would mean her death. If her father found her, he'd kill her.

He promised to if she ever tried to run away or tell anyone what went on in the Family.

He had guns. Lots of them. And knives. He knew people everywhere. People who would bring her back to him.

He promised her that.

Once, when she had tried to run, he held her down, one

hand around her throat, and the other pointing a finger at her, poking it against her forehead over and over like it was a gun.

"No one even knows you exist. Do you realize that? There are no records of your birth. I delivered you and Sadie so there are no birth certificates in your name. If you ever run away, if you ever tell anyone anything about me, I'll kill you. Like I killed Sadie. And your mother."

She had been a slave, and that was that. When she left, she knew she had to leave for good. She had to escape completely, take on a new life somewhere else where he couldn't find her.

Somewhere new.

CHAPTER THIRTEEN

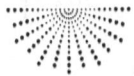

WHEN MICKEY WALKED UP, Tess looked him over, trying not to show any response to the way he appeared.

He was a big man, heavy-set, with huge arms and a big gut sticking out over his belt buckle, which was silver and thick. He reminded Tess of an old grey-haired motorcycle gang member, with tattoos covering his arms and longish silver hair in braids.

He was scary, in other words.

"Tess McClintock?" he said in a soft voice, his hand extended.

Tess stood and they shook. "Nice to meet you. Thanks for agreeing to talk with me."

"My pleasure," he said and sat on the chair beside her. "You want to know about Rachel. Rachel and little Sadie."

"Yes," Tess replied and took out her recorder. "Do you mind if I record our conversation? It ensures I don't misquote you or anything."

"I'd rather you didn't quote me at all," Mickey said, a dark expression on his face. "Don't need any more bad press than we're already getting."

"I understand," Tess said. "I promise I won't quote you or mention Mickey's Bar and Grill except what's already been put out there in the news. This is all just background to my piece on the case. I'm friends with Craig and Rachel and so I'm just looking for as much detail as I can get. Paint a picture of her as you knew her."

Mickey nodded. "Okay. As long as you don't quote me or mention my name in the article. You can use what I say as background. Don't need any more bad press."

Tess turned on the recorder and placed it on the table between them. She cleared her throat and began her questions.

"Tell me about Rachel. When did you first meet her?"

"Rachel?" he said and settled back, staring off into space like he was remembering. "I think the first time I saw her was on one of my runs with the truck, back in 2014. I parked under the bridge on Aurora. She was with a group of kids, homeless, runaways, and came to the truck for some food. I tried to talk her into going into the foster care system, but she said she had a family in town through the Catholic Charity but wasn't living at home at the moment. Said she didn't trust the government-run foster care system." He laughed. "Which is ironic, when you think that I used to be the biggest hater of the government around but there I was, trying to get her to go into state care."

Tess raised her eyebrows at that. "So, you think the state's good for something," she said with a slight grin.

"Yeah, even I have to admit that kids shouldn't be living on the streets and should be in some kind of care. Foster home, communal living arrangement. Especially a fifteen or sixteen-

THE GIRL WHO RAN AWAY

year old girl with a child. I hated to think that she was maybe turning tricks at her age to support her habit."

"She was in foster care, though, right? A Catholic charity."

"She was, and things were good for a while. A couple of sisters who lived together took her in. They helped raise Sadie while Rachel tried to go back to finish her high school. Things looked like they were doing okay. But Rachel," he said and shook his head, "she started running around with a crowd from the streets. I saw her around when I took the truck out, and was afraid she'd lose Sadie, but she eventually got cleaned up. She was lucky that Candace and Leslie were so good to her, looked after Sadie while she went wild."

"What do you know about her background?"

Mickey made a face, shrugged. "Not much. She was pretty tight-lipped about her family back in Montana. Said her father was one of those sovereign citizen types. They lived off the grid and were prepared for World War Three. The kids were home-schooled. Pretty secretive, from what I could find out when I did some research on sovereign citizens in Montana."

"Do you know the names of her parents?"

Mickey shook his head. He rubbed his chin and glanced at Tess like he was sizing her up. "She didn't want anyone to know. Said that she'd be in danger if she ever revealed it. No matter what anyone did, she wouldn't crack and tell us where she came from, who her parents were. She just told us her name was Rachel. Rachel Martin from Montana. She had some ID with that name. I tried calling up Martins in Montana, but there's a shitload of them and I don't have the time, frankly. I guess neither did Candace and Leslie or the folks at the Catholic charity who sponsored her. They just wanted to help her which is what I felt. She needed help. We were there to offer it. That was good enough for me."

"Were Leslie and Candace nuns or something?"

He shook his head. "Candace was, for a while, I guess. She taught at the local public school and neither of them ever married or had their own families, so they did a lot of fostering. Girls who were pregnant. That sort of thing."

Tess nodded in understanding. They were probably anti-abortion advocates who took in pregnant girls and helped them when they kept their babies.

"Were they still close recently? Did she keep up contact with Candace and Leslie?"

"Far as I know," Mickey said. "I heard Rachel talk about her and Sadie having turkey dinner at Candace's house. Craig went, too."

"So, as far as you knew, there were no problems between Rachel and Craig?"

"Not that I knew. Based on what I saw and heard, they were happy as larks. I knew she was going on a trip, take some time off, but not moving away like Craig said to the police."

"What do you think happened?" Tess asked, hoping to get Mickey's gut instinct on the case. "You met Craig. You saw them together. Do you think he could have hurt her and Sadie?"

Mickey shook his head. "If he did, it was completely out of character. He was pretty shy. Quiet. He seemed pretty gentle." He was quiet for a moment, glancing around the bar. "I've seen people go from gentle to violent though. I was in the army a few years. I've seen people become killers. It happens. Give a man the right motive, and he'll kill. Right or wrong, we can all kill, if we're in the right circumstances."

"I know that as a fact," Tess said, thinking about her own experience with Eugene. Only a few very determined pacifists would resist defending themselves. Most people would lash out if it was to protect themselves. Some to protect their sense of self. Tess believed that was what happened when men killed their intimate partners and children -- to protect their ego. They were fragile and couldn't withstand the hit to their sense of self-worth when their partner threatened to leave or did leave.

"Can you give me the full names of Rachel's foster parents? I'd like to speak with them, if possible."

"Sure," he said and rubbed his chin. "I'll look it up in my records and send it to you in a text when I get home. Right now, I have to pick up supplies for the truck. We go out on a run Friday and Saturday nights so the kids can get some food into them and maybe have a shower."

"That's a really great service you provide," Tess said softly. "I'm sure the kids really appreciate it."

"They do," Mickey said and stood. "I know it."

"You told police that Rachel had asked for some time off because she was going on a short trip. Did she tell you where?"

"No, just a drive to get away for a while. I didn't ask. All I cared about was filling her shifts, frankly."

He shrugged.

Tess looked over her questions and then exhaled.

"Thanks for speaking with me," she said and tucked a lock of hair behind her ear, giving Michael the signal that she was done and would be heading to the washroom before she left. "Can you tell me where the washroom is? I need to visit before I leave."

"Sure thing," Mickey said and pointed an alcove in the middle of the room. "Behind that divider is the ladies."

She shook Mickey's hand and went to the washroom, using the facilities to give Michael time to pay his bar tab and leave, get into his vehicle and watch, just in case someone followed her. Aurora Avenue was notorious in Seattle for pimps hitting on any new girl or woman they saw on the street or in the bars.

She spent about five minutes in the washroom, and then left, checking out the other patrons on her way out to ensure Michael got her signal and was already gone. Luckily, he was so she went right out to her vehicle and got inside. She glanced around and saw his Jeep still across the street where she last saw it and felt a sense of relief.

When she drove off, she watched and saw that he pulled out and did a U-turn when she was a block away. He followed her all the way to the restaurant, keeping a couple of cars between them, just to be safe. She drove until she found a parking spot in the lot behind the restaurant. She waited until Michael also drove into the lot and parked in a slot beside hers.

He got out and came over, opening the door for her.

"How'd it go?"

"Fine," she replied and locked her vehicle before putting her arms around his neck. He pulled her against his body, and they kissed warmly. "I was glad to see you there, to be truthful. Mickey seems like a really nice guy, but there were some pretty scary looking people in the bar. Biker types."

"Yeah, I noticed. Luckily, I look just disreputable enough to pass as one of the usual patrons."

Tess smiled and brushed a hank of his hair off his brow. "You do. You look a bit roguish."

He raised his eyebrows suggestively. "Oh, I am. The clean-cut all-American former FBI Special Agent persona is just an act."

"I knew it," she replied, and they walked hand in hand to the restaurant entrance. They waited for the hostess to seat them and then, once they were alone and the waitress had taken their drink orders, they held hands across the table.

"So, tell me what you gleaned from your interview with Mickey? Anything useful?"

Tess nodded. "I got the name of her foster mothers and Mickey's going to send me their contact info so I can call and see if I can arrange an interview. I imagine the cops have already spoken with them, right?"

"I'll have to check and see where they are in the investigation. Usually in a missing persons case, we speak with as many family members and friends as we can, so we can get a picture of the missing person's life. There are often hints about trouble in their personal or professional life which may provide evidence of motive, if there's foul play suspected."

"Mickey thought Craig seemed harmless, but he admitted that anyone could turn violent, given the right incentive. What he did say suggests she escaped a bad family life in Montana, if that's where she's really from. He knew she had fake ID, but neither he nor the Catholic charity cared. They just wanted to help her out during her pregnancy, so no one ever pushed her for her real identity. Until we have that, how can we know what threats she might have been facing? Craig said she was afraid of her past catching up with her and needed to leave because of it. I wonder if someone from her family or her past found out she was in Seattle and was coming for her."

"You'd think she'd have told Craig the truth about the threat, if she was really afraid."

Tess nodded. Why hadn't she told Craig about whatever threat from her past she was afraid had caught up with her?

"Oh, I have something," Michael said and made a face of pain. "You're not going to like it."

"What?" Tess asked, a surge of adrenaline in her.

Michael exhaled. "The blood from the car came back as belonging to Craig."

Tess grimaced. "His blood?"

Michael nodded. "Yes."

"What does that mean?" She stared off into the distance, her mind working furiously. "He could have hurt himself when working on the car," she offered. "Changing a tire -- who knows what -- and some of his blood was left on the steering column. It doesn't mean he killed Rachel and Sadie."

"No, it doesn't, but I can bet you a thousand dollars that there's none of your blood in your car, nor is there any of my blood in my car. It's suspicious. Not to mention that the car was abandoned near a shallow grave with the partially-exposed skeletal remains of a child and contained the handbag and belongings of two missing people, both of whom lived with him."

Tess sighed. "You're right. It does look bad. So, what else is on your agenda?" she asked, wondering what he was working on.

"Just the double murder upstate," he replied.

"Double murder?"

"Yes. Cabin east of Deming. Two victims, both men in their forties. Both murdered. One man was killed and dumped in the outhouse pit, head first. The ME thinks the man was still alive and likely smothered in the shit."

Tess cringed at the image. "Oh God. That's horrible."

"It appears that the men were making some pornographic material."

"What?" That piqued Tess's interest. Not that it was shocking that men were making porno in a cabin up north, but the fact that they had been murdered. There were many reasons for them to be killed -- people in the porn business were often also involved in other illegal activities. Drugs. Prostitution. Organized crime.

"Yes, there were several camera tripods and camera equipment in the bedroom. The cameras had their memory cards removed so we have no idea what they were recording, but of course, I'm suspicious right away. Especially since there were children's toys found in the cabin."

"Who are the men? Any IDs?"

"No ID. The cabin was broken into. There's no record of anyone renting it," Michael replied. "We'll have to rely on DNA or dental records to ID them. But if they were making porn, I'm curious as to whether they were linked into the ring we uncovered in Paradise Hill. There were links to the Bellingham area from what I read but Hammond had his tentacles all across the state."

Tess bit her lip as a surge of adrenaline went through her. Two murdered men who might have been making porn from an area connected to the ring operating out of Paradise Hill. A missing woman and her eight-year old daughter, gone without a trace, their vehicle left near a set of skeletal remains. The woman herself a runaway, who spent time on the streets.

"That just sent a shiver down my spine," she said quietly.

"I thought that would interest you. I'm trying really hard to stay totally objective about things, but I can't help but jump to conclusions."

"Remember what you told me," Tess said. "Withhold judgement until you have more evidence. Don't draw conclusions too soon or you'll cut off possible avenues of investigation. Keep an open mind..."

"I know. I'm trying, but my mind goes to certain places," Michael replied.

For the rest of the dinner, they spoke about the case, going over each detail. When they were finished with their meal, Tess and Michael walked hand in hand out to her car. She would go home while Michael went to the police department to talk to the detectives involved in the missing persons case. They probably wanted to go over the plans for the search of Craig's apartment the next morning.

"If you're tired, don't wait up for me. I might be late," Michael said while she sat in the driver's seat, the car door still open.

Tess nodded and Michael bent down to kiss her before getting in his own vehicle.

Once home, she took off her jacket and boots and sat down at the desk in her office, her mind still going. She stared at the photos she had of Craig, Rachel and Sadie.

What the hell happened on that dark lonely road in the shadow of Mt. Baker?

CHAPTER FOURTEEN

Michael drove to the local police office and met with Mark Chambers, the detective in charge of the missing persons case, to talk about the search of Craig's apartment the next day. When he arrived, it was just before nine o'clock, and there were still several detectives at work along with some tech types, sitting at computer terminals. The scent of burnt coffee greeted him.

"Hey, what's up?" he asked when he got to the kitchen were Chambers and another officer were standing.

"Just going over our checklist for tomorrow morning."

While Chambers made a fresh pot of coffee, he and Michael discussed the case and they went over what they already knew about the timeline. Despite having an early morning, Michael stayed late and went over the details so it would be clear in his mind the next morning. By the time he arrived back at the apartment, it was nearly one in the morning and Tess was asleep. She'd left a note on the kitchen island.

Wake me up when you get in if there's anything new you can tell me.

He felt like talking but it was already way past the time he should be asleep, so he didn't. Instead, he got ready for bed and crept into bed beside Tess, doing his best not to wake her.

She kept sleeping, and he lay awake for quite a while despite being physically tired. His mind just wouldn't let go. The double murder case up north was pretty close to where they'd found Rachel's abandoned car.

His mind fought not to join them, but it was a battle he knew he was losing. He couldn't help go back over the crime scene and the possible evidence of another child murder. Some men couldn't stand the thought that someone else might have their woman and children. Some parents couldn't face not having control over their children and killed them as a kind of revenge. A woman was at her most vulnerable when leaving a bad relationship. Some men just couldn't accept that their partner no longer loved them or wanted to be with them.

Michael didn't feel that kind of possessiveness towards Tess or Julia, but he understood it in an intellectual sense. He was more of a stoic when it came to emotions. He tried to keep everything even-keeled and not let himself get carried away with anger or happiness. Even with Tess, he tried to be sensible, although he could have let himself fall very hard for her. He knew that wouldn't be good for either of them. He wanted to be with her and no one else. She was pretty much everything he wanted in a woman. More, even.

But he wasn't going to try to possess her.

At least, he was going to fight that kind of emotion, even if he felt it now and then. He'd seen too many women and girls dead and abused because of male possessiveness to let it happen to himself.

He wanted to marry Tess, one day, after the divorce was final, and if she wanted. But they had a lot of living to do in the meantime. He had to get his life in order, go back to school and she had to go to Quantico, if she was accepted.

Maybe then.

The next day, Michael got up early and had a quick shower before leaving the apartment while Tess slept. It was just starting to get light outside and as much as he would have liked to speak with her, Tess didn't have to be in the office until much later, so he let her sleep.

He got in the car and drove through town to meet Chambers and search Craig's house, stopping at the coffee shop for his usual morning cup of takeout coffee. He pulled up to the building where Craig lived and parked his Jeep, walking over to the other officers who were standing on the front sidewalk, talking. He slipped his identity badge around his neck, showing that he was an investigator with the District Attorney's office and joined them.

Chambers turned to him and nodded. "There you are," he said, all business. "We're ready to go in."

"Lead the way," Michael said and pointed to the front entrance. "I'm just along for the ride on this one."

Chambers nodded and walked up the path to the front entrance. The building was older, built in the 60s era, and had a small entry with a panel listing all the apartments, small buttons beside each name.

Chambers buzzed the number beside Craig's name and waited, but there was no response.

"He's probably an early bird," Chambers said. He ran his finger down the list of names and came to the one marked Building Manager and buzzed.

In about twenty seconds, a man's voice came over the speaker.

"Yes?"

"It's Detective Chambers from the Seattle PD. Who am I speaking with?"

"Jeff Glover, the building manager."

"Mr. Glover, I have a warrant to search the premises of Craig Lang. He's not at home and I'd like if you could open the apartment for me."

"I'll be right down," Glover replied.

Chambers turned to them as they waited for Glover to appear. Within a couple of minutes, a middle-aged bald man exited the elevator, wearing what looked like a janitor's uniform -- dark blue, matching pants and shirt. Work boots. Sleeves rolled up like he'd been busy doing some repair work.

"Detective Chambers?" Glover said after he opened the door to the lobby, admitting the three men.

Chambers nodded and held out the search warrant, which Glover took and looked over after slipping on a pair of reading glasses.

"You arresting him because of Rachel?"

"This is just a warrant to search his apartment and take possession of his electronics. It's not an arrest warrant." Chambers stated.

Glover nodded and motioned for the three men to follow him. They followed Glover down to an apartment at the end of the hallway. Glover pulled out a ring of keys that was attached to his belt and opened the door to Craig's apartment. He held the door open.

"Be my guest."

Chambers nodded and the three went inside. Michael slipped on his protective gloves and watched as the other two police officers did as well.

"We'll let you know when we're finished," Chambers said.

"I'm on my pager. Got a sink to fix. Here's my number," he said and handed Chambers a business card.

"Thanks."

They went inside and divided up the apartment, each person taking one room and going through, looking for evidence that might be relevant.

Michael went into the bedroom first. He searched a large chest of drawers in the corner. Half the drawers were empty, and he assumed they had once been used by Rachel. When he was finished, he went to the bedside table and opened the drawer, seeing a box of condoms and a tube of lube. There was also a small manual alarm clock and a couple of containers of baby wipes. He next went to the closet and searched the boxes on the top shelf, looking for anything that might be pertinent. Just old photos from what looked like Craig's past, faded Polaroids of an older couple and children playing in a park. Backyard barbecues. Christmas scenes with kids sitting around the tree, opening presents.

Nothing suspicious. Just pictures like he'd find in his own closet and photo albums.

"Got the laptop," Chambers called out from another room. Michael left the bedroom with nothing in his hands and went to another bedroom where Chambers was standing over a desk. He was wrapping up a power cord and slipping the computer and cord into a large brown paper bag.

"I guess he uses this as a darkroom," Chambers said, pointing to the black paper on the windows. There was a large rubber strip that went around the door, to prevent light from seeping inside. On a table against one wall was a series of trays, used to process print photographs and a projector that created the images. Craig still processed his photos by hand using chemical processing. Some of them had been included in displays at local art galleries.

Michael checked out the bookshelf, but there was nothing suspicious. Just books on photography and history of old Seattle and the mountains. Old cameras and lenses were stacked on the shelves. Craig seemed to be a collector.

Chambers was rifling through a filing cabinet, flipping through files.

"This is interesting," he said and gestured for Michael to come over. "A nude woman in various suggestive poses."

"Looks more artistic than pornographic to me," Michael replied. "Like something you'd find in the 19th Century. Not very explicit."

"I guess you're right," Chambers replied. "I'll keep looking. Maybe they get more explicit."

In the end, after a solid hour going through the apartment, they left with nothing much in the way of evidence. The search warrant was pretty narrow and focused only on electronics and any other evidence that might be linked to the disappearance.

All they had was an apartment that looked like a woman had decorated it and signs of a man who had fallen apart in her absence. At least, that was how Michael saw it. The sofa was covered in old newspapers and the coffee table was littered with empty takeout food containers. A pizza box sat open on the stove, a few crusts remaining. Dirty clothes were piled in the bathroom on the floor -- men's clothing. Dirty dishes in the sink. The garbage was overflowing. The bed unmade. Otherwise, the place was pretty ordinary.

It appeared that Craig stopped looking after himself and the apartment when Rachel disappeared.

The crime scene techs were busy collecting fingerprints and hair samples, dusting doorknobs and other surfaces. It wasn't a crime scene, but there might be something found that helped them understand what happened.

If there was a smoking gun, they didn't find it.

CHAPTER FIFTEEN

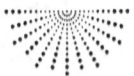

THE MORNING SICKNESS passed after the fourth month and from that point on, Rachel actually felt pretty good, all things considered.

She was living at the Sisters of Mercy shelter, she was taking classes towards her high school accreditation, and she slept at night without fear of anyone coming in to hurt her. Her belly was starting to swell, the small mound growing by the week, but otherwise, she had never been happier since before...

Before her father started to take a special interest in her.

She shoved that thought out of her mind. She'd been going to counseling sessions with a therapist and was learning how to push bad thoughts away, using her mantra.

I am good. I deserve to be happy. I am safe. I am free. No one can hurt me now.

Whenever a bad thought would pop in her head, and they did frequently, she'd look at her surroundings, and remind

SUSAN LUND

herself that she was no longer living with him. He had no idea where she was.

She was safe.

The only thing she had to worry about was staying healthy, taking her prenatal vitamins, sleeping a full eight hours a night, eating well, and doing her school courses.

The baby would come and then she would be a mother. She would have a child to care for. The Sisters promised to help her find a place to live on her own, once she'd finished her high school classes and could get a job. Then, she and her child could make a life for themselves.

The Sisters would be there along the way when she needed them.

She wouldn't make the same mistake her mother made -- get caught up in drugs and prostitution. That was what led to Rachel and Sadie. That was what led to all the suffering.

Rachel wouldn't make that same mistake.

When the time came for her to give birth, Rachel was afraid.

"You're a healthy young woman," Sister Jean said, patting Rachel on the back as she bent over in pain during a contraction. "Girls used to get married when they were twelve or thirteen and give birth soon after. Humans are meant to give birth early. Relax. Soon, you'll have a baby girl or boy to look after and your life will have real meaning. You'll be a mother. Having a child is the greatest gift God gives a woman."

Rachel panicked. The pain was incredible. It was unbearable, and with each contraction, she grew more fearful. Her only consolation was that it would be over in twenty-four

120

hours, if she was like most new mothers. Then, she would know whether she had a boy or a girl.

She hoped she had a boy.

Boys didn't suffer the way girls did.

Boys were strong. They ran the world. A boy would protect her when he grew up. A girl would need protection.

She didn't want a girl, although she'd accept it if she had a daughter, but she hoped it was a boy.

"Just accept what God has chosen for you. He has a plan for us all."

While Rachel crouched over, groaning in pain during a particularly painful contraction that made her think her insides were going to be ripped out of her body, she wondered what God's plan was for her.

Had God planned for her to be tortured by her father and the men her father took her to serve?

If so, she wasn't sure if she accepted God's plan. When she asked Sister Jean about that, Sister Jean only answered that it wasn't for us to understand God's plan for us, but to accept it. Rachel had suffered, as women suffer in childbirth. It was pain that gave us the gift of life and the gift of motherhood.

All Rachel could think of in the middle of a contraction was for it to end.

When a contraction was done, there was nothing but an end to pain. No wisdom, no greater strength.

"Just think-- with each pain, you are closer to having your baby," Sister Jean said encouragingly.

Rachel tried to use that as a mantra during her contraction, but the pain was so strong that all sense fled her, and she could only groan like an animal.

"How much longer?" she asked Doctor Alvi, who came by each hour to check her progress.

"You're still a long way off," Doctor Alvi replied with a smile. "You're only two centimeters dilated. When you're ten, you can push."

For the next six hours, Rachel walked around the shelter, up and down the hallways. The Sisters prepared a delivery room for her and had all the equipment in case she needed special care. Sister Jean was a midwife and would know if Rachel had to be taken to the hospital for an emergency C-section. That scared Rachel the most -- having to go to the hospital. She had no identification. She didn't want to go and for some social worker to force her into the system. She was afraid they'd find out her real name and send her back.

Luckily, when the time came for her to push instead of blow, Dr. Alvi was able to deliver her safely in the shelter's medical treatment room. Rachel got up on the examination table and pushed until the baby came out in a huge gush of amniotic fluid and blood. Dr. Alvi and Sister Jean took the baby to a separate table to check it out while Sister Maria checked Rachel for the afterbirth.

The pain stopped miraculously once the baby was out and Rachel wept, relieved that it was over and that she didn't have to go to a hospital after all.

Dr. Alvi came over with the baby and handed it to Rachel. "You have a beautiful baby girl," she said and placed the tiny girl on Rachel's bare chest. "You should put the baby to your breast and get your milk started," Dr. Alvi added. "It takes several days to come in fully, but until then, there's special milk that gives the baby special immune properties."

Rachel did as she was instructed, struggling to put the baby onto her breast. When she and Dr. Alvi finally managed it, Rachel held the tiny baby in her arms.

"What will you call her?" Dr. Alvi asked, while she checked Rachel out for any tears or bleeding.

"Sadie," Rachel said. "I'll call her Sadie."

"That's nice. Is there a middle name? What's her last name? I need it for the birth certificate."

"Martin," she said, thinking of the name her mother had told her was her grandmother's maiden name.

"Sadie Louise Martin. Louise was my mother's name. I'll name her after my mother."

Dr. Alvi took care of the paperwork while Rachel held little Sadie and tried to be happy about having a girl. Most of all, she didn't want Sadie to have to suffer what she had or what the first Sadie had suffered.

Rachel was determined that no one would ever hurt Sadie.

No one.

If anyone ever touched Sadie, Rachel would kill them.

Rachel moved out of the Sisters of Mercy shelter and into a private foster home with Candace, a former nun and her sister Leslie. They lived together and fostered girls with babies. They were determined to save such girls from lives on the streets or in prostitution or crime.

It was their calling in life and they saw Rachel and little Sadie as just what they needed to prove their commitment to being pro-life in all things.

Candace was the former nun. Tall and strong, with short steel-grey hair, she was formidable. Leslie was her smaller softer sister. The two of them dedicated their lives to caring for unwed mothers.

So, during the first couple of years of Sadie's life, Rachel was surrounded by women who mothered her the way Rachel had never been mothered. It helped her learn what a mother was supposed to do, and how a mother was supposed to behave, for Rachel had only ever seen her mother hide and shrink away from her father, who was the head of the household and made all the decisions. The moments of love and affection and care with her own mother had been rare -- moments of such bliss that Rachel could cry that they were so infrequent.

Children needed a mother's love, Candace told her. Rachel would have to lavish love and affection on Sadie to make up for the love she missed as a child.

When Sadie was two years old, they convinced Rachel to attend a special school for teens who had been unwed-mothers so she could socialize as she finished her high school diploma. She was smart and had learned fast, completing several years of high school in half the usual time. She felt finally able to learn and perform, now that she was safe.

But she did miss having a friend. She missed having a childhood and she missed out on having a normal teenage experience of friends and video games and movies -- all the things she read that girls her age took part in.

So, she reluctantly agreed to attend the special night school, where she and other unwed mothers could take classes to get their diploma.

Once she was done, she could get a part-time job. She

might even consider college if she could qualify for a scholarship.

That became the whole reason for Rachel's existence, outside of caring for Sadie -- she would get the best grades possible and would go to a university to study psychology. One day, maybe she could help other girls like herself, fleeing a home of violence and abuse.

Then she met Emma and it all went downhill from there.

Emma seemed fine at first -- another unwed mother a couple of years older than Rachel, and wiser in the ways of the world.

Emma had actually gone to high school -- a real high school with both boys and girls -- and she had made it through her freshman year and then part of her sophomore year before getting pregnant. Her boyfriend was a senior and one of the druggies, who sold pot and Molly in the school yard.

Rachel didn't even know what Molly was, assuming it was a girl he sold.

"No, silly. *Molly*. MDMA. You know, the love drug. It makes you happy. It makes you horny. All the kids take it at raves."

Rachel felt so out of touch with the rest of her generation. She'd been drugged before, but it was stuff designed to make her zone out and not care what the men were doing. It didn't make her happy. It made her throw up hours later. She didn't want to do drugs ever, but Molly sounded good, like it made your life better.

Emma was so pretty and wore makeup and short skirts with leggings underneath and Doc Martens. She had blue hair and a pierced nose and eyebrow.

SUSAN LUND

She was the coolest girl Rachel could ever imagine.

"Talk your foster parents into letting you come to my place," Emma said.

"They'll never let me. I'm not sixteen until November. I have a curfew. I have to be home right after class."

"Oh, crap. That sucks. As soon as you turn sixteen, you should come and live with me. You'll be an adult then and can do what you want legally."

Rachel didn't want to break the house rules or anger Candace or Leslie, but she did want to have a life eventually. One day, she wanted to take Molly and go to a rave.

She wanted to be happy.

She wasn't sure about a boyfriend, because she didn't want to think about sex ever again, but she was lonely. Most of all, she wanted a normal life.

So, after her sixteenth birthday, when Sadie was almost two years old, Rachel told Candace and Leslie that she was going to visit with a friend for coffee.

That was the start of her downfall.

CHAPTER SIXTEEN

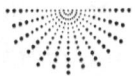

Tess spent the day waiting for Michael to report back on how the search of Craig's apartment went. The morning passed slowly for her, and so she spent her time going over the missing persons cases from the time period that might cover when the child was buried. She went back several years and added up all the children aged between five and ten who went missing during the twelve-year period from 2002 until 2017, just two years earlier. That was a lot of ground to cover, and she figured she'd have quite a number of missing children who fit the description, but she was wrong. Most missing children under the age of ten were found and taken off the database. They were abducted by the non-custodial parent and were located quickly.

There were only three children in the correct age range in the database who went missing and stayed missing over the past two decades.

She wrote down the names and pulled whatever other details she could off the NamUS site.

One of the missing children, a girl named Julia, had been murdered by her mother, the girl's body thrown into the river. The body had not yet been recovered, but the mother had been convicted and put in jail. Another had been abducted by the non-custodial parent. There was a warrant out for his arrest but that was several years earlier, and the child was still missing. That left only one case where there was no apparent conviction of anyone and no information on a possible non-custodial parent abducting the child. A girl, aged nine, who went missing in the middle of the night, with the only signs that the child had gone being an overturned bench under an open window. No one had heard anyone enter or leave the house, and the family's dog had not barked. The child just vanished. That was the oldest case and was from thirteen years earlier.

The ME said that the body could have been in the ground for as short as two years or as long as a decade, so it could have been her.

That would mean that someone either abducted her in the night, or one of the family members killed her and concocted a story. The family was located in Bellingham, which was less than an hour's drive from the location of the body.

Tess wasn't sure that it was a good fit, but it was possible. According to records, there were three other children in the family, including an older sister and two younger brothers.

She printed off the photograph of the girl and created a case file.

It was the first possible victim.

Tess wondered if perhaps the skeletal remains had been someone Rachel had known. Possibly a friend or sibling and that was why her car was found at the site. But if Rachel really was from Montana, why would she know someone who was buried near Mt. Baker? In the end, there were only two possibilities: either Rachel's abductor had taken her there for a reason, or Rachel had gone there for a reason and both reasons seemed to be the buried body of a child.

Had Rachel gone there to see the location of the body? Had she dug up the grave, knowing it was there? Or did her abductor go there to gloat over the kill? But then why leave the vehicle there? And why leave the evidence there for anyone who searched the area to find?

She had so many questions, and tried to sort through them logically, to get some kind of order out of the disparate pieces of evidence.

Next, Tess did the same for Idaho and Montana. Rachel had claimed to be from Montana, and so Tess wondered if the body of the child had been someone she once knew -- or a family member. But why would someone bury a child in Washington State if they were from Montana?

There were only two cases in Montana that fit the age range and possible interval. One was a boy who went missing when he and a group of children were swimming in a river and the other was a girl who went missing while on her way home from a friend's house. Tess printed off the case files and photos and posted them on a cork board beside her desk.

It wasn't much to go on, but it was all she had.

Three children who could be the victim, who went missing in the appropriate time period and who had never been located.

Of course, it was possible that none of the potential victims were right. The dates and locations were based on speculation and a story Rachel told Craig and Mickey about where she was from. Tess didn't even know Rachel's real name or where she was really born. She could have been from anywhere in the US for that matter -- or even from Seattle itself. Until they identified her correctly, it was all speculation.

Michael called her later that morning, while Tess was out getting a fresh cup of coffee. She stopped on the street on her way back to the *Sentinel's* offices and sat on a bench so she could answer the call.

"Hey, there," Michael said, his voice warm.

"Hey," she said back and smiled. "What's up?"

"We searched Craig's apartment," he said. "Nothing really to be found of interest, except some old clothes and possessions of Rachel's and Sadie's, which were taken into custody. Fingerprints taken, and Craig's laptop and a cell phone were also taken to see what websites he had been searching. There's really nothing else to report at this point. Once the evidence has been processed, we might have more to go on but there was nothing glaring that I could see in the apartment."

"No cache of child porn or links to Satanic cults?" Tess replied, a hint of sarcasm in her voice.

"No. Nothing like that. The place seemed pretty ordinary, just a little messy. Craig isn't very good at taking care of himself."

Tess had been only joking of course, and then felt bad.

"I shouldn't joke," she said guiltily. "I feel sick about this. I always liked Craig and if he's innocent, he's really hurting right now. If he did it, I hope he burns in hell. Was he there while you searched?"

"No. He was at work, so the landlord let us in. It makes it a lot easier to do a search when the suspect isn't present."

"Poor Craig," she replied, imagining poor Craig when he arrived home after a long day at work. "He'll come home and discover that the police were there searching through his possessions."

"He was called and arrived at the apartment within an hour," Michael said quickly. "By then, we were finished. Did you know he came from a wealthy family, and inherited a bunch of money? He's been living well-below his means ever since. He's given half his money away to homeless shelters since his parents died."

"No, he never talked about himself."

"Well, he's wealthy, but you wouldn't know it from his apartment."

Tess took a sip of her coffee before replying, her mind working, trying to square this new information about Craig. "His parents are dead?"

"Yes, they were older, and he was an only child, born to his mother when she was in her forties. His mother was a professor at Washington State University, and his father was a judge."

"That's so strange that he never talked about his family. I feel bad for him that all of this is happening. He seems like the least able to deal with all the publicity and contact with the police. Did you leave the house in a mess?"

"We did our best to return the apartment to its pre-search state, which was pretty clean except for a mound of Craig's dirty clothes on the bathroom floor and his dirty dishes in the sink. Oh, and newspapers all over the sofa and empty food containers on the coffee table. Of course, we removed the computer and any other electronic devices we discovered."

"Poor Craig. He must be so afraid for Rachel and Sadie. Any update on the skeleton? DNA results?"

"No. I don't expect the DNA results from the bones for a while. They take a bit longer. The ME has to extract the DNA and then process it before it can be put in the database to look for matches."

"Can you estimate how long?"

"Dr. Keller said late this week or early next week. She's prioritized the case and hopes to get us a profile to use as soon as possible."

"What about the blood in the car? Have you talked to Craig about it?"

"We did. He said he cut himself when changing a tire. We checked and Rachel did in fact have a flat and was driving on the spare, so that checks out. We also found blood on the jack. Just a bit but some. It backs up his story. But when I see blood on a jack and know there's a missing woman and child? I get nervous."

"I just don't see him killing anyone," Tess said, feeling despondent at the prospect that Craig had done it.

"I don't see him for it, but as you know and I know, we can't always rely on our gut instinct."

Tess sighed. "Don't I know it. I hope we're both right and he's innocent," she said, imagining Craig entering his apartment and seeing police there.

"We'll see what a search of his laptop and cell shows. Until then, who can say whether he's a likely suspect?"

Tess shrugged. "I know. Well, I gotta get back to the office."

"Okay," Michael replied. "See you for supper."

"Bye."

Tess entered the *Sentinel's* offices and went to her desk by the window, determined to focus on Craig's case. Michael seemed concerned about the blood found in the car but like her, didn't see Craig as the proper suspect.

Whatever the case, she had work to finish, and needed to go over the final draft of her latest article on missing and murdered women and girls in Washington State.

CHAPTER SEVENTEEN

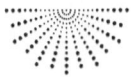

Michael sat at his desk and pondered the evidence.

The police were moving forward with their case against Craig Lang, the photographer, and boyfriend of Rachel Martin, the woman missing along with her daughter, Sadie. They were gathering evidence, testimony from everyone who knew the trio. Combing through their past lives.

They'd come up against a brick wall with the woman.

There was no one named Rachel Martin matching her age on any registry in either Washington State or Montana. Rachel was a unique enough name for a woman, that he had gotten a number of hits when he searched databases for women named Rachel. But there were no birth certificates issued with the name Rachel Martin from either Washington or Montana.

She had a fake ID.

He had no idea what her real name was and neither did her boyfriend. Or if he did, he wasn't telling.

They'd taken trace evidence from the apartment -- hair and fingerprints -- in the hopes of identifying her that way, but none of the hairs they found had a follicle, so they were out of luck. Her prints weren't in the database, despite her living on the streets for several years. She had never been arrested for drugs or prostitution.

It was as if she just didn't exist.

And now, she and her daughter were gone.

Michael drove to visit Rachel's foster caregivers and ask them about her.

The two women, Candace and Leslie Abbot were frequent foster parents to young girls who were pregnant and keeping their babies. They were well-known to the Catholic Family Services folks and had a good solid reputation for helping out girls who were down and out.

One of the two women met him at the door and introduced herself to Michael as Leslie. They went into the kitchen where she had a pot of coffee brewing.

"Have a seat," Leslie said and motioned to the small kitchen table. "Candace is out at the moment shopping."

He sat and took out his notepad, wanting to take notes on what she said.

"Tell me about Rachel. How did she come to live with you and your sister?"

Leslie brought over two mugs filled with coffee and a tray with cream and sugar and spoons. They both fixed a cup of coffee and then Leslie exhaled, her hands curled around the mug.

"Rachel?" she said and took in a deep breath. "Rachel was a good girl who had a terrible home life and ran away when she got pregnant. She went to the shelter and that's where we met her. After she gave birth, she came to live with us and we helped her raise the baby. It's what we do. We believe in supporting these girls so they can get on their feet, make a decent life for their children if they decide to keep them."

Michael nodded. "What do you know about her family?"

Leslie shrugged. "Rachel didn't want to talk about them. Not even in confidence. It was that bad, so we didn't push her. She told us that her father abused her and that her mother neglected her. She ran away from home and she was trying to forget her parents and her past. She wanted to make a new start and look after her baby as best she could. Finish high school. Get a skill and then find a job."

"She did pretty well," he said, going over what he knew about Rachel. "She had a job and was taking night classes at the community college. Why would she up and leave all of a sudden?"

"I have no idea," Leslie said. "Everything seemed to be going so well for her. She had some serious problems for a while, like many kids her age. She used drugs and alcohol for a few years, but she managed to get clean and stay clean. She finished high school and started to work. She met Craig," Leslie said and smiled. "She seemed to blossom after that. He really provided stability for her. I just don't know why she'd leave all of a sudden like that. Especially without Craig."

"You know Craig pretty well?"

"Yes," Leslie said, taking a sip. "He's a strange guy. Asperger's, you know. But he's really sweet underneath the awkwardness."

"Do you think he could have hurt Rachel and Sadie?"

"What?" Leslie said. "Craig? No. Of course not. He was a stabilizing influence in her life."

"He was the last person to see her and Sadie alive."

Leslie shook her head in disbelief. "I know police always think it's the boyfriend or husband, but I will never believe that he hurt her. He *loved* her. You could see it when they were together. She loved him. He loved Sadie and Sadie loved him. They were a family."

Michael wrote a few notes, thinking that merely being a family wasn't good enough. In his experience, families often ended in bloodshed.

He didn't bother saying that to Leslie. She appeared very upset at the prospect that Craig was a suspect.

"You have to understand that when a woman goes missing, we always look to their home life first. It's often where she's at greatest risk."

"I know that," Leslie said, twisting a paper napkin in her hands. "But in this case, I think it's safe to say that Craig couldn't have hurt either Rachel or Sadie. It's just not possible."

He exhaled softly, not willing to push her any further since she already was so close to the edge.

"She never mentioned any names of her family? Her father or mother? Anything we could use to trace her, see if she went back to her home town?"

"She said she was from Montana. That's it. She said she hitchhiked to Seattle from Montana and that she came right to the shelter."

"How did she know about the shelter?"

"She said her mother was here back in the day and so it was the first place she came after she arrived in Seattle."

"Does the shelter have records back far enough to check for someone matching her mother's description?"

"Not that I know of. They probably threw out all the old

paperwork. They only have to keep records for eight years for tax purposes."

Michael nodded. Obviously, Rachel hadn't told her foster family any real details about her past -- no names or locations. Montana was a big state and without any other evidence, there was really nothing he could do to find her.

"Was there anything she ever said to you about places she liked to visit or wanted to visit?"

"She said she loved the mountains. Montana has a lot of mountains and rivers. Great fishing and hunting. She said her father was a mountain man. He was a prepper. You know -- one of those kind who keeps a bug-out shelter full of canned goods and batteries, camping equipment in case the SHTF." Leslie smiled. "She said he was a nutcase. That's all. She never said his name, or her family name, or the town where they lived. Nothing." She shrugged and made an apologetic face. "That's all I can tell you."

Michael closed his notebook. "Thanks for your help."

"She may have gone back to Montana. Maybe she wanted to reconcile with her family."

Michael stood up and pulled on his jacket. "Do you think that's possible?"

"In my experience, people always want their parents to love them. Even after years of abuse and neglect. It's a very strong instinct and desire. I've counseled kids who have kept going back in hopes that their father or mother will finally love them. It's very sad, because usually, it's an impossible dream. Rachel never expressed any desire to me or my sister about going home and trying to reconnect with her father or family. Never once."

At that moment, the front door opened and a middle-aged

woman with graying hair came in, two paper shopping bags in her arms.

Leslie stood. "Candace, this is Michael Carter, an investigator with the District Attorney's office. He wanted to ask us some questions about Rachel and Sadie."

Michael went to her and reached out to help her with the armloads of groceries. "Can I help you with that?"

Candace smiled at him and handed over the bags. "Thank you." Then, while Michael carried the bags into the kitchen, Candace removed her rain jacket and boots.

Leslie took over in the kitchen and began unpacking the bags.

"Would it be possible to speak with you for a moment about Rachel and Sadie? I already spoke with your sister but wanted to see if I could pick your mind for details about them."

"Sure," Candace said and came into the kitchen, a nervous smile on her face. "Ask away. I'm sure I can't tell you anything different from Leslie. But go ahead."

Michael sat back down at the kitchen table and waited for Candace to sit down as well. Once she was settled, he took out his notebook and went over the questions he asked Leslie. Candace had nothing to offer in addition to what her sister said, saying pretty much the same thing.

"They were happy as two peas in a pod," Candace said, shaking her head. "I just can't believe that he would hurt her. Something bad must have happened to Rachel and Sadie. Why else would her car be abandoned? Why wouldn't she call one of us to let us know she's safe?"

"Did she ever tell you anything about going up north? Any family up there?"

Candace shook her head. "No. She said she was from

Montana. She never mentioned anything about anyone up north where the car was found. I just don't understand why she'd go up there. She said she was from Montana, her family was still there, and she never wanted to talk to them again. She said her father was abusive and her mother was neglectful. She said her sister died young and she was alone. She never went to school. She was homeschooled. The family was a bit nutty like that."

Michael nodded. "Yes. Your sister said something about that. Is there anything else you can think of? Anything about her plans for going away on vacation or anything? If we knew where she was going, we might have an idea of who she might have been meeting."

"No. Nothing. We talked now and then, but she's been really busy with school and work and of course, her life with Craig. We have a new girl now, but we keep in touch."

Michael stood. "I appreciate the time, so thank you. If you think of anything. Any detail about her past or her family that might be interesting, please call me."

He handed them a card with his name and number at the DA's office.

Then, he said goodbye.

His talk with them had turned up nothing of use, but it did paint a picture of a young girl escaping a bad family life and wanting to forget it completely.

She'd left a bad home life and started an entirely new life in Seattle. He wondered if she wasn't doing exactly the same thing again, but somewhere new.

CHAPTER EIGHTEEN

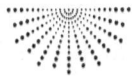

EMMA EDUCATED Rachel in the ways of the world outside her little life.

"Candace is a lesbian," Emma opined one day when they were debating whether Rachel should sneak out late one night and come to a party.

That fact didn't bother Rachel. She understood that some women did not like men. They liked other women.

Emma had explained it all to her after they met, and she took on the education of Rachel in all things she lacked.

"I hate men," Emma explained. "But I don't like women so it's a man I'm looking for. Women need men to survive and you have to find the good ones who will look after you. That's what every girl needs -- a good man to look after them. Give them sex when they want it, and in return, you get a nice apartment, and your food and clothes paid for. I can do that."

Rachel could have hated men, after what she experienced at home and at the warehouse, but she realized that not all men were like that. In fact, Sister Jean said that most men were good. Only a small number of men were evil.

"God made us fallible," Sister Jean said one day when Rachel went for a visit. "Some more than others. Find a good man and marry him. Be true to him and your life will be happy."

Rachel wasn't so sure. Her mother had married and had tried to be a good wife, but her father was just evil. Rachel knew that now. Her father was just the way Sister Jean said.

Evil.

If Rachel ever met a good man, she would consider getting married, but there was a lot of living for her to do before then. Rachel enjoyed the freedom that living with Candace and Leslie afforded her, looking after Sadie while Rachel went out with Emma to parties and dances, and occasionally, they let her sleep over and babysat Sadie.

That was the first time in Rachel's life where she felt somewhat normal. She had an allowance and bought clothes with Emma -- clothes that were fashionable and made her feel pretty.

"You're so skinny, kiddo," Emma would say. "You need some meat on your bones. Guys like a little booty. You should start working out. Squats," she said and performed a few. "Do squats."

Rachel didn't care about being skinny. That's just the way she was, but she did want to look normal. Even just wearing jeans and a hoodie, some Doc Martens like Emma, and some makeup, a streak of pink in her blonde hair, made her feel like she fit in.

Finally, Rachel fit in.

At a dance one night, she finally took Molly, and it was the very best feeling in the world. For the first time in her life, she felt actual happiness. She was so happy, she cried. She hugged Emma and everyone else she met. She loved everyone and everyone loved her.

From then on, whenever she could, Rachel took Molly. It was her go-to drug of choice. While Emma smoked pot and sometimes drank alcohol, Rachel only wanted Molly. She hated alcohol, because it reminded her of her father and the men at the warehouse, who drank so much, they'd puke in buckets.

Then, one night, when she slept over at Emma's place, she tried a line of white powder that Emma was snorting.

"It's Oxy," Emma said. "If you think Molly is good, try this."

Rachel tried it, and Emma was right. If Molly made her happy, Oxy was pure bliss. Oxy was this great enveloping warmth of pureness that chased away all the sadness and bad memories.

Then, she slept.

One of the older guys at the party, she couldn't even remember his name, tried to climb on top of her, and in truth, she didn't even care. She felt so blissed out, she didn't fight. Emma was sober enough to pull him off, but even she eventually succumbed to the effects of the Oxy.

Rachel woke up later to the feel of the guy thrusting inside of her. Her clothes had been partially removed and he was on top of her. Her only thought wasn't the fact he was raping her. It was whether he'd seen the faint scars from the stab wounds and would think she was a freak.

She didn't really care about the fact he was having sex with her. It wasn't anything she hadn't felt many times before in her life, and at least the Oxy took away all the pain.

When he was done, he threw a ten-dollar bill onto the bed beside her.

"He liked you," Emma said when they had both sobered up enough to sit and stare at the bill in Rachel's hand. "You didn't even ask, and he gave you money."

"If I take it, it means I'm a prostitute."

"No, silly," Emma said and pushed Rachel's shoulder. "Prostitutes always negotiate up front and get paid before they have sex. Randy gave you money because he liked you."

"I didn't tell him it was okay," Rachel said doubtfully. "At least, I don't remember saying yes. The nuns said that consent is important in a healthy relationship."

"Randy is a good guy. He wouldn't rape you. You must have said yes and just don't remember because of the Oxy."

Rachel nodded, because she couldn't remember anything after she did the line of crushed Oxy except a warm feeling of bliss and hands on her, touching her.

Nothing about it felt the way she used to feel back at home or in the warehouse.

It couldn't be abuse in that case...

Over the next year, Rachel's life gradually fell apart.

She tried to keep up with her night classes, but in truth, she stopped going altogether, spending her time at Emma's place, high, sleeping with whoever might take a fancy to her because at that point, she didn't care. They always left money and it was only about three months into the arrangement that she finally understood that she was a prostitute.

She and Emma had become prostitutes, working for Randy.

He never forced her, but he gave her money, he gave her drugs, and he had sex with her whenever he wanted.

Leslie and Candace cared for Sadie, and while they encouraged Rachel to get help, to go to a detox center and get clean, they never forced her. She would roll in early in the morning after a night spent at Emma's place, and sleep it off, have a shower, eat some food and play with Sadie for a while, before going out late that night to start all over again.

Leslie stopped her one night before she left.

"You should eat before you go."

Rachel shook her head. By then, she needed her drugs before she could eat.

"I'll be fine," she said and waved Leslie off. "I gotta go."

"You need help, Rachel," the older woman said, a hand on Rachel's shoulder to stop her. "You're in trouble. I can tell. Candace and I are happy to look after Sadie, but she needs her mother."

Rachel looked in Leslie's eyes and knew what the woman said was right, but by then, she needed to get high to simply get through the night.

"I know," Rachel replied, tears coming to her eyes at the realization. "I'll try."

"You'll lose Sadie if you don't," Leslie said softly. "This can't go on forever."

Rachel wiped her eyes on her sleeve, but she had to leave. She needed a hit.

"I'll be back later," Rachel said. She stopped by Sadie's bed and bent down, kissing the sleeping baby goodnight. "Good night, sweet baby," she whispered. "Mamma loves you."

Then, she went out into the night, her body aching with need. Once she had her first hit, she'd be okay.

. . .

Her life went on like that for the next year, with Leslie and Candace becoming more and more insistent that Rachel get help and Rachel spiraling down deeper into addiction.

Sadie seemed a happy baby despite the fact her mother was an addict and prostitute. She was starting to crawl, and Rachel had been away or unconscious for all of Sadie's big milestones. The first time she sat up on her own was with Leslie. The first time she crawled was with Leslie. Her first words were spoken to Leslie and Candace, not Rachel.

The first time she stood on her own, Rachel was passed out in her bedroom, the blackout drapes pulled against the daylight.

Leslie opened the door and stood in the doorway, the expression on her face clearly upset.

"Rachel," Leslie said angrily. "Your daughter just started to walk. You should be the one watching her."

Rachel rolled over and pulled the blanket over her face. "I'm sick," she said weakly. "I need to sleep."

"You're always sick. You need help, girl. If you don't clean yourself up, you'll lose Sadie."

"Yeah, yeah, yeah," Rachel said dismissively. "I will, I will. Just shut the door."

Leslie stood in the doorway for a long moment, then Rachel heard her sigh heavily. Finally, the door closed, and the room was cast back into darkness.

Rachel wept silently, for she knew what Leslie said was right. She should have been the one watching Sadie, encouraging her first words and steps. But Rachel needed her hit to just get through the day now. She needed to work to keep up her habit.

One day bled into the next, and it was all a huge blur of intoxication, sex and sleep. There were only a few moments of sober reflection on the state of her life and how close she was to losing Sadie.

What changed everything was one of the girls Rachel knew going missing.

Rose Clarke, fifteen, a pretty brown-eyed girl originally from Tacoma, who had been brought up to Seattle to work for Randy.

She went missing one night. Never showed up the next evening to stand on the corner and wait for dates. The last time anyone saw her was after she got into a truck with some John.

"She ran away," Randy said, shrugging. "She probably went back to Tacoma. She was always complaining that she missed her sisters."

But it didn't feel right to Rachel, who had spent a lot of time with Rose.

When they found her body in a dumpster at the edge of town, Rachel knew she had to do something, or she'd end up like Rose.

So, when a reporter and camera man came around, asking for any information about Rose, Rachel told them what she knew. She was afraid again, the way she'd felt back when she lived at home. Afraid for her life.

That was when she met Craig.

He'd come around with a reporter from the *Sentinel*, asking questions about missing street prostitutes. He kept his eyes downcast when he spoke with her, offering her a cigarette when they stood in the cold winter night while the reporter-lady spoke to one of the other girls who didn't want to be on camera.

Craig was a sweet man, who couldn't make eye contact except through the lens of his camera.

Strangely enough, they fell easily into a relationship. It seemed he could see right into her soul with the lens and asked if he could come by and take some photos of her for his private collection. At first, she was suspicious that he was some kind of weird pornographer, but he wasn't.

He did portraits of street people. He told her that some of his photographs were on display at a local coffee shop and when she went to see them, she was honestly touched.

They were haunting portraits of some of the people she knew from the streets. Homeless old men in black and white, their skin filthy, their wrinkles showing them aging far too soon, toothless, rheumy staring off into space.

Even the prostitutes he photographed had a quiet dignity that was hard to give to women who sold their bodies for drugs.

"Why do you want to photograph me?" she asked one night when he paid her just to talk.

"I can see your pain. I want to preserve it, so everyone knows."

She shook her head. "No one can know," she replied softly. "No one can know who I am. I'm trying to escape my past."

"Just for my private collection, then. Maybe one day, you'll feel safe enough for me to show them."

She finally agreed and met with him in the park during the day. He took hundreds of photographs of her while she sat and smoked, talking about her life before she came to Seattle. She never told him the real truth, of course, because that was too ugly, but she tried to describe the few patches of color in an otherwise black and white life.

He photographed her with Sadie, on the days she had her and was getting better in rehab.

When she was finished with her six weeks detox and therapy, they began a relationship.

She felt he really saw her when he pointed the camera at her.

It was the strangest thing.

It also made her want to stay clean for the first time since she started doing Oxy. She wanted to spend time with him, and he didn't do drugs. He barely even drank.

Craig was a normal, if somewhat strange guy who didn't want to have sex with her. At least, he didn't only want that.

Craig saved her life.

She was sure of it.

CHAPTER NINETEEN

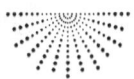

WHILE MICHAEL WAS WORKING LATE at the DA's office,
Tess decided to take a drive to the strip to Mickey's and see if
she could talk to a few of the staff about Rachel. She felt more
comfortable going there after being there once before so she
didn't need Michael to go along.

She drove along Aurora Avenue, the busy street in North
Seattle where a lot of the street hookers plied their trade. It was
a pretty seedy part of town and she was surprised that Mickey
continued to operate his bar there, considering. But perhaps he
was being loyal to his original clientele and wanted to help out
as much as possible by keeping business in the area.

He was an interesting case in himself. Former Army.
Former biker. Former drug addict. Involved in petty crime.
Went to prison. Got out and went clean, worked at the bar,
then bought it and took it over. Now, he had a charity that
provided food and clothes and showers to the homeless and
street kids who lived under Seattle's bridges and other

locations where they could pitch a tent or park their cardboard box for the night.

While she was driving, she saw Craig across the street, walking along the sidewalk. It was raining lightly, pushing most of the normal street traffic indoors. She could see women standing in dark doorways, dressed in short skirts, with warm bomber jackets against the cool night air and rain. Nights like that would be hard for them and Tess felt lucky that she'd had such a good life in comparison.

She knew that most of the hookers started out as runaways, with drug habits and pasts filled with abuse and neglect.

What was Craig doing walking down Aurora Street after dark in the rain?

She parked her car and watched for a moment. He stood in one dark doorway and spoke to someone hidden from sight, his back turned to the street. Was he trying to pick up a prostitute?

If he was, she had to really re-think her view of him. How could he be out looking for sex when Rachel and Sadie were still missing?

She followed along for a moment and then decided to park her vehicle and follow him, talk to him. She found a spot and after crossing the street, she walked up to where he stood under an awning, sheltered from the rain. He was talking to two young women who were obviously street kids, their clothes ratty, their hair knotted and messy. They looked to be around fifteen or sixteen.

He had something in his hand -- a piece of paper of some kind.

She walked up, her hands in her pockets.

"Hey," she said and gave Craig a smile. "What's up, Craig?"

He turned to her, his hair wet from the rain, drops dripping off the end of his nose.

"Tess," he said and didn't smile back.

"What are you doing?" she asked, unable to keep a note of disapproval from her voice.

"I was just asking people if they've seen Rachel."

He handed Tess the piece of paper. It was a flyer, showing Rachel and Sadie standing together, Rachel's hands on Sadie's shoulders. Rachel and Sadie were both smiling. Beneath it was a caption:

MISSING
Rachel and Sadie Martin
If seen, please contact Craig at:

The number was for Craig's cell.

"You seriously think she's still in town?" Tess asked, frowning. She handed the piece of paper back to Craig.

"I don't know what to think," he said, his voice emotional. He gave the flyer to one of the girls, who tucked it into her jacket pocket.

Craig cleared his throat. "Ask your friends about her. If you or anyone sees her, call that number."

The girls nodded and Craig turned to leave. Tess followed him.

"Are you going to keep walking up and down Aurora in the rain?"

"What else can I do?"

She grabbed his arm and stopped him. "At least wait until the rain stops. Have you eaten?"

He shook his head. He was pale and he looked terrible.

"Come and have a coffee with me. We can talk."

He exhaled and finally nodded. "I have to do this first," he said and walked to a piece of plywood that was covering a storefront window. The store had been closed and its windows boarded up. Craig took out another flyer and a staple gun from his backpack and stapled the sheet to the plywood. He stapled another about three feet away from it.

"Let's go," he said. "I can't really put them up when everything's wet."

She slipped her arm through his and led him down the street to a small diner.

They took seats in a booth by the front window and put in an order for coffee and Craig ordered some food.

"I need this," he said finally when the waitress brought around the coffee pot and poured for them. "I haven't eaten since breakfast."

"Craig," Tess said with a frown. "You have to look after yourself."

He shook his head. "It's hard to do anything, thinking about Rachel and Sadie. My stomach feels sick most of the time."

"What do you think happened," she asked, unsure of what to say.

"It's my fault," he said softly. "She ran away because of what I did."

"You said that before. What *did* you do?"

"I poked my nose into her life where it didn't belong. Then, I wouldn't go with her when she asked me. If I had, we'd probably be somewhere in Oregon and she and Sadie would be with me now."

Then he covered his eyes and his shoulders shook.

He was crying in front of her.

"I have a bad feeling," he said. "I have a bad feeling that they're dead."

She reached out and laid her hand on his, trying to comfort him. She just couldn't believe that he was faking it.

"Craig, you don't know that they're dead."

He met her eyes finally.

"Her car was abandoned in the middle of the forest on the side of a volcano. What else can I think but she was abducted. Both of them. Their suitcases were still in the trunk. Rachel's bag and her cell." He shook his head. "When people abduct women, they kill them. Even I know that. I've covered enough cases to know that."

Tess couldn't reply, because even she figured the two were dead. It looked like someone followed her to the location or forced her to drive up there. Then, they took her and Sadie. There were no footprints leading deeper into the forest. There were only tire tracks to and from the scene. Rachel and Sadie had not left the site on foot.

She knew, from Michael, about the skeletal remains found near the vehicle, but she couldn't tell Craig about them until the information was released publicly. Besides, would that comfort him or make him feel worse?

It was impossible to know why Rachel had driven to that location. Was she going there because she was told to, or was it by choice? That made all the difference, but she had no idea and she was sure the police didn't either. Not enough was known about Rachel to tell.

Craig finally got control over himself and wiped his eyes with a paper napkin. "I'm sorry," he managed. "I just wish she'd let me know that she's okay, if she's alive and not being held captive."

"You think she might be hiding?"

He shrugged and glanced out the window when the waitress brought their food. "She might be. Maybe someone met her there and took her somewhere safe. I don't know what to believe."

They sat in silence for a while and Tess watched Craig, trying hard to see any hint of deception. She'd watched the faces of men who had killed their wives or partners while they lied and cried on camera. You wouldn't necessarily know they weren't telling the truth. They were convincing.

When you went back afterwards and studied the men's faces closely, you could imagine seeing the deception in the way they held their mouth or the look in their eyes, but she didn't always feel it the first time she saw the men. Now, she routinely suspected any man whose partner or wife went missing.

She had to suspect Craig, too.

He seemed so genuinely afraid...

"If there's anything she said about her past -- anything the police could use to identify her and find out who she really is, that would help."

"I told the police everything I know. All I know is that she used to live in Montana and that they used to come to Washington for fishing and hunting. I took a picture of hers up to Bellingham because it had been developed at this little camera store there. The guy behind the desk said he didn't know who worked at the store back when it was processed and there was no way to find out except to go back to the archives. They'd probably thrown out the old receipts so there was no way to trace whoever paid for the photos to be developed."

He shrugged.

"What was the name of the camera shop?" Tess asked.

"Bird Camera and Photography. I told the police all about it."

Tess nodded and made a mental note of it. If nothing else, it might be a way of tracking down the story she knew she would be writing about Rachel and Sadie.

Two more to add to the dozens of women and girls from Washington State who went missing, disappearing without a trace.

CHAPTER TWENTY

MICHAEL SPENT the evening at the office, trying to keep the various bits and pieces of evidence separate, but they were starting to come together in his mind. He had learned to trust his gut while in the FBI. His gut didn't always tell him what was right, but it did tell him when something was off. For example, John Hammond as a serial child killer -- back in Paradise Hill, his gut told him that was off as a theory of the case. Sure, John Hammond was guilty of one hell of a lot of perversion, but he wasn't the killer they were searching for.

Now, he had two cases and while they were being treated as separate, unconnected, his gut told him that wasn't the right way to look at them. His rational mind wanted to keep them apart, but his gut said no.

A young woman and her daughter go missing after an argument with her boyfriend about moving out of state and starting a new life. Her car is found abandoned with her purse and their suitcases still inside, a dozen feet away from the skeletal remains of a child -- obviously murdered or her accidental death hidden. The woman had been using a fake identity for the past eight years, since coming to Seattle as a pregnant runaway, living in a Catholic shelter and spending some time on the streets while her foster family cared for her daughter. She got clean, finished school, got a job and a relationship, then disappeared into the night with her daughter, after saying her past was catching up with her and that's why she had to move.

In the other case he was working for the DA's office, two John Does were found stabbed to death at a remote cabin at Silver Lake, not too far from the site of the abandoned car. They had filming equipment set up in the cabin, but all the memory chips had been removed. There were children's toys at the cabin. Michael's mind fought going there, but he did. He figured that the two men were filming child porn. There were drugs and alcohol at the scene including what the ME identified as ketamine. Probably used to drug the child or girls. There must have been a fight -- possibly with one of the other men involved, who killed the two and took off with the evidence.

The ME was processing the two bodies at the moment, and all the forensic tests weren't back yet, but it was clear that both men had been stabbed by someone using a knife with a three-inch blade.

No murder weapon was found at the scene.

One thing the ME said was that the men had been dead for a week to ten days based on the amount of decomposition. Rachel and her daughter Sadie went missing in the same time period.

His mind tried to put the two together because the car was found ten miles west of the town of Deming on an old logging road in the shadow of Mt. Baker. Less than half an hour from the location where they'd found the bodies of the men. It wasn't like Whatcom County was a hive of crime and for two big cases to occur so close in time with each other forced Michael to put them together.

However, the police in the Seattle Major Crimes Unit were laser-focused on Craig as their main suspect. The Whatcom County Sheriff called in the Seattle PD to assist with the case of the abandoned vehicle given the link to the missing persons case in Seattle. They called in the FBI to deal with the double homicide case because of its apparent link to child porn.

The two cases just begged to be put together.

Michael thought about Craig. He was strange -- there was no doubt about it. He had Asperger's or some degree of Autism Spectrum Disorder and had difficulty looking at people in the eye. As a consequence, he appeared rather shifty, like he was guilty.

He *looked* guilty.

When being interviewed by police, he seemed either emotionless when describing Rachel or he cried. Michael watched the videotape of the first police interview. It was almost painful to watch the man break down, weeping openly. Was it all an act? If so, the man was a consummate actor, but when Michael spoke to the psychiatrist who often consulted with the DA's office, Dr. Granger said that people with Asperger's often had difficulty expressing and disguising their emotions. They could come off as cold or uncaring or overcome with emotion. When they talked, they often droned on, discussing their pet topics without recognizing that others weren't as interested as they were. They had trouble reading other people's emotions and knowing what to say -- or what not to say -- in equal measure.

Craig seemed either stoic, with no emotion, or totally broken, weeping openly.

Dr. Granger watched the video with Michael and nodded his head throughout.

"Watch him talking about his latest project. He's talking without any emotions, describing the subject matter in detail. His voice is monotone. Later, watch him describe Rachel and Sadie. He's very upset. Having trouble speaking. He's either really afraid that they've been harmed or he's putting on an act. But it doesn't ring true for me. If he truly has Asperger's, it's rare for them to become violent. They do, of course, but they are no more likely than others to do so. When they do, it's often explosive."

"If she wanted to leave and he didn't want to, would that be a good-enough reason for him to lose his temper?"

Granger pursed his lips. "Often they have difficulty changing. They don't like abrupt changes in plans. He could have been upset at the prospect of moving away. I spoke to a few of his colleagues and he was never volatile. Never showed any propensity to getting upset or showing anger. In fact, they all described him as harmless."

Michael nodded. "They're holding a press conference tomorrow morning to update the public on the case. Apparently, Craig is going to make a public statement, asking whoever has Rachel and Sadie to let them go. Asking for anyone who saw them to come forward."

"That should be interesting," Granger said. "My suspicion is that he won't do well on television. He'll either come off as stilted and stiff or overly emotional and putting on an act. Why are the police having him do the press conference? They must know he won't do well. Does the man not have a lawyer yet?"

Michael shrugged. "I have no idea. He should, if he doesn't."

Michael made a mental note to look into whether Craig had a lawyer. Given the police's intense interest in him as a potential suspect, which Michael fully accepted as normal, and even smart, he should have representation. It was of course, logical to focus on Craig, given the fact that most women who were murdered were at the hands of their intimate partners. It would be foolish not to start with the boyfriend. Still, there had been a few cases in Michael's experience where police had fixated on the most likely suspect only to be totally going in the wrong direction.

Eugene was a prime example.

Even Michael had been convinced that John and/or Garth Hammond -- and possibly Daryl Kincaid -- were the serial killers the FBI was seeking.

No one -- no one -- thought for a moment about Eugene.

Now, police were focused on Craig. It was still very early on in the case's history and there was enough time to rule him in -- or out. It all came down to the evidence, but Craig's behavior would be under very tough scrutiny. If he did anything wrong, if he appeared to be putting on an act, if he was caught in an unguarded moment smiling or laughing, his status as the prime suspect would be cemented.

"Thanks for your help," Michael said and shook Granger's hand.

"Any time," Granger replied and returned to his own offices.

He really enjoyed his work with the DA's office. It was

possibly the best substitute for his former job with the FBI. He was able to get right into cases, read the evidence, talk to police, and come to conclusions, but he wasn't the one responsible for arresting suspects and all that entailed.

In fact, it was a job he could do permanently if he wanted.

He wasn't sure yet what he wanted to do for the rest of his life, but he knew it would have to be in law enforcement in some capacity. Fighting crime, even if only as an investigator, was in his blood.

He and Tess were alike in that way, their personalities and temperaments forever changed by the experience in Paradise Hill with the disappearance of Lisa. While Tess waited to learn if she was accepted into the FBI, he would have to decide if he enjoyed working for the AG enough to continue in that capacity.

Working the two cases was almost as fulfilling as being an FBI Special Agent. It wasn't exactly the same, but it was close enough that he felt almost like he was back in the saddle again.

CHAPTER TWENTY-ONE

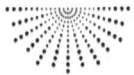

Everything was wonderful.

And then it wasn't.

For three years, everything was great between them and in their little family.

From the time she was eighteen and had finished high school, she was happy. She worked on a diploma in hospitality from the local community college with the hopes of, perhaps, one day opening her own bookstore and coffeeshop. During that time, she and Sadie had lived with Craig in his two-bedroom apartment in a better part of town.

Craig took on the role of step-father with delight. He felt comfortable with children, he said, because they were like kittens or puppies. They didn't judge you or think you were weird. They accepted you for what and who you were, unquestioning even when they questioned everything. They simply accepted that their reality was natural. Their questions were totally innocent and only about how the world worked and not hurtful questions about why you were so weird.

Craig learned to play through his experiences with Sadie. He said he'd never played in his life, having been an only child cared for by servants and nannies, and had always been more interested in books and machines. He'd always found other people confusing and frightening. But with Sadie, he seemed to brighten.

It was weird because Craig was strange, according to everyone else who met him, and yet she only felt at home when she was with him. She felt like she could be her true self.

Craig wanted that. He saw her for who she really was -- someone with a sad dark past, trying to escape it, who only wanted to be happy.

"Be happy with me," he said and pulled her into his arms. "I'll be happy with you. Maybe for once, we can both be happy -- together."

He admitted that she was his first real girlfriend. Girls found him awkward and he never felt he could ask a girl out even if he liked her, because he just couldn't force the words out. It was only after he photographed her enough and knew enough about her that he asked Rachel out for coffee.

She had to make all the first moves, which was actually a good thing for a girl like her who had always been the victim.

But he had to go and screw everything up.

He had to ruin things, and now everything wasn't wonderful.

Everything had gone to shit.

She never told him any details about her past, wanting to forget it as much as possible. She didn't keep much from her earlier life and had only a few items from before she moved to

Seattle. In fact, the only item in her possession from her past life that could identify her was a photo of her and her mother, sitting together on the shore of the lake up near Bellingham where she was really from. The only clue to her past was in that photograph and while she knew it could probably identify her, she couldn't part with it. It was the only proof that she even had a mother.

It was after Sadie died, when she and her mother were alone with him, her father the monster. They'd gone to the lake that day to stay at the cabin. Her father liked to stay in that area. In the photo was a sign that gave the location away -- Silver Lake Lodge.

Craig asked her about the photo when he found it one morning while he stood getting dressed and saw it on her dresser, the corner tucked under the lace cloth that covered the surface. He pulled it out and glanced at it, studying the photo. He turned it over and then back again.

"Is this you and your mom?"

She jumped up and grabbed the photo from his hand, not wanting him to look too closely at it. On the back was the name of the camera store where her father worked. It was also where the film was processed.

"Yes," she said for how could she deny it? It was clearly her and her mom. They both had the same platinum-blonde hair and fine bones.

"Silver Lake," Craig said. "That's in Whatcom County, isn't it? I thought you were from Montana."

Rachel tucked the photo into her handbag, glancing at it quickly before she did. She made up a lie on the fly. "We lived in Montana. Visited Bellingham for several weeks in the summer one year. I was born in Helena, but after my father got into trouble, we moved to rural Montana." Of course, it was a bald-faced lie. They lived in Washington her entire life. They lived in North Seattle. That was where he met her mother. He got in trouble and moved to Maple Falls, changed their name, and tried to start a new life. He worked at the camera store in Bellingham. He took her to Bellingham with him on the weekends, to the warehouse, where she was given to rich men who liked young girls.

He killed Sadie.

"Montana, huh? I've never been there. Maybe we could go sometime. I heard it's pretty nice."

"Why would you want to go to Montana? Washington's just as pretty," Rachel said, not wanting Craig to start digging into her past only to find out it was all a big fat lie.

"That's your mom?" he asked, staring at her in his way, like she was the most interesting subject he could ever study. "She looks just like you. Fine and fair."

Fine and fair.

Rachel didn't feel fine or fair except with Craig. He made her feel that way.

"I'm a lot like her, except I got away," Rachel said.

"You got away?"

She nodded. "From him. I was the lucky one."

"Don't you miss her?" Craig asked, his eyes on her, checking for truthfulness.

Rachel shrugged. "I do, I guess. She was my mother. But she couldn't mother me. She could barely look after herself."

"Is she still alive?"

Rachel shook her head. "No. Dead."

Rachel didn't want to keep talking about her mother. It made her sad to think about the woman who gave her birth and who did so little to protect Rachel and Sadie. Rachel's therapist said that she had to understand that her mother loved her but was unable to protect herself. She couldn't look after Rachel and Sadie because of it.

When Rachel was growing up, she used to blame her mother for everything. If only she'd been a stronger woman, a better mother, a better wife, maybe her father would be nicer. Maybe none of it would have happened. For a while, she hated her mother, but then, after Rachel had run away, and after years of therapy, she realized her mother was as much a victim as Rachel and Sadie.

The only thing to do was forgive her mother for being too weak and move on. She had to focus on the future and what was currently good in her life. That's what Rachel tried to do -- to forget the past. To focus on the now. This current moment.

Her current life was good. Craig was good. She knew he meant well, asking about her past. Sadie was happy in her school. Rachel was happy working at Mickey's and going to class at the community college. That was good enough.

Then, everything went to shit when he found the damn photograph...

She tucked it into a pocket in her handbag, hoping that he didn't ask any more questions about it and her past. Then, she turned to him, a smile on her face. "I don't like to talk about my past. You know that. It was bad. I had some problems and left. That's all you need to know."

"You can't hide from your past," he said. "It's still inside of you." He came over and pulled her into his arms, hugging her tightly. When he pulled back, he kissed her tenderly and then stroked her cheek. "Your past is in here," he said and tapped her head lightly, smiling. "You have to accept it and own it and move forward."

"It's easy to do when your past is good, but not when it's bad. When it's bad, you just want to tuck it away in some dark corner of your memory and hope you never run into it again."

"If you do, it'll always be there waiting. What's so bad in your past that you can't tell me about it, the man who loves you with all his heart?"

"I just don't want to even think about my past," she said in a quiet voice, her throat choking closed at the thought of it. "All you need to know is that bad things happened to me and so I want to forget it completely."

"But you keep this photograph so you can remember your mother."

She nodded. "It's the only photo with me alone with her. This was the only one of us by ourselves."

"Tell me about her."

She shook her head. "All you need to know about me is that my mother is dead. My sister is dead. I left home because I wanted to start a new life somewhere else. That's all you need to know."

Craig frowned and stared into her eyes. "You can tell me. I won't ever tell anyone. I thought you'd know you're safe with me by now."

"It's not that," she said, glancing away nervously. "It's that I want a new life and now I have it. I don't want to talk about my family, okay?"

He hesitated. "I don't like the idea of hiding from your past."

"I like it this way," she said, trying to sound light. "I'm independent. I have a new life and that makes me happy."

"Okay," he said finally, pulling her against him again. "If you're sure."

"I am. My family just doesn't exist anymore. You and Sadie are my family now."

She should have been more truthful and then maybe he wouldn't have tried to find out about her past. Instead, she downplayed the real reason she wanted to hide from her previous life. And he took it upon himself to find out who she really was.

And now, everything was shit.

It was all because of that damn photograph of her and her mother. Developed at Bird Camera and Photography store in Bellingham, where her father worked. The cabin in which they lived near Maple Falls, where she never wanted to step foot again. Where they lived until Sadie died and where it all happened.

There was a stamp on the back of the photo with the name and address of Bird Camera and Photography in Bellingham and that was what led Craig to the place.

When she found a receipt for gas that he'd bought from a local Chevron station in Bellingham, she knew he'd actually gone there in person to check. She stood at his chest of drawers and stared at the receipt, her heart racing.

He'd actually gone to Bellingham...

What would he have discovered while he was there?

Her past was there. Some of the only good memories she had were there -- from before it all happened. Before he killed Sadie, when she and her sister were happy, playing together at the cabin, swimming in the lake.

Her mother even seemed happy then, too. At least, happier.

She and Sadie had thought they lived the perfect life. Unlike the other kids, they didn't go to regular school. They were home-schooled, taught what good citizens should know instead of all the lies the government-run schools taught. According to her father, they lived good natural lives, off the grid and off the land as much as possible, growing their own food when they could.

Their father hunted and fished with his brothers and with the other men in the area. Sure, the cabin they lived in was small, and they didn't have running water or electricity, chopping wood for fuel, using candles for light at night, but back then, she and Sadie didn't know they were missing out. They were just two happy peas in a pod.

That's what their mother always said.

Two peas in a pod.

She had been happy once, until things changed. Until Sadie and her father started going off alone together. At first, she was jealous of Sadie for spending more time with her father.

Why Sadie and not her?

But then Sadie seemed unhappy and talked about wanting to run away.

"Why do you want to run away?" she asked, upset that Sadie had been out all day with her father, leaving her alone with her mother to do chores. "Seems like you have it so good, going to town with Father..."

"I wish it was you instead," Sadie had said in a tearful voice. "You could go with him."

Sadie went to the tiny room they shared at the back of the cabin. Her face was wet.

Rachel followed. "Why? Why are you crying?"

But Sadie would never tell her.

And then, Sadie was dead, and it was all too late.

CHAPTER TWENTY-TWO

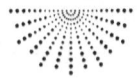

Tess worried about Craig.

She went to his apartment that morning before the press conference, agreeing to attend the event with him for moral support.

It made her feel a bit guilty because she was also writing an in-depth article about the case, due of its natural link to her work on missing and murdered women and children in Washington State.

But he was also a friend and colleague, even if they didn't socialize, and they worked closely on many stories and she felt a real affection for him.

She arrived at the apartment building and texted him that she was waiting outside.

CRAIG: I overslept and have to have a shower. Do you want to wait in the car or come up?

Tess considered. She'd usually demure and stay in the car, but she wanted to check out the apartment. She felt guilty for doing so, but it was all information she could use to understand what the hell was going on.

TESS: *I'll be right up.*

CRAIG: OK *I'll buzz you in.*

She left her car and went to the front entrance, pressing the button beside his name on the panel. He buzzed the door and she went to his apartment and knocked on the door. When Craig answered, he looked terrible. His hair was a mess, falling in his eyes, which were bleary and red, and he had a considerable growth of stubble.

"Come in, Tess. Thank you for being a friend."

"Don't mention it," she said and entered, hanging her coat on a hook on the wall.

"Have a seat. I'll be quick."

"Thanks," she replied and went into the living room. There were empty boxes of pizza and half-eaten takeout containers of Chinese on the dining room table. A dozen newspapers littered the floor and sofa. The place was a mess.

She picked up the boxes and cartons and took them to the kitchen, where she emptied them into the appropriate containers under the sink for recycling and composting. After she was done, she loaded the dishwasher and found the detergent. She turned it on. At least Craig would have some clean dishes. It looked like he hadn't done the dishes since Rachel left. There were also some dirty pots that couldn't fit in the tiny apartment sized dishwasher, but she wasn't going to scrub them.

Instead, she piled them neatly into the sink and wiped off the counters.

Then, she went back to the living room and collected up the newspapers, folding them neatly and placing them in recycling where other newspapers were waiting for recycling day.

She glanced into the main bedroom and saw that it was also a mess, with the bed covers all tossed in a heap, and dirty clothes on the floor and covering the chair by the closet.

He'd really fallen apart.

She sat down on the sofa and took out her laptop, writing down a few notes based on her assessment of his apartment. This was not the apartment of someone who was celebrating finally being rid of a girlfriend he no longer wanted. This was the apartment of a man who was broken, who was either overcome with guilt and remorse over his actions or was truly brokenhearted at the disappearance of his beloved and her daughter.

Craig emerged from the bathroom about ten minutes later, freshly showered and dressed, rubbing his hair with a towel.

"Feel better?" she asked, forcing a smile, closing up her laptop.

"No," he said.

She frowned and kicked herself. He couldn't play the game of pretending to be fine. He wasn't fine and couldn't pretend otherwise.

"I'm sorry. Of course, you're not better."

"I just have to brush my hair and we can go."

She nodded and collected her things, stuffing the laptop into the bag.

They slipped on their coats and boots and she followed him out to the parking lot.

"Do you want to come with me?" she asked. "I can take you there and bring you back home, if you'd rather not drive."

"Yes, thanks," he said. "I'm so tired. I can hardly think straight."

She drove to the police station in the north precinct, which was located next to City Hall, and found a parking spot about a block away. They walked together to the entrance and checked in at the reception desk. They were escorted to a waiting area. At that point, Tess stayed in the waiting room, while Craig met with the detective in charge before the event.

She had press credentials, so was allowed to cover it for the *Sentinel*, but she had to wait with the other members of the press, and it was about forty-five minutes before the press conference began. Tess went to the room where the press conference was being held and saw that they had blown up a photo of Rachel and Sadie, which was on display behind the lectern. To each side of the lectern sat a couple of other staff from the Seattle PD, and on the far left, Craig. He looked broken, sitting there, avoiding eye contact with everyone and anyone.

Tess felt a pang of sadness for him. He was a mess.

The Detective in charge, Mark Chambers, started off by giving a description of the case, and how Rachel and Sadie had gone missing after they were supposed to go for a short vacation together. Craig hadn't reported her missing for a week, because of that. Chambers noted that Rachel had told her employer that she was going on a trip and would be gone for the weekend and maybe longer. He'd cleared her shifts for the five days she expected to be away. Chambers went over the details of finding the vehicle abandoned on a remote logging road near Mt. Baker and how their possessions were still in the vehicle, including suitcases and Rachel's handbag and cell phone.

Finally, the time came for Craig to speak. He stood up and walked to the lectern. He had a single piece of paper folded up in his shirt pocket and unfolded it carefully, like he was using the time to gather his courage. He cleared his throat, and then glanced at the reporters gathered in front of the lectern.

"Thank you for being here," he said, his voice cracking. "Rachel was -- is -- my life." Then, he broke down right away and had to cover his eyes for a moment. Tess thought that wasn't a good sign. He said 'was' at first. Did he think she was dead?

He got hold of himself and cleared his throat again. Then, he read from the sheet of paper.

"If you have Rachel and Sadie, please let them go. They deserve to live. Rachel had a very hard life before she came to Seattle. She has worked so hard to provide for Sadie. Both of them deserve to live. Rachel, if you ran away to escape from someone or something, please let us know. People here will protect you. Just come home."

He turned away and sat back down at his place.

Detective Chambers got up and thanked everyone, repeated the phone number for the tip line, and then closed the press conference.

That was it.

Tess waited until everyone else had left the room and then went over to where Craig stood lifelessly, alone near the back door to the conference room. The police detectives and staff spoke together while the members of the press left the room.

"How are you?" Tess asked when she got to Craig.

He shook his head, seemingly too upset to speak.

"Let's go, unless they want to speak with you more."

Craig turned to Detective Chambers. "Can I go?"

Chambers gave Tess the once-over, checking out her press pass, probably wondering about her. They'd never met before, but she was a bit notorious, given her experience in Paradise Hill shooting Eugene and rescuing Elena.

"Don't leave town," Chambers said firmly. He turned away, dismissing Craig.

"Let's go," Tess said and took Craig's arm, wanting to comfort him. He allowed Tess to lead him out, her hand on his elbow, guiding him down the hallway to the exit.

They drove to Craig's apartment and Tess parked in front of the building.

"Will you be all right?" she asked.

"I don't know," Craig said. "I don't know."

He got out of the car and stood on the sidewalk for a moment, like he was thinking of what he should do next.

"Call me if you need anything," Tess said.

"Thanks," he replied and then he closed the car door and walked up to the building without looking back.

He was like a zombie, she thought as she watched him disappear into the darkened building entrance. He came off as an extremely exhausted and emotional wreck at the press conference.

Did the police find his performance appropriate or acceptable? What was their thinking, putting him up in front of the cameras like that?

CHAPTER TWENTY-THREE

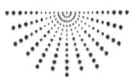

MICHAEL WATCHED the press conference with interest, not having attended because of a previous meeting with Nick about a new case, but he was curious to see how Craig performed and what the purpose was of putting him in front of the cameras.

Usually, it was to encourage citizens to send in any tips they had on the missing person's whereabouts. Seeing a distraught relative or loved one break down on television elicited sympathy in viewers and led them to call in with tips. It often took a public event to tweak people's memories and motivate them to call in with information. As soon as a press conference was over, the police tip line would be flooded with calls -- most of them bogus sightings and musings of people on what happened. But there was almost always a tidbit of truth here and there that helped move the case forward.

Sometimes, it was to encourage citizens to call police with what they knew about the suspect. Seeing a suspect in the case in front of cameras acting all upset would lead to a tip that helped close the case -- someone remembering an event in the suspect's past that helped build a case against them -- or exonerate them.

That might be Chambers' thinking in this instance.

If he was honest, Chambers had to be as uncertain as Michael was, because Craig did not feel like a killer. Perhaps Chambers just wanted to show that he was working the case and really hadn't decided to pursue Craig to the exclusion of all other suspects. There were enough sex offenders in the Metro Seattle area to keep them busy following up on everyone's whereabouts for days. Michael had spoken with a few of the other detectives in the department and knew they had their minds made up that Craig was responsible for the disappearance of Rachel and Sadie and all that was left was building the case.

There were a number of strikes against Craig: he didn't report them missing, and only confirmed they were gone when police questioned him hours after their abandoned vehicle was discovered. A neighbor in the building said she heard Craig and Rachel arguing the night she left and saw Rachel and Sadie leave the apartment building alone. The neighbor didn't report seeing Craig leave the apartment, but she went to bed soon after and he could have left without her knowing.

So, it was still possible that Craig followed Rachel up to the location, killed them both and left the vehicle there. Who could say where he might have buried the bodies?

There were thousands of miles of old logging roads in the northern Washington area.

Unless they found a crime scene that had blood evidence showing that Rachel and Sadie had been murdered, all they had were two missing persons cases and a lot of suspicions.

It was at that point that Michael thought about Mickey and decided to go have a chat with the man.

He'd been dissatisfied with Tess's discussion with Mickey. Maybe it was time to really push him for information about Rachel and her past. It was a big empty box and there was nothing he or the police could really go on to build a theory of the case outside of Craig being the main suspect, killing her and Sadie out of jealousy or anger.

He got on the phone and called Mickey's bar, asking to speak to Mickey. He identified himself as an investigator with the DA's office and waited while the hostess found Mickey.

Finally, the man came on the phone.

Michael introduced himself again and asked if he could come by and speak with Mickey about Rachel.

"Sure," Mickey said, and he didn't sound at all upset at the prospect of being questioned. "Always glad to help the investigation. When would work for you?"

"I can come by in fifteen."

"Okay but don't come to the bar. I'll meet you farther down Aurora at the donut shop. I don't want police in my bar. The employees will worry that I'm in trouble."

"You're not in trouble, Mickey. I'm just filling in some blanks in my file."

"I understand," he said finally. "See you in fifteen."

"See you then." Michael ended the call and pulled together his files, looking over the evidence collected to date, deciding on his approach to Mickey. How could he get Mickey to give up more background on Rachel than he already had? Mickey had a pretty rough past, had been in prison, involved in a motorcycle club. He'd found Jesus and turned his life around and was now apparently a saint.

He looked on Rachel as one of his children, as a success story. The man would want to do whatever he could to find her, if that was the case.

He drove along Aurora Avenue to the donut store a few blocks south of Mickey's Bar and Grill and parked on the street about a block down from the entrance. He glanced around and saw Mickey walking down the street towards the store. The man was looking around nervously, and then ducked into the donut shop. Michael got out and went in after him.

Mickey was at the register ordering a coffee and donut when Michael arrived at his side.

"Hello, Mickey?" he said and extended his hand.

Mickey turned to look at Michael. "You're Special Agent Carter with the CARD team? I remember you from the case in Paradise Hill. It was all over the news back in January."

"Not a special agent anymore," Michael replied. "I'm working with the DA's office as an investigator." He pointed to his right shoulder. "I had an injury that keeps me from shooting. Can't be trusted with a gun any longer." Michael smiled, trying to make light of it.

"That's too bad," Mickey said. "I'll go grab us a booth."

While Michael ordered his own coffee, Mickey took a booth by the window and waited. Once his coffee was ready, Michael joined the man, still wondering how he should approach Mickey.

"Look," Michael said after taking a seat. "I'll get right to the point. I'm hoping to save Rachel and Sadie's lives. We need to know everything that anyone knows about them so we can find them. Everything. Good or bad. If her life is in danger, we need to know who might be a threat. If she and Sadie have been harmed, we need to find who did it and bring them to justice."

Mickey took in a deep breath and sat back. "I'm just as anxious as you are to make sure Rachel and Sadie are safe. Those two are like a daughter and granddaughter to me. I'd do anything to keep them safe. I hope you understand that. Anything."

"That's good to know. So according to your report to the police when they questioned you, Rachel called in and said she was taking a vacation and needed some time off. Is that right?"

"Yes. She said she wanted to take Sadie on a short vacation. Didn't know how many days. I needed to find someone to cover for her shifts. I always make the schedule up a week ahead and I'd already made it up. I'd have to cover her three shifts the following week."

"That must have been inconvenient for you."

"It happens."

"Straight up." Michael said, wanting to get to the point. "What do you think happened? The police are leaning towards Craig as the prime suspect, but I want to know what you think. Do you think it was Craig?"

"Straight up? No, I don't think it was Craig. I think she was afraid of someone from her past and ran away."

That surprised Michael. "You didn't tell that to police."

"I took her at her word that she was taking a short trip with her daughter, but when the car was found, maybe she wasn't telling me the truth. After her car was found abandoned with her luggage and handbag still inside, I had to consider that maybe, someone had it in for her."

"So, you think she was afraid and that's why she left. Not because she wanted a vacation."

Mickey nodded. "Maybe someone she was afraid of found her. All I know is that it wasn't Craig. Of that I am certain."

Michael made a mental note of that. Someone who knew her well was certain that the main suspect wasn't guilty. There was no reason other than the man didn't think Craig did it.

"What can you tell me about Rachel's past? I understand she was a runaway and came to Seattle from Montana."

Mickey took a bite of his donut and chewed for a moment before responding and in that hesitation, Michael felt the man was trying to decide what to say -- or how much to reveal.

"She had a very bad, abusive past," Mickey said. "Father was a monster. A real scumbag. From what she told me, he abused her, sold her to pedophiles. Finally, he started using a knife when he raped her, and she ran. I mean, this was a thirteen-year-old girl. What a horrible life. She told Craig that she was afraid her past was catching up with her. Well, that might be what she was running from."

"Did you tell this to police?"

Mickey shrugged. "I told them she had a bad past. They didn't dig any deeper than that."

Michael shook his head in disgust. "I knew she had a troubled past but had no idea it was that bad. Was this in Montana?"

"Yes, but there are links to Washington State. You should be looking up north, Bellingham area. There's a big network across the three states, and they operate in Washington as well. Bellingham. Rachel mentioned it once, if I recall correctly. Her father used to travel there. They may have spent some time in the area when she was growing up."

Michael frowned. He knew there were pedophiles operating online across the country, and who sought out children for sex, preying on street kids and the children of addicts. But Bellingham? It wasn't like it was a known hotbed of pedophiles.

"Her father was into child porn as well. He took pictures, made porno films. Photography was his specialty. He was into cameras. You should be checking it out."

Michael nodded. "We will. This is really helpful. I'm surprised the police didn't ask you this. Why didn't you tell them?"

"I did but they didn't dig any deeper."

They spoke for a while longer, but there was nothing else Mickey could tell him about Rachel's past.

He shook Mickey's hand and they parted, Mickey walking north to the bar and Michael to his Jeep. He drove back to the office, an unsettled feeling in his gut. Mickey had a lot to say about Rachel's past that he hadn't told police. Police didn't seem interested in what Mickey had to say.

Michael intended to check out anything he could find on pedophiles operating in the Bellingham area. Someone into cameras and making child porn. Mickey appeared to suggest that was who might have taken Rachel and Sadie, if anyone did.

It wasn't much, but it was something.

And it seemed to tie in directly with his double murder case...

CHAPTER TWENTY-FOUR

"I TOLD you not to ask me about my past," she said to Craig. She held up the credit card receipt and stared at him, frowning, a hand on her hip. "Why did you have to go to Bellingham?"

He came over to her and took the receipt out of her hand, looking at it with a guilty expression on his face. "I want to know your past," he said softly. "Besides, you shouldn't be snooping in my things if you feel such a need for privacy." He tucked the receipt into his pocket and exhaled in frustration.

"You shouldn't be snooping in my life," she replied. "I'm trying to forget it."

He took hold of her shoulders, his eyes on hers. "Tell me why."

She shook her head.

"Why won't you tell me?" he asked, frustration in his voice. "If we're going to be together, I need to know."

"Why do you need to know?" she protested. "It's bad. That's all you need to know. Of all people, you should understand.

You don't do this," she said and pointed to the faint scars where she'd cut herself when she was younger, "if you were happy and had a good childhood. I had a bad childhood, okay? My family is bad. I ran away from home because of it. I don't want to talk about my family, I don't want to see them, I don't want to ever hear about them or where they are, or what they're doing."

"I should know what happened," he said softly. "In case I need to know for some reason. I can keep a secret, Rachel. I can protect you."

She gave him a look of disbelief. "You couldn't protect me. Not from *him*."

She should have shut up at that point, but she couldn't.

"Why not?"

She shook her head, intending to stop talking, but unable. "Because he's strong. He's big. He's mean, and he has every kind of weapon you could imagine."

"We could go to the police," Craig said and led her over to the sofa. He took her hand and pulled her down beside him. She sat on his lap, trying to avoid his eyes. "We could tell them what happened, and they could arrest him, if it was as bad as you say. He hurt you. He made those thicker scars on your breasts and stomach. He made those, right?"

She shook her head quickly, not wanting to tell him anything. "I'm not talking about it."

"It's okay," he said and exhaled slowly. "You don't have to tell me anything you don't want to tell me. One day, if you want, you can tell me everything. I won't judge."

He wrapped his arms around her, and she felt his warmth and tenderness. He had never once hurt her. He had never once forced her to do anything. It made her heart almost burst with love for him that he was so good, so patient. He wanted to protect her, but she knew he couldn't ever hope to.

Her father was just too evil.

No one could protect Sadie or her mother from him. She knew that even Craig or the police couldn't protect her from him either.

She wanted to tell Craig the truth about it all, get it off her chest, unburden herself of the pain of her past, but she knew it would only lead to badness. The fact that he went to Bellingham to find out about her was dangerous. All she could do was hold it in and beg him not to look any deeper.

"Don't go back to Bellingham again," she whispered against his shoulder. She glanced up in his eyes. "If you do, you'll put me in danger. He can't ever know where I am. Ever. That's why I ran away."

He nodded and she hoped he finally understood.

"Well, the first thing we're going to do is get you feeling safer," Craig said. "There's a self-defense and personal protection class at the community center run by a retired cop. It teaches you how to protect yourself from being attacked or abducted. You should take it. We could take it together, if you want. That way, if the past ever catches up with you, you can stop it from harming you."

Rachel exhaled. She was glad he was turning his focus on protection instead of knowing more about her.

"Okay," she said softly. "I'd like to learn how to protect myself. I'd like to teach Sadie as well."

"When she's old enough, she can take the class. I think it's for age twelve and up."

Rachel nodded and put her hand on his arm. "No more snooping, okay? No more questions."

He nodded. "No more snooping or questions until you're ready."

"I won't be ready until he's dead," she said in a quiet voice.

"Oh, *Rachel*," he said, and his voice cracked. He pulled her into his arms once more and she let him hold her, needing his warmth to chase away her sadness. She sighed and tried to put the receipt out of her mind, but she feared he'd opened a hornet's nest.

For the next few weeks, she went to the class down at the local community center. Once a week at the fitness club, she learned how to walk with confidence to discourage anyone who might be following her. She learned how to spot danger and how to avoid being abducted. She learned how to escape from different approaches and holds. She learned where to hit and practiced hitting a punching bag, kicking the bag in the nuts, ramming her fingers into imaginary eyes, elbowing necks. She learned how to escape zip ties and various restraints.

She even practiced shouting, which was hard for her. She was short and had a slight build. She had barely any voice, having always been so passive, but Danny, the police officer who taught the course, said that attackers relied on women being quiet and fearful.

"You have to scream," he said firmly. "You have to yell. You should be angry that someone wants to harm you. The man who is trying to grab you is counting on you being nice. He's hoping you'll be too polite to scream or yell but that will only get you dead. You have to get *mad*. Never ever get in a car with anyone. Never ever let them put you in the car, in the trunk. Once they have you, they'll take you somewhere they can control you and no one will find you. You can't let that happen. You have to scream, you have to run, you have to kick and yell when you're still in public and there are people around. Once you're out in the countryside, you're dead. Save yourself before that happens. Once it does, the odds are against you."

She promised herself that she'd never let any man take her, get her into a trunk and drive her into the forest. So, even though she was tiny and thin and had a soft voice, she tried to get mad. She'd bitten back her anger for so many years, she could barely remember how it felt. Instead, she'd taken drugs or drank away her anger. She'd swallowed it and turned it into small cuts on her thighs and arms alongside the ones *he* made.

The stab wounds that finally drove her to run away.

She wasn't going to let silence or fear make her an easy target.

She practiced yelling when she did kickboxing. She screamed into pillows when she was alone, when Craig was at work and Sadie was at school. She stood in front of her mirror and held her knife in her hand, practicing stabbing whoever tried to abduct her, always imagining his face when she drove the blade down.

It felt surprisingly good.

In the end, the course and the kickboxing were great antidotes to her fear. After the six weeks were up, and she got her certificate in self-defense and personal protection, she felt a lot better about things. She didn't want to get a gun, like Craig suggested. Guns frightened her and she worried about Sadie finding it and accidentally shooting herself or someone else.

Instead, she got a Kershaw Natrix XL pocketknife and ankle holder.

From that day on, she wore that concealed knife whenever she went out. She'd drive to the campus at night for her class, park in the parking lot, and feel completely safe. If anyone dared to try anything with her, she'd simply bend down and pull it out. One of the things the police officer who taught the self-defense course made them practice was aggression.

She had to learn to yell and scream and punch and hit.

All the things he'd beaten and threatened out of her.

So, she took up kick boxing. Three days a week, she went to the fitness club with Craig and learned how to kick box. Craig smiled, watching her with her gloves on and helmet, the mouth protection, while she kicked and punched and grunted. He seemed really proud of her. She even put on a bit of muscle during those months after she'd found the receipt.

"Look," she said and held up her arm, tensing her bicep to show how much bigger it was. "I'm getting stronger."

"You are," he said and pinched her arm to feel the muscle. "Pretty soon you'll be able to take me."

She laughed because Craig was so tall and thin, and so harmless. She couldn't imagine him hurting a fly.

In fact, she laughed once when he opened the window in the apartment just so he could let a fly outside instead of killing it with a folded newspaper, the way she was going to.

"Don't kill it," he said and shooed it outside. "It has a life. It has a place in the ecosystem."

"As long as it doesn't have a place in my apartment," Rachel said and smiled at him, watching as he tried desperately to shoo the fly outside. The stupid thing kept coming back in and Craig would have to chase it back out

THE GIRL WHO RAN AWAY

again. Finally, after many attempts, Craig managed to get the fly to leave.

He seemed really happy not to have to kill that fly.

He really was harmless. Maybe it was him who should take the self-defense class...

Still, she worried that Craig going up north would alert her father that she was still alive, and someone was looking for him. To be safe, she started to hoard her money, saving it in case she had to leave again. She went to Mickey one day and asked him if he could get her and Sadie fake ID that could be used to cross into Mexico if she needed.

"I know people who can get you what you need, but do you really want to go down that route?"

"I might have no other choice," she said. "Can you help me out? I'll pay whatever it costs."

He finally nodded and sighed audibly. "Okay, but I don't like it. You deserve to be happy, and so does that little girl of yours. After all you've been through. What names do you want, if you have any preferences?"

Rachel shrugged. "For me, just something that starts with R, so it's easier for me to remember. For Sadie? How about Elsa? That's her favorite character from the movie Frozen. She'll like that. Can you do that?"

"I can try. If Craig is being bad to you, I'll talk to him, straighten him out."

"No, I'm happy," she said and smiled. "Craig is great and I love what I'm doing. This is just an insurance policy in case my past catches up with me."

Mickey came through with the fake ID for her and Sadie and Rachel tucked the documents into a lock box she bought at Walmart. Soon, she had a tidy sum put away in the event that the shit hit the fan, as her father used to say. In her case, that meant her father finding out where she was.

So, she really felt safe for a while.

She grew more confident in general because of the self-defense class and the knife tucked into its holder on her ankle. She walked down streets at night and was no longer afraid. She didn't need drugs or alcohol to numb the pain. Instead she practiced kicking and yelling and stabbing. She had learned to use her own innate desire to protect herself.

Life went on as normal, with Sadie at school and Rachel taking classes and working lunch shifts at Mickey's, taking the occasional evening shift when Mickey needed someone to stand in. Craig worked taking photos for the *Sentinel*, and he worked on his personal projects, photos of downtown, the waterfront, and occasionally, of mountains. He started doing film projects as well, and used drone shots, stringing together views of the city with free music he found on the internet. They even went into the mountains to take shots of the Cascades.

He was really an artist at heart, which was strange, since he was so interested in the science of things.

Their relationship was good. She felt safe with him. She trusted him with Sadie, never worried that he would abuse her even when the two of them were alone.

They were a happy little family of choice -- not one of birth and blood.

And then...

One day a month later, she felt like someone was following

her. It was nothing at first, just a person ducking into a doorway when she turned around to check behind her.

No, it couldn't be...

She was just creeped out after Craig told her about a case in the interior of Washington State of a child porn ring that had been operating for years under everyone's noses. It had state-wide tentacles and was linked to the sex trade. When he told her about the case, she tried to act nonchalant, as if she wasn't interested. Of course, she thought about her father and his friends right away, because they used to take pictures of what they did to her. When Craig told her there had been murders of children up in Bellingham and in Idaho and Montana, and that a child serial killer was operating in Washington State, she had trouble sleeping at night for the first time in a long time.

It made her think about Sadie and what happened way back when.

She began to feel the hairs stand up on the back of her neck when she walked alone to her car late at night after her class was over or after a shift at Mickey's. She thought about her knife, tucked in its holder down beside her ankle. She thought about what she'd do if someone tried to grab her from behind -- how she'd twist around and jab the man's eyes out. How she'd knee him in the balls. How she'd elbow him in the throat. How if she had to, she'd reach down and grab her knife and stab him.

She always thought her father would come after her, try to kill her for leaving. She never thought her father would take little Sadie in the middle of the day.

But that's what he did.

CHAPTER TWENTY-FIVE

TESS WATCHED as Michael slumped down onto the sofa, his head on one arm rest, his feet on the other. "I'm exhausted," he said and let out a long sigh.

She sat on the sofa beside him. "Tell me. What's exhausting you?"

He pulled her down for a quick kiss and then stroked her arm. "I met with Mickey today. He told me a horrific story about Rachel and the abuse she experienced as a child."

Tess frowned. "I knew she had a hard life but didn't know any details."

"This was more than hard. Based on what he told me, it was hell."

"Tell me," Tess said and settled in beside him. "Tell me what you can off the record, of course."

Michael exhaled as if the prospect was hard for him. Of course, he'd developed PTSD after dealing with child sexual abuse and murder and so she understood that another case of child sexual abuse would be difficult for him to deal with.

"If you don't want to talk about it, I understand," she said softly and laid her hand on his arm. "I know it's difficult for you."

He shook his head. "No, it's just tiring to hear story after story. I was so lucky to have grown up in a good family. It sometimes surprises me to face evidence of a bad one. How children survive is a miracle."

"They're resilient, at least, most of them. Some can't adapt. They turn to drugs and alcohol."

He nodded and told her about his trip to meet with Mickey. She listened with rapt attention as he detailed his trip to the donut store on Aurora, and how Mickey wanted to avoid him showing up at the bar.

"Sounds like she really was afraid of someone from her past," Tess said, lying down beside Michael and getting comfortable.

"She was," he said. "One thing Mickey was certain of was that Craig wasn't the kind of guy who could do this and that there were no problems that he knew of between them."

"How would Mickey know that?" she said doubtfully, even though she felt the same way from her own experience with Craig. "With a lot of couples, you have no idea until they break up or announce their divorce."

"You're right but I think he was pretty close with Rachel. He saw her as a kind of surrogate daughter. He's quite the character and has seen the rougher side of life, of people," Michael said. "I read up on him after the interview. His past is pretty storied. Army, biker gang, petty crime, major crime, then redemption, the mission," he said with a sigh. "He seemed really upset at what happened with Rachel's and Sadie's disappearance."

They lay in silence for a moment, both of them thinking about the case. Finally, she sat up.

"Hungry?"

He nodded. "I don't feel like cooking, but I sure could go for something hot. Kung Pao?"

"Sounds like just what the doctor ordered. And a beer," she added.

They drove to their favorite Chinese restaurant closer to downtown Seattle and were sitting at a table in the window, watching the pedestrians go by when Michael got a call on his cell.

"Hello, Michael Carter speaking," he said shifting his cell to his shoulder while he scooped some of the Kung Pao onto his plate.

His eyes widened and he glanced up at Tess.

"That's curious," he said and picked up the phone after putting the spoon down, his attention now focused on the call. He listened some more, his eyes on Tess. "Thanks for calling. I'll be in bright and early."

He ended the call and placed his cell down on the table.

"The ME identified one of the dead men in my case up near Silver Lake. It's a William Sutton from, get this -- Bellingham."

"Bellingham?" Tess said, her own eyes wide. "Where have I heard that mentioned before? Oh, right. You just mentioned it because Mickey mentioned it."

"Precisely," Michael said and sat looking at the dish of food in front of him. "One of the two murdered men was from Bellingham -- a place that has been identified by a witness as a place Rachel was linked to and people she feared. They identified Sutton from prints and dental work matches up. He's also on the national registry. Tier Three."

"Holy hell," Tess said. "I guess we were right about the filming equipment. They weren't just doing a video for their blog on hunting and fishing."

"Nope," he replied. "He's supposed to verify his address every ninety days. Was convicted of abduction and rape of a child under twelve and sentenced to prison. He was released about five years ago and has been complying with the terms of his parole -- at least with respect to reporting in. He was obviously breaking those terms, if our interpretation of the evidence at the scene was correct."

"Which was?" Tess asked, knowing Michael could only tell her so much.

"There were children's toys present. Girl's dolls, clothes. Like what a pedophile would use to lure a child or keep them amused." Michael shook his head. "Sick fucks."

Tess watched Michael's face as he poked at his food. She could see he'd lost his appetite by the way he pushed his food around on his plate.

"I know you're not in favor of the death penalty in general," he said and glanced at her, "but sometimes you wonder if it wouldn't be the better option for some of these hard-core pedophiles. They're not going to change. Ever."

Tess nodded. "I might make an exception. These kinds of people screw up children for the rest of their lives. And they won't stop. It's just that we can't always catch them breaking the terms of their parole until after the fact."

She sighed and leaned back in the booth, her own appetite now gone. "It's good to have one ID on your victims, but it kind of tears at you. A convicted child kidnapper and rapist is murdered. Do you celebrate or feel a need to get justice for him?"

"Always justice," Michael said. "By finding out who did this, we might uncover even more crimes that we can close, and bring a murderer to justice."

Tess nodded. "You're right. Sometimes, I get so mad at the stuff I read about pedophiles that my sense of justice is temporarily dampened, but you're right. Even a creep like Sutton deserves justice, even if only to take his killer off the streets."

Michael pushed his plate away. "I've stuffed myself enough for now. Let's go get a couple of beers and go home."

"Lead on," she said and smiled, although she didn't really feel it. She found it hard to celebrate when there were murders and disappearances that demanded to be investigated, murderers brought to justice.

The next day, she and Michael got up and went for a run before Michael showered and ate his breakfast, intending on getting to the DA's office early. Tess planned on going in to the *Sentinel* to work on her articles. She had a meeting with Kate to talk about the most recent article on Paradise Hill, which focused on how police in the local department, especially Chief Joe, had missed the serial killer under their noses.

She felt bad for the Chief and his wife. They must feel responsible in some way for Eugene, despite the fact that when they adopted him, the seeds of his psychopathy were already laid down. He was abused, physically and sexually, before age five and had likely inherited defective genes from his psychopath father Daryl. No matter how good of a home the two provided Eugene, they hadn't been able to overcome that early experience of abuse. If anything, Chief Joe would have made Eugene even more effective as a serial killer by feeding him tidbits of information about the cases, allowing Eugene to evade detection for decades.

Tess tried to be as objective as she could, but it was difficult. She had developed an affection for Chief Joe over her time in Paradise Hill and it made her sympathetic to him. She didn't want to write anything critical of him but neither did she want to whitewash the case. He was clearly blinded by his family ties to Eugene and didn't catch the signs that his adopted son was a psychopathic serial child killer.

Most people didn't figure out they had a serial killer under their nose until they read about it in the news.

"What are your plans for the day?" Michael asked as he poured his thermos of coffee. "More work on the article?"

"I was just thinking about Chief Joe," she said and leaned against the kitchen island. "I wonder how he's doing."

"He's living in paradise," Michael said and went over to her, his thermos of coffee in hand. "He and his wife are in a retirement village, with manicured lawns and a restaurant and golf course. I imagine they're doing okay, considering."

"Don't you feel bad?"

"Of course," Michael said and pulled on his jacket and boots. "The man was like a mentor to me when I was younger and considered joining the FBI. Everyone was totally blind about Eugene. He was that good at covering his tracks."

"He was. He killed all those cats. He broke into all those homes and stole all kinds of trophies. He knew where all the security cameras were located so he knew where he could get caught and where he was safe."

"He told his mother that all the stolen property he amassed was all from flea markets or pawn shops. He knew what to say because he read every serial killer case in the library," Michael added. He grabbed his briefcase and then Tess went to him and gave him a goodbye kiss.

"Want to go out for supper tonight?" she asked. "Maybe go for Happy Hour somewhere and get some bar food?"

"I'll see what's on the agenda for the day. I'm meeting with the ME about the double homicide up North in the late afternoon, but I should be able to make Happy Hour."

"Give me a call," she said and watched him leave, closing the door to the apartment when he disappeared down the stairwell.

CHAPTER TWENTY-SIX

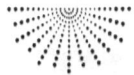

ON RACHEL'S way home on that Friday afternoon, she was listening to music on her iPhone, her ear pods in her ears. She'd just finished a lunch shift at Mickey's and was feeling mellow because her tips had been especially good, as they always were on payday. She wanted to buy something nice for supper -- maybe some steaks that Craig could grill on the new barbecue they had on the patio.

She was driving down a long stretch of street about a dozen blocks from home, arriving at the playground to pick up Sadie.

She saw the group of kids who hung out after school, waiting for their parents to pick them up. They were out early, and Rachel was a few moments late, but Sadie knew not to leave.

She was supposed to be waiting for Rachel to pick her up.

That was the rule -- wait until Rachel came to pick her up. Do not leave for any reason.

Every day, it was the same: Rachel finished her lunch shift

at Mickey's. She drove to the bank and deposited her tips, keeping some left over for the lock box and for her and Sadie to get a drink at 7-Eleven before going home.

Rachel drove up to where Sadie was supposed to be waiting.

Where was she? Why did she leave?

She knew not to leave...

Rachel parked her car and got out, walking over to where Cecile and Dana were sitting on swings.

She stood with her hands on her hips. "Where's Sadie?"

"We got out early today. While we were waiting, her grandpa came. He said that he had to pick her up because you had to work an extra shift at Mickey's."

Rachel felt like ice had gone through her veins.

"What did he look like?"

Cecile shrugged. "I don't know... Like a grandpa? He was old. He had grey hair and a beard."

"Did Sadie go with him willingly or was she abducted?"

When Dana and Cecile frowned, Rachel understood that the girls had no comprehension of the concept.

"I mean, did she seem happy to go with him?"

"I don't know," Cecile said, shrugging one shoulder. "He said you couldn't come and pick her up. That he was her grandpa."

Rachel walked back to her car and got inside. She didn't know what to do -- it had to be her father. Who else would pretend to be Sadie's grandpa? Who else would have just walked up to the playground and taken Sadie like that? Considering Craig had been up poking around Bellingham recently, it had to be her father...

Rachel checked her watch -- she wasn't late, but they'd

gotten out early. The school was supposed to tell parents when their kids were being let out early.

Why would Sadie leave with a man she didn't know? Over the years, Rachel tried to make Sadie as aware of danger as possible without making her afraid. She had obviously not gotten the message that she wasn't supposed to ever leave with a stranger.

Rachel had drummed it into Sadie's head that she should always wait at the school playground until she or Craig picked her up. She was never to leave and go to a friend's house unless they had already made plans and it was arranged beforehand.

She was *never* to get into a car with a stranger.

And yet, she got into the car with a man who claimed to be her grandpa?

Craig's father was dead so it couldn't be him...

Her hands started to shake. Panic finally filled her, and she screamed silently into the car's steering wheel, gripping it tightly.

A text message notification chimed on her cell. It was from a number she didn't recognize.

She's such a sweet girl. I'm touched that you called her Sadie. Why don't you come and join us? We'll have a little family reunion. You know where. It'll be so nice to see you again. Like old times, hey little girl? Like old times. If you cooperate, you and she will be home by Sunday night.

That changed everything.

You know where...

Rachel knew one thing: she had to go to the police. If he was where she thought he'd be, he could see for miles. He could watch her drive up the road leading to the cabin. He'd know if anyone was with her. But there had to be a way for the police to get to the cabin. She couldn't get Sadie by herself.

She had to go and do whatever she could to get Sadie out, away from him.

He didn't count on the new Rachel -- the girl who knew how to fight and kick and stab. That girl wouldn't let him hurt her or Sadie.

She was going to drive to the police and make a report, but before she could, a man opened the car door and sat in the passenger seat. He was an older man, maybe in his fifties, with gray hair pulled back in a ponytail and dark glasses. She didn't recognize him, but he had a bearing that said danger.

"Don't make a move," the man said in a guttural voice. He pulled out a small handgun from his jacket pocket and stuck it into her ribs. "Give me your cell."

She handed him her cell.

"Open your messages."

She did as she was told, her mind fighting to remain in control, every moment thinking of ways she could get out of this, but he had a gun pressed into her ribs. She remembered what Danny the police officer told her about what to do if you were already in a vehicle with someone intending you harm.

"Stop at the first set of lights and jump out. You're better off getting scraped up than being taken to some remote location."

Except her father had Sadie...

"Send your boyfriend a text. Hold your cell phone up so I can see what you're doing while you're doing it."

She did as she was told, her hands shaking so badly, she wasn't sure she could type. He dictated a message and she entered it exactly as he said.

I'm taking Sadie and going for a short trip. It was spur of the moment, but I got a lot of tips and decided to take her to the coast. I know you're going to be busy with the shoot tonight, so we won't be in your hair this weekend. See you later. Love you.

He watched her enter the text and send it, taking the cell from her and tucking it into his pocket. "Good girl. Now, follow the white van ahead of you. Your dad has your daughter and if anything happens to me, or we stop following, you'll never see her again."

Rachel glanced down the block and sure enough, there was a white service van, the kind used in business rather than a family van. Inside was her father and Sadie.

All her training in self-defense and personal protection went out the window. She couldn't use any of it to avoid being abducted.

None of it.

She could cry about it all, but she didn't. She remembered what Danny said -- use your anger to give you strength. The bad guys count on you being afraid. They rely on you being cooperative, on you not wanting to make a scene. She'd make a scene all right... When the time was right. Until then, she had to cooperate if she wanted to get Sadie back alive.

She had nothing but her knife and her righteous hatred, but she hoped that would be enough. If she knew her father, and she thought she did, he'd probably kill them both so there would be no one alive who knew his secrets. He must have found her after Craig went nosing around the shop in Bellingham. Did her father learn of Craig's visit and find out where she was?

He'd changed his name after he'd had some problems in Bellingham and decided to move the entire family to Maple Falls, near the Canadian border. They all changed their names, and he decided to live off the grid, slowly becoming part of a prepper radical group of sovereign citizens. He'd worked at the store at that point, Bird Camera and Photography and built a pretty functional cabin in the forest outside town about an hour's drive up near Maple Falls.

It was there that Sadie happened.

It was there that all of it started.

She knew that's where he'd be going -- with her little Sadie. With his daughter. With *her* daughter.

She'd kill him.

She followed the van along Highway 9, avoiding the Interstate. Bill didn't talk much to her on the way, but he did read the emails on her cell, probably checking to see if she'd written anything about her father, but she never mentioned him. She didn't have time to send an email or text to anyone between the time she spoke with the girls and the man stepped into her car.

They drove through Maple Falls, and she had a moment of grief at seeing the old town. They took Silver Lake Road north to the cabin, which was just northeast of Silver Lake, arriving just before six o'clock.

When she stopped the car, parking behind the van, she was sickened to see the cabin. It brought back both good and bad memories of when she was a child -- when it all started and she still thought life was good, her father loved her and she and Sadie would be friends forever. Her father hadn't started to hurt Sadie yet, and her mother was still present, even if she did have a sickness that sent her to her bed to lie in darkness for hours, and sometimes, days. She and Sadie had been five years old. They lived in Maple Falls for three years before it started. Before it happened.

The door to the van opened and a thin older man with grey hair and a greying beard got out. He was holding hands with Sadie. Sadie smiled when she saw Rachel and it wasn't lost on her how the man -- her father -- had a knife in his hand, just inches from Sadie.

"Mom!" Sadie called out, sounding happy. "Grandad invited us to the cabin for the weekend."

She stared at the man, taking him in, how tall he was, how heavy, sizing him up as an opponent. He was small of build, like her.

"I know, sweetheart," Rachel said, trying to sound light despite the fear that made her heart pound. "Are you okay?"

"Yes," Sadie said. "Grandad was showing me all the little animals he made with his whittling knife."

Rachel nodded, not trusting her voice. She finally made eye contact with him.

"Hello, *sugarplum*," he said in an overly-sweet voice that didn't fool her for a moment. "Good to see you again. I see you met Bill. If you and Sadie play nicely with me and my friend, you should be on your way after the weekend is over."

Then he turned to Sadie. "Go on inside with Uncle Bill," her father said, shooing Sadie into the cabin. "Your mom and I have to have a little heart to heart."

Sadie went into the cabin with "Uncle Bill", apparently unharmed and unafraid. Once Sadie was inside and the door closed, her father walked over to her, the knife still prominently displayed. She understood what it meant.

Fight me and I'll kill you and harm Sadie.

"What have you done to her?" she said, her voice wavering with emotion, barely able to conceal her anger.

"Nothing yet," he said, humor in his voice. "We just got here. But I have plans to get to know her much *much* better."

"What do you want from us?"

"Just want to catch up on things, you know," he said. "We have some unfinished business. I want you to know how hurt I was that you ran away. Can you imagine the luck of that boyfriend of yours coming to Bird Camera to see if he could find out about your real identity? Can you imagine my luck that Bill was working that day and was able to find out who he was and where you were?"

She shook her head. "He meant well. I never told him anything about you."

"Too bad for him, but what a stroke of luck for me. Why, old Bill came right to me and told me about this young man looking for your father and family. I knew what I had to do."

He smiled, and she saw that same broken-tooth in the front that so tormented her for the years after he killed Sadie and he took her instead to the warehouse and did his perverted things to her.

At that moment, she hated him so much, all the anger and disgust almost overwhelming her. She'd tried for so long to deny it, to hold it back, to push it deeper down into her mind so she wouldn't remember but it all came flooding back. He was a disgusting monstrous pig of a man, who used her for his perversions. He'd killed Sadie when she resisted and her mother when Rachel told her what he did.

"Why don't you come inside?" he said in a voice laced with gloating. "We have everything ready for a fun weekend."

He pointed to the cabin with the knife. She knew she

wouldn't be able to fight him with the knife at her ankle. By the time she'd have freed it, he'd stab her.

She'd have to play along, find her moment.

Her only hope, her only prayer, was that it would be before Sadie was harmed.

CHAPTER TWENTY-SEVEN

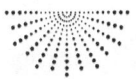

THE NEXT DAY, Tess spent the morning at the *Sentinel*, and met with Kate to discuss her series of articles. When the meeting was over, she went to Mickey's before lunch to see if he or his staff would speak with her about Rachel. Michael got quite a lot out of the man and Tess hoped to tweak his memory or that of his staff even more if possible. He seemed like a really nice person. Someone who had seriously turned his life around and was now trying to give back and make up for all the harm he did when he was younger.

She walked into the bar, which was pretty slow considering it was almost lunch hour. There were a few customers, but otherwise the place was empty. She walked over to the bar and took a stool.

Landon, the bartender, came over and placed a coaster in front of her. "What can I get for you?" he asked.

"I knew Rachel," she said and showed him her press credentials. "I work as a reporter with the *Sentinel* and was hoping to speak with staff about her disappearance."

"You knew Rachel?" he asked, his eyebrows raised.

"I'm a friend of Craig, her boyfriend. I interviewed her for an article I was working on."

Landon gave her a once-over and pushed the coaster towards her. "I'd be happy to talk to you, but if you want to sit at the bar, you have to buy something."

"Will a soda qualify?"

"I suppose," he said with a shrug.

She ordered a diet soda and took out her notebook and pen.

"What can you tell me about Rachel? What were your general impressions of her as a person?"

"I thought you knew her," he said, sounding skeptical.

"Yes, but just as an acquaintance. Like I said, we talked about my work on missing and murdered women and girls in Washington State. It was after Rose Clarke was murdered."

"Oh, yeah. Rose. Rachel knew her." He glanced off into the distance, leaning against the bar. "Rachel was someone who seemed like she could break in half at any time and was fighting hard to keep it all together."

Tess nodded and wrote down a few notes on what Landon said. It jibed with what Tess had thought herself when interviewing the younger woman for her articles on street kids who had gone missing as part of her overall work.

"Go on," Tess said, hoping to encourage him.

"She was a hard worker," he said and took a bar wipe and wiped the chrome along the bar top. "She always took an extra shift if she could get a babysitter. She told me she was saving up for a trip to California so she could take her daughter to see the redwoods and then maybe to Mexico."

Tess wrote that down because she figured that might be a

good way to personalize her article on the woman so readers could get a good mental image of her as a person and a mother.

"She told me she fantasized about working on a cruise ship, and traveling around the world, but because she had Sadie, she couldn't do that but she still wanted to take Sadie traveling. Make up for her own childhood."

"Was she a good mother?" Tess asked.

"She was. She was determined to give Sadie the best childhood she could. Rachel used to say she missed having a childhood and so she wanted to make sure Sadie had a good one. Rachel never went to public school and was home schooled, so she missed the social life other kids experienced. She said she always felt like an outsider as a result."

That confirmed what Tess already knew about Rachel, and she wrote as much of it down as she could, glad that he was painting a more personal picture of Rachel that corresponded with her own. Landon seemed to know quite a lot about Rachel, and even talked of her time at the Sisters of Mercy shelter.

All in all, the picture he painted was of a girl who survived a personal hell, rose above it, and was thriving -- all things considered. Why would she just up and leave?

"Did she ever complain about her relationship with Craig? Mention any problems?"

"No," Landon said, shaking his head. "She seemed really happy with him. He's kinda strange, but she said he was just shy."

"Do you have any staff photos of her?" she asked.

"I think so," Landon said, frowning. "We had a few staff nights on Sundays. We'd cook dinner for everyone and party.

There might be some in the staff room. I can go look, if you like. It's pretty dead."

"Sure," Tess said and waited while he left the bar and disappeared into the back. She sipped her soda and listened to the music, which was old gold from the 70's. *Listen to the Music* by the Doobie Brothers was currently playing. Her father's music era.

The door to the back opened up and instead of Landon, Mickey himself came marching towards her.

"Hello, Tess," he said and stood beside her, his hands on his hips. "You here for more background?"

"Yes," Tess said. "I hope you don't mind. I just popped in when I was driving by and thought I might ask the other staff a few questions about Rachel. We really don't have much on her past."

"She ran away from her past and started a new life," he said. "She didn't want to talk about her past. She didn't tell us much about it."

"I was hoping for impressions of her as a person and what she's like."

"You met her. She's a very sweet lady, and a hard worker," Mickey said and he almost seemed angry at Tess for being there.

"Yes, that's what Landon said, and it confirms my own impressions."

Some more patrons entered the bar, and Tess glanced at her watch. It was almost noon. Landon came back behind the bar and placed a sheet of paper on the bar top in front of Tess. "That's a picture of Rachel when she won Staff Member of the Month. I thought you might like it. I could scan it with the printer in the back, if it's okay with Mickey."

Mickey shrugged. "I'll do it. Looks like the lunch crowd is coming. You better get back to work." With that, he took the photo and went to the back through the staff door.

Landon nodded and gave Tess a wide-eyed expression before he went over to a couple who sat at the far end of the bar.

When Mickey returned a few moments later, Tess accepted the scan of the staff photo. "Thanks," she said. "I didn't mean to intrude."

"No, you picked a good time. We start getting busy at noon and then stay busy all afternoon. Now, unfortunately, I have to get back to work, too. Rachel was one of my lunch staff and I'm short today because she's not here. Hope you got what you needed."

He gave her a quick forced smile and she took that as a broad hint she should leave.

"Thanks," she said and held up the scan. "I'll let myself out."

Mickey disappeared out the back of the bar, through the staff door. Tess finished her diet soda and then got up from the bar to leave, with the distinct impression Mickey wasn't happy that she'd been there. She would have liked to get more from Landon, but he was now busy serving customers and she didn't want to make Mickey angry with the man.

Landon waved at her as she passed him and before she was able to leave, he came around the bar and met her at the front door.

"Before you go, I wanted to make sure you knew she came in the night she left town," Landon said, his voice soft.

Tess frowned. "Mickey said she called. She wanted to tell him that she was going out of town."

"No, she came in. She must have come in the back entrance. I saw them in the office when I went to get some beer from the cooler. I think he left with her," Landon said, almost whispering. "When I came back, they were both gone."

"Really?" She frowned at that. According to what Tess knew, Rachel had called to tell Mickey she wouldn't be in for a few days because she was taking a short vacation.

"He didn't come back for a long time. Just before closing."

"Did you tell police?"

"No one asked," he said with a shrug. "I assumed Mickey told police what happened when they came by. You're the first person to talk to me or any of the staff. They talked to Mickey, but not us."

"Thanks." She reached into her bag and pulled out a business card with her work number. "If you can think of anything else, call me." She turned to the door. "Leave a message on the answering service if you don't get me."

"I will," he said.

She watched as he went back to the bar and continued serving customers.

So, Mickey left the bar after speaking with Rachel. He was gone for hours and didn't return until just before closing...

Michael would be very interested in hearing that.

CHAPTER TWENTY-EIGHT

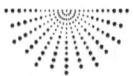

MICHAEL POURED coffee from his thermos into his cup.

"What?" he asked, not sure he heard Tess right. On the other end of the line, Tess repeated what she'd just said.

"Landon, the bartender who was working the night Rachel went missing, said that she came in to tell Mickey she was going on a short vacation. He said he thinks Mickey left with her and he didn't come back for a couple of hours."

Michael leaned against the counter and considered this new bit of evidence. "Mickey never told me that or the police."

"I thought you should know," Tess said. "I just left the bar after getting the distinct impression Mickey wasn't happy that I was speaking with Landon about Rachel."

"Well, this is news. Mickey never said anything about leaving the bar that night," Michael said. "In fact, he said Rachel called him. He didn't say she came into the bar."

"Maybe she did call him, but he omitted the fact that she also came in. So, he was partly telling the truth. They were in the back of the building, in the office. Landon saw Rachel when he went back to get more beer out of the cooler. The staff might not have known she was even there if she came in through the back entrance."

"Why didn't the bartender call police with this information?" Michael asked, frustrated. "That means that Mickey, not Craig, would be one of the last people to see her before she disappeared."

"I know," Tess said. "He said no one from the police department spoke with any of the staff. They all spoke with Mickey and since he said she hadn't been in that night, I guess they didn't feel it was a good use of their time."

Michael rubbed his forehead. "They were focused on Craig. Still, I'm surprised the bartender didn't speak up."

"Mickey seemed upset that I was asking questions," Tess said. "He more or less stopped the interview and was too busy to speak with me again, so I left without talking to him. I got the distinct impression he wasn't happy to see me poking around."

Michael nodded. "Thanks for calling. I might have to drop by and speak to Landon myself. Maybe bring Mickey in for questioning. Clear up a few questions I have about his whereabouts the night Rachel went missing. I may have to reschedule my meeting with the ME."

"You don't think Mickey is responsible?" Tess said, her voice sounding dismissive. "He seems like such a sweet man."

"I don't know, but if he left with her, I want to know why he didn't tell us."

"It is highly suspicious," Tess offered. "Landon didn't seem to want Mickey to know he knew. He only told me just before I was leaving, so I think he was hoping to keep it quiet. He seemed afraid of Mickey."

"I have to confront Mickey about it, so I hope Landon is prepared to speak with police," Michael said. "The fact that Mickey misled police by withholding information about Rachel coming into the bar the night she went missing is serious. If he actually left the bar with her, I need to know where he went and why. I also need to know why he lied to me and to police, if that's the case. That's considered a gross misdemeanor and while we don't usually prosecute people for lying to police, if it materially hinders a police investigation or a prosecution, he could be charged."

Tess exhaled. "I was hoping he was a good guy," she said, and Michael could hear the pain in her voice.

"He may still be, but I need to know why he didn't tell us. Then, we'll know if he is a white hat, or black. Look, I have to go and speak with Nick about this. See what our next move is. I'll see you later."

"Okay," Tess said. "When you get off work, maybe I'd like a beer or three."

"Sounds like a plan."

He ended the call and walked right down the hallway to Nick's office. He knocked and waited for Nick to respond.

"Come," Nick said.

Michael opened the door, poking his head inside. "Do you have a moment?"

"Any time," Nick said and waved Michael inside. "Have a seat. Something up with the Martin case?"

"Yes, actually," Michael said and sat in the chair across from Nick's desk. "Tess, my partner, who works for the *Sentinel* on the crime beat, went to speak to staff at Mickey's Bar this morning. Apparently, Rachel came in to the bar on the night Craig says she went on a vacation. She spoke with Mickey and they left the bar together."

Nick leaned forward, his interest clearly piqued. "Oh, really? Isn't that something..." He leaned back and ran his hand through his hair. "Would have been nice if Mr. Mickey Howell had told police that little detail. It kind of sheds a whole new light on the situation. Did he say where they went?"

"Tess didn't speak with Mickey about this. This was from Landon, the bartender. He was working when Rachel came in that night. The other staff may not have known because she came in the back entrance and was in the office with Mickey when Landon went to the back to get beer from the cooler. When he came back, they were gone. Mickey didn't get back until after midnight. Just in time for closing."

"I think you better call Mickey up and speak with him so he can answer a few questions. Do you think he'll be compliant? If I recall the file, he has a record."

"He's been clean for the past decade, according to my research."

"You might swing by and ask him what the hell's going on. If he doesn't cooperate, we may have to bring him in."

"Should I take someone with me?"

Nick shook his head. "Keep it low profile. We don't want to scare him off. If you think he's being deceptive, we'll bring him in. Otherwise, I like to let people show us who they are."

"Gotcha," Michael said and stood up. "I'll drive by now before Happy Hour in case it gets too busy and Mickey uses that as an excuse."

"Good thinking," Nick said. "Let me know how it goes."

"Will do," Michael said and rose, leaving Nick to his files.

. . .

Michael drove north on Aurora to Mickey's Bar and Grill. He didn't call first, just in case the man was guilty and decided to run. Instead, Michael parked on the street and walked into the bar casually, his hand in his pocket. He went up to the bar and took a seat. A young man with spiky black hair came over and placed a coaster in front of Michael.

"What can I get for you?" the young man asked. His name tag read *Landon*.

Michael reached into his pocket for his identification and replied. "I'll have a soda and lime. I just spoke with Tess McClintock and based on what she said, I have a few questions, if you don't mind."

Landon took the ID from Michael and read it over. "Tess called you already?" He shook his head.

"She cares about Rachel and Sadie. This is a big deal for her. Her whole career has been focused on missing and murdered women and children."

"Yeah, she said that," Landon said and picked up a clean glass, filled it with ice and then poured some soda out of a bar bottle. He garnished the glass with a lime slice and placed the glass on Michael's coaster. "Ask away. I have nothing to hide. I know Mickey might be upset with me, though."

"If you're telling the truth, there's no reason for Mickey to be upset."

Landon shrugged. "Yeah, right."

Michael took a sip of the soda and then focused on Landon. "You told Tess you saw Rachel in the bar on that Friday night she supposedly was going out of town."

"Yes, she must have come in the back."

Landon then relayed pretty much verbatim what Tess had told Michael.

"Thanks," Michael said. "Depending on how things go, I may need you to come down to the station and give a report." He reached into his pocket and gave Landon one of his business cards. "Call me if you can think of anything else about Rachel on that night or anything that you think might be important."

"I will," Landon said and eyed the business card. "You work for the DA's office?"

"Yes, I'm a special investigator on the major crimes unit."

"Cool," Landon said. "I got to--" he said and pointed to the other end of the bar where a cocktail waitress stood, a tray of empty glasses on it. She'd placed a bar order on the counter.

"Go ahead. Is Mickey in the back?"

"I think so," Landon said. "Customers aren't supposed to go back there without an escort..."

"I'll be fine," Michael said and walked to the back, pushing the swinging door open that admitted him to the rear of the building. He passed through a prep section where there was a dishwasher and some refrigerators. A short hallway led to the back door and beside the exit, a door with a window, showing the interior of what looked like a business office. Inside, Michael saw Mickey sitting with his back to the door, his laptop open.

Michael pushed the door open. "May I come in?"

Mickey turned around and his eyes widened when he saw Michael.

He visibly slumped in his chair. "I wondered how long it would take before you dropped by."

CHAPTER TWENTY-NINE

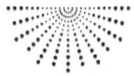

Rachel stood inside the door and looked around the cabin. It was the same as she remembered from years earlier. A wood stove sat in the middle of the living room and behind it was a huge picture window. The stove offered the only heat in the entire place and at night in the spring, the bedrooms got really cold. Water froze in the basin where they washed themselves in the mornings, but her father always said it was good for them. Hardship built character. There was a rudimentary kitchen on one side of the main living area, a rugged oak set of cabinets with a laminate countertop and one sink. There was no running water in the place, so they used bottles of water when they stayed at the cabin. Her father chopped wood out back, and her mother kept the wood stove stoked to heat the cabin.

Now, there was electricity from the solar panels on the roof. That meant there was a stove and refrigerator as well as electric lights. It wasn't nearly as rudimentary as when she was a child and came here with her family.

The picture window looked out over the valley below and her father was right -- he could see any vehicles coming up Silver Lake Road from the cabin's vantage point. At night, she remembered him sitting by the window, watching the countryside with his scope. He'd brag he could see everything -- people coming and going up the road closer to the cabin.

She spent the first few moments trying to figure out how to kill him.

Her father took Sadie over to the dining room table, where a collection of carved animals sat next to a pile of shavings. She could make out a bear, an eagle with its wings spread, and a wolf.

Sadie was smiling as she examined the wooden carvings.

"You like them?" her father said, standing beside Sadie, stroking her long fair hair.

"They're pretty," Sadie said in a voice filled with awe. "Can I have one?"

"I made them when I knew you and your mom were coming up here," he said. "Which one do you want the most?"

Sadie picked each one up and examined them, finally settling on the wolf. "It looks like Rex from down the street. I want this one."

"Consider it yours," he said and gave Rachel a smile. "Do you have a kiss and hug for your old grandpa?"

Sadie turned to him and without hesitation, threw her arms around his neck and kissed his cheek when he bent down to her. He squeezed her tightly and glanced over at Rachel. The expression in his eyes told her everything she needed to know.

He planned to use her in his perverted ways. And he was going to make Rachel watch.

Bill stood by the door, his hand in his pocket. Rachel could see the outline of his weapon.

She knew that she and Sadie would never get out alive. Her father was counting on her being the same passive girl she used to be, cowed by her fear of him, but he was wrong.

While she watched, her father went to the small refrigerator beside the kitchen counter and opened it up, reaching in to get a bottle of juice.

"Here's some juice for you, sweet stuff," he said to Sadie. "Like I promised. I know you're thirsty. Drink it all up like a good girl. We're going to have fun tonight, the four of us."

A jolt of adrenaline went through Rachel. Her father used to drug her when he took her to the warehouse. It didn't stop her from knowing what happened, but it did stop her from resisting. She didn't know what he gave her back then, but it was something trippy that seemed to put a screen between you and what was happening to you. Ketamine probably. Depending on what he gave Sadie, the drug could take up to an hour to take effect. Whatever the case, she knew she had to assess the situation and try to figure out how to escape.

While she watched, her father rolled up his sleeves and sat beside Sadie, taking one of his half-finished carvings and starting to carve it once more.

"Why don't you sit down?" he said to Rachel. "Sit over there. Bill will sit with you. He worked as an enforcer for a bike gang and knows how to keep the peace, don't you, Bill?"

"I surely do," Bill said and moved his hand in his pocket.

Rachel frowned. Had Bill been brought along to control Rachel while her father was with Sadie? She glanced at Bill and felt sick to her stomach. He had a mean look in his eyes, which were beady, dark and flat, like the only emotion he felt was hatred. She sat on the sofa and Bill sat close beside her, pressing against her, his hand in his pocket poking the gun into her ribs. He turned on a radio on the side table and was listening to some talk show, going on about the end of the world. One of the prepper nutcases who had radio shows talking about end of days.

After about fifteen minutes, while her father talked to Sadie about the animal he was carving, Sadie began to yawn, rubbing her eyes.

"Mommy, I don't feel very good," she said and glanced over to where Rachel was sitting.

"Oh, honey, I'm so sorry. Do you need to go to the bathroom?"

"I feel sick," Sadie said and before Rachel could even move, Sadie proceeded to throw up whatever she'd had to eat, including most of the juice she drank. It came back up and out, splashing onto the wooden floor.

"Jesus *Christ*," her father said, pushing away from the table. "Get over here and clean this up." He pointed to Rachel, who was only too happy to go over and help Sadie.

"What did you give her?" she hissed, and by the time she got over to Sadie, the girl's eyes were rolling around in her head. "She's passing out!"

"Just a sedative," her father said. "It's not supposed to make her throw up."

Rachel picked Sadie up and was going to just leave, get into the car and drive away, but of course, her father was having none of it.

"Wipe off her mouth and lie her down on the sofa. We got work to do."

"You *monster*," Rachel said under her breath, staring at him while she cradled her semi-conscious daughter. "I won't let you touch her."

"Put her *down* on the sofa," her father said, jabbing a finger in front of her face, "or I'll slit her throat like a pig and let her bleed out in front of your eyes."

Rachel sobbed, unable to fight back. She laid Sadie down and wiped off the girl's mouth, laying her on her side in case she vomited again.

"Now, come here and clean up this mess," her father ordered. "She ate some damn Cheetos on the way here. I can't stand the stench."

Rachel went to the kitchen sink and found a bucket underneath, and some wash cloths. She filled the bucket with hot soapy water and took a roll of paper towels over to the floor where Sadie had vomited. While the two men worked setting up some tripods for cameras and recording equipment, Rachel cleaned up, but she was also plotting out how to escape.

She was not going to let them do anything to Sadie.

When she was finished cleaning, she dumped the water down the drain and was eyeing a set of knives in a butcher block on the counter. She could grab one and run at her father with it. What would Bill do? If he really was a former enforcer for a motorcycle gang, he wasn't likely very passive. She couldn't hope that he would cave once he saw her father was dead. She'd have to kill him, too.

Her heart pounded as she contemplated what to do.

Before she could grab a knife, her father was behind her, punching her in the head. The impact of his fist knocked her sideways and she fell to the ground, her head hitting the floor before she could protect herself.

Then, darkness...

CHAPTER THIRTY

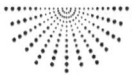

MICHAEL SAT on the chair beside Mickey's desk and removed his notebook and pen.

"Why don't you tell me what happened on the night that Rachel came into the bar -- the night she went on vacation."

Mickey sighed and leaned back in his chair, and Michael could almost see his mind working, trying to figure out the best way to tell his story.

"She called me around nine and asked if she could come in and talk to me. I said sure. We weren't too busy yet. I usually take the truck out for a few hours on Friday night, get the kids food and a shower. So, I had some time to speak to her, before I fixed the truck."

"You took the truck out Friday night after you spoke to her in the office?"

Mickey nodded. "Yes. She came in, told me she might be moving away from Seattle and wanted to let me know I'd have to find someone else to take her shifts."

"She said she was moving away? That wasn't what you told Detective Chambers when he came by to question you."

"She didn't want people to know she was moving away. She said her past had caught up with her and she needed to leave. I understand that kind of trouble, given my past. It caught up with me as well back in the day before I got sober."

"Why didn't you tell police she was planning on moving away?"

Mickey shrugged. "She asked me not to. She wanted to keep things up in the air in case she changed her mind. So, I told staff she was taking a short vacation to explain her absence from the bar. Look, she was afraid of her past, okay? I was only trying to help the girl."

"You lied to the police," Michael said firmly. "You lied about seeing her, you lied about what she told you. How could telling the police that she'd been in the bar and was moving away be harmful to Rachel?"

"When they found her car, I thought that maybe something happened to her. You know, she was abducted or something. It would make me look guilty. Isn't that what's happening? People now think I'm somehow guilty because I spoke to her the night she went missing?"

"Think how much less guilty you would look if you had told us the truth."

Mickey sighed and rubbed his beard thoughtfully. "I did what I thought would help her out. You have to realize she's like a daughter to me. All these kids -- they're like my kids. I'd do anything to help them get off the street. Get clean. I was only doing what she asked me to do. That's all."

"I'm going to have to ask you to come in and make a statement to that effect."

"You can't just write it up yourself? Do I have to actually physically come in? I have a bar to run and it's a busy afternoon. Happy hour coming up..." Mickey said with a shrug.

"Yes, I'm going to need you to come down to the office and provide a written statement. I'll need the names of some people we can contact who can back up your story about taking the truck out to confirm your whereabouts that night."

Mickey sighed. "Okay. When? Does it have to be now? Can I come in tomorrow morning? It would be better for me."

"You don't have someone who can manage the place while you're gone? It will take less than an hour."

Mickey ran his hand over his head and seemed to be considering. "I can call in my relief bartender. He's done some floor managing for me before. Let me call him."

Michael waited while Mickey flipped through and old rolodex on his desk and then picked up the landline and called a number.

"Yeah, Bob, can you come in and manage the place for an hour or two for me over the dinner hour? I have to go somewhere."

Mickey listened and nodded. "Thanks, man. I owe you a big one. I'll be gone, so just come in and take over when you get here. There's a special on draft so I expect we'll have a busy Happy Hour crowd tonight."

Mickey hung up and turned to Michael. "Shall we?"

Michael stood and they left the office. "My truck is out back. Should I meet you at the DA's office?"

"I think Detective Chambers will want you to go to the precinct."

"Okay. Are you coming along?"

"I'll follow you," Michael said.

"Got it," Mickey said and Michael followed him down the hallway and out through the front of the building. Mickey's truck was parked in front of the bar. Michael got into his Jeep and followed Mickey once he pulled out into traffic.

They drove through the streets to the Seattle police headquarters and found parking slots in the visitor's area. Michael got out of his Jeep and went to where Mickey was parked.

"Lead on," Mickey said.

Michael led the way into the precinct, and they took the elevator to the third floor where Chambers and other detectives on the major crimes unit and homicide detectives had their offices. Once they were in the main reception area, Michael showed the admin his ID and led Mickey to a back office where Detective Chambers met with the public to conduct interviews.

"Wait in here," Michael said and Mickey went inside. "Detective Chambers will be with you in a moment."

Then, Michael found Chambers, who was meeting with his lieutenant.

When Chambers was finished, he came right over to Michael. "What's up?"

"Mickey's in Interview Room 1. He's ready to provide a revised statement on the Friday night Rachel went missing."

"Yeah, your boss over at the DA's office called and gave me a head's-up that you might bring him in. Thanks. You sticking around?"

"Not unless you need me. I have a meeting with Dr. Keller and then a date with a bottle of beer and some buffalo wings."

"Go eat some wings for me," Chambers said. "Oh, and thanks for this."

"Don't mention it. Glad to help."

Michael left the building and went to his Jeep. When he got inside, he checked his cell and saw that Tess had sent a message.

TESS: *Is Happy Hour on?*

He texted her right back.

MICHAEL: *I just brought Mickey in for questioning. Now, I have to meet with the ME. Can we push back that drink until six?*

TESS: *You brought Mickey in?*

MICHAEL: *As a matter of fact, he's in Detective Chamber's meeting room right now, giving a revised statement so it went pretty well by any measure.*

TESS: *Good. Hopefully, he can provide police with a better idea of what happened with Rachel the night she went missing. Do you think he was involved in her disappearance?*

MICHAEL: *We'll see. Maybe the ME will have something to tell me. She said I'd be really interested in her findings, so I'm preparing myself for surprise.*

TESS: *Sounds intriguing. Meet you at The Barrel at six. Text me if you're delayed.*

MICHAEL: *Will do.*

Michael drove off, taking side streets to avoid the traffic so he could get to the ME's office in a reasonable amount of time. If the meeting was as interesting as Keller promised, he was definitely excited.

CHAPTER THIRTY-ONE

WHEN RACHEL WOKE UP, she was lying on her side on the floor against the back wall. Her hands were zip-tied above her head to a metal pipe that carried water into the house from a cistern outside.

A bank of lights shone brightly into the living room where Sadie lay on the sofa. Rachel could just make out her body, her feet bare. The two men were naked and were moving video cameras around. They were drinking, passing a bottle of bourbon between themselves while they prepared for whatever it was that they intended to do.

Rachel knew.

She had memories of such a setup from her own childhood -- vague memories of lights and sounds, of men looming over her, naked, grinning, laughing, doing things she didn't understand. Making her do things she didn't want to do but had no ability to resist.

She would *not* let that happen to Sadie.

Luckily for her, her father and Bill had no interest in her and were having trouble getting their camera set up just right. They fussed and fiddled and had to tear down their set up and then re-set it up again, adjusting the lighting and taking shots to see how it looked.

"The lighting *sucks*," Bill said, watching some video her father had shot as a test.

"We're wasting time," her father said. "This will just have to do."

Rachel knew that she had to act now. She moved her legs forward as far as she could, still lying on her side, and was able to move her ankles up near her zip-tied hands, glad that neither man had interest in her for any sexual purpose. They were far more intent on getting the cameras set up properly for whatever perversions they planned on filming next. She managed to pull up the pant leg of her jeans and worked on getting the folding knife out of its holder without making a sound, but it was slow going and she had to hold her breath to prevent herself from grunting from exertion.

When she finally had the knife loose, she pulled down her pant leg and tried to cut the zip-tie that held her wrists together. It was nearly impossible, for she had to turn the blade around, and hold it in position, then move it against the zip-tie on her wrist without cutting herself. She managed to slide the blade between her skin and the plastic, then began a sawing motion with her fingertips. Finally, the blade cut through the plastic tie with an audible pop, but luckily, both men were intent on pouring the bourbon down their throats and adjusting the camera angles. Bill glanced over at her once or twice, but she had been careful to stop her movements, so it looked as if she was just lying in the same position as they had left her in.

Her escape was made even more important when she saw Bill climbing on top of Sadie.

She tried not to think about what he was doing, what they would do if she didn't get loose and stop them. She focused instead on getting free of her restraints. Once her other wrist was free, she didn't hesitate. She jumped up, knife in hand, and threw herself on top of Bill from behind, her arms around his shoulders, her legs clasped around his hips. She jabbed the knife down into the side of his neck, slicing through the flesh where she knew the carotid artery was located.

She screamed as she did and it so shocked her father, who was trying to move a camera into a different position, that he tripped backwards in shock. Bill tried to stand up, his hands at his neck, and then she and Bill crashed into her father before he could react. They knocked him against the counter, and he hit his head on the corner as he fell.

Luckily, both men had enough bourbon in their bloodstreams that their reaction time was longer than normal. Blessed with a surge of adrenaline and pure hatred, Rachel stabbed Bill a half-dozen times in rapid succession, the knife plunging into his back over and over. The blade went into his body the full three inches to the knife's hilt, and finally, he lay still. She crawled off him and lurched at her father, who was struggling to his feet. She stabbed him in the gut, ripping him open before he could reach down to his clothes on the floor and grab the gun from the pocket of Bill's jacket.

He crouched in on himself, holding his gut protectively as blood seeped through his fingers.

"You fucking *bitch*," he half-growled half-screamed. He glanced down at his belly, removing his hand to reveal his gut, which had been cut open, something bloody pushing out, blood oozing out around the knife wound.

On the floor, Bill groaned, his head turned to one side, the blood gushing from the wound in his neck, one hand clamped over it trying to stop the bleeding. Soon, he was silent, and she knew he'd lost consciousness from blood loss.

She turned to face her father, who backed away, one hand on his gut holding his wound, the other bloody hand held out, trying to stop her.

"Don't," he said. "Don't..."

He turned and tried to run, making it to the door, throwing it open and stumbling down the steps. Light spilled out into the yard, shining on the outhouse. She followed him, wondering what he was thinking. Was he going to try to make it to the car?

She ran over and blocked his way, holding the bloody knife out.

"Don't even think of it," she hissed.

He backed away, naked, blood running down his groin.

"I'm bleeding to death," he said, his voice almost a sob. "You fucking stabbed me!"

She lunged at him, wanting to finish the job, and he stumbled away towards the outhouse, a trail of blood shining on the wet grass, visible in the light from the cabin.

Did he think he was going to hide in there?

She almost laughed when he threw open the outhouse door and tried to close it, lock himself in.

Before he could, she pulled it open, glad it was on a hinge

and not hung like a proper door. She pushed inside and stabbed her father twice and then three times with her knife, the blade plunging into his neck and chest. He screamed like a girl each time the blade made contact. Finally, he slumped against the seat and she stabbed down again and again, losing count how many times her blade met his chest and gut and genitals.

Then, he lay still, leaning sideways, his eyes closed. He slumped onto the floor and she hoped he was dead. She panted while she watched him, her own body covered in blood that had sprayed out of him.

She decided to put him where he belonged -- in the hole. The hole filled with shit and piss.

He'd killed Sadie -- the first Sadie. He'd killed her mother.

He'd abused her for years afterwards.

He'd hurt *her* daughter Sadie. He'd done things to Sadie while she was trying to cut the zip-ties. She knew he'd done worse to other little girls over the years and was thankful that her Sadie appeared to be unconscious.

He deserved to die in a pile of shit and piss.

It was a struggle, and he was pretty much a mass of wiry muscle and bone, but she finally managed to open the bench, which was on a hinge, revealing the open pit below. She dragged and lifted and pushed him up and he fell head first into the darkness. He fell down about four feet, but the hole wasn't large or wide enough to take all of him. His feet stuck up, their white skin stark against the dark wood of the outhouse wall, the soles red with blood.

On her part, Rachel was covered in his and Bill's blood. Her hands were slippery with it and it got onto her clothes and in her hair. She wiped her mouth with the back of her hand and stood there for a moment, admiring her work.

Her mind was crystal clear on what she had to do next.

She went back to the cabin, closed the door, and set to work.

CHAPTER THIRTY-TWO

MICHAEL SAT in the ME's office and jotted a few notes in his notebook. Dr. Keller flipped through a file, examining the evidence, giving her thoughts on the case.

"They were both stabbed multiple times. Both had a considerable amount of alcohol and other drugs in their systems. The John Doe in the outhouse didn't turn up any hits on the system when we fingerprinted him or any dental records. In fact, he had perfect teeth. One of those flukes of nature who either grew up in a fluoride-rich water source nearby or had really good genes. The other victim was identified in the National Registry as William Sutton, and was a Level Three offender, convicted of raping a girl under age twelve and served seven years in prison for it. It was his third conviction, so he was hard-core."

Michael shook his head. "Someone killed both those men. Looks like they were in the middle of filming something. Both men were naked. Since there was no film in any cameras or memory cards, we can't tell what but given Sutton was a pedophile, I can guess what they were filming."

Of course, Michael put his two cases together, imagining that it was Rachel and Sadie there at the cabin, being filmed. He tried not to put them together but couldn't help it.

"Can you tell anything about the murder weapon?"

"It was a wide blade, so it wasn't a switchblade. More like a tactical knife used by police or military. Also, by the nature of the wounds, the blade was curved, and the wounds were inflicted from above, like Sutton was lying down when he was stabbed. The John Doe had slash marks on his belly, some of which were deep enough to penetrate the abdomen. He also had stab wounds on his neck and chest and abdomen, twenty-three in all."

"Overkill," Michael said.

"Yes," Keller replied. "Whoever killed them both was angry. Very angry. Other than that, there wasn't anything of note in the autopsy or the toxicology report. Two middle-aged white men, stabbed to death, with alcohol and other illegal substances in their bloodstreams. Apparently, filming either gay porn or child porn, I'd suspect. The children's toys could have belonged to one of the previous renters, or else they could have had them to lure children." Dr. Keller shrugged. "Either way, it was a pretty violent way to go. Neither of the two men were in any shape to defend themselves, given their blood alcohol levels. Not pass-out drunk, but given the drugs and alcohol, they were pretty stoned."

Michael nodded, writing down a few notes in his book. "Wonder if it wasn't someone who was with them who got into a fight over drugs, or something to do with filming."

"Who can say? That's beyond my pay grade, Detective."

"Not actually a detective," Michael said with a smile. "Just an investigator."

"Whatever they call you," she said, smiling back.

"As long as they pay me and let me investigate, I honestly don't care what they call me. So, this is interesting, but you said I'd be really surprised."

"You will be." Keller's eyebrows raised. "I found something very interesting in addition to the basic facts of the two victims," she said and pulled open another file that was on the edge of her desk. "Something very curious."

"I'm all ears," Michael said. "Did you identify the Jane Doe skeletal remains?"

"No," Keller said and held out a sheet of paper, removing it from the clip that held it into place. "Take a look. We matched the DNA sample to this one. There's a 99% chance that the remains of the child belong to a first degree relative of the John Doe at the cabin."

"What?" Michael grabbed the sheet of paper from Keller and read over the report. He'd seen DNA reports before, and understood the basics, so he zeroed in on the analysis.

Sure enough, the results indicated that the skeletal remains were that of a young girl of about eight years of age. They ran a DNA analysis against the database and the only hit came back to the DNA of the John Doe from the double homicide in Whatcom County.

"I knew those two cases were linked," he said, his heart rate raised. He glanced up at Dr. Keller. "Father - daughter, right?"

"Yes."

Michael shook his head, still fighting to comprehend the immensity of the results.

"Do we have any DNA results back from the apartment of

the boyfriend?" he asked, sitting with the sheet of paper in his hand.

"We were able to create a profile," Keller said. "The woman must have been a clean freak and cleaned up before she left. Our technicians checked the hair brush for hair with follicles, so we could pull a profile from that, but no luck. The garbage had been taken out before she left, her toothbrush and makeup were gone, and even the sheets had been washed recently. She was a good housekeeper, that's for sure. Luckily, we had her samples from the vehicle."

"And?"

Keller pulled another sheet out of the file and handed it to Michael.

"What am I reading?"

"Perfect match between Rachel's profile and that of the skeletal remains. At first, I thought there was a screw-up in the work and I actually raised my voice when I went to question the techs on duty. But we went over everything several times and tested other items in the vehicle. The skeletal remains belong to Rachel's sister, her identical twin."

"My God," Michael said, a surge of adrenaline sweeping over him. "It was her identical twin? She must have gone there to visit it before she left the state. Or she was taken there." Michael frowned and his mind went there. "Was she at the crime scene near Deming?"

Keller smiled and pulled out a third sheet of paper.

Michael's jaw dropped open. "Let me guess -- you pulled Rachel's profile from the scene."

"Not her," Keller said and handed Michael the sheet. "It appears that someone tried to clean up the crime scene, so if she was there, we don't have her profile in any of our samples, but we found the profile of yet another child of the John Doe."

"What?"

Keller nodded. "We pulled a profile from some vomit in the cushion of the sofa. Someone tried to clean it but didn't succeed completely."

Michael shook his head. "What do you mean?"

Keller must have seen the confusion on Michael's face and spoke slowly. "We matched the DNA profile to Rachel's, and it comes back as a parental connection. The DNA profile we pulled from the crime scene belongs to Rachel's daughter, Sadie, who was John Doe's daughter by incest."

A shudder passed through Michael. Immediately, his mind went to what he'd learned at the bar. Mickey had left the bar with Rachel the night Craig claimed she left on her vacation. He was reportedly gone for hours. Mickey said he was out with the truck and had people who could back him up, but was that the case?

Was Mickey the killer?

Had Sadie been abducted and taken to the cabin? Had Rachel enlisted Mickey's help to get her back, resulting in Mickey killing the two men and Rachel and Sadie leaving the state?

"This is," Michael said, hesitating to put it into words. "Unbelievable."

"It's rather novel, actually. When this is all done, I'm going to write it up for a journal article." She smiled. "Besides the DNA, we also have evidence that there were at least two other men at the murder scene, based on footprints in blood the forensic team was able to collect. Both prints were definitely men's boots, one with a particular tread that we've identified as a Doc Marten, size ten. The other looks like a work boot of some kind. We ruled out the security guard and any of the other attending police officers and forensic investigators. Two men were either at the scene when it happened or shortly after."

"That's good to know. One of them may be the killer. The other may have been a participant who left after the murder. Or," he said and thought back to the original police report. "Maybe the anonymous tipster who called in the first report of something going on at the cabin."

Dr. Keller nodded and closed her file. "I hope you're sufficiently surprised."

"Oh, I am," Michael said with a rueful laugh. "But at least we're that much closer to closing the case."

After he thanked Keller for the briefing, Michael left the ME's office, his mind was still numb about what he'd learned. He sat at his desk in the DA's office and stared at the file in front of him.

Sadie was Rachel's daughter with her father. The skeletal remains belonged to Rachel's identical twin sister.

He called Tess.

"You won't believe what I just learned," he said, his voice low.

"Tell me," she replied, and Michael could hear hesitance in her voice.

"I can't. Not here. We better meet for a beer. I think it might be a multiple tequila shots night."

"Should I be upset or happy?"

"Don't know yet. Be prepared to have your mind blown."

"Can you give me a hint at least?" Tess said, her voice sounding frustrated.

"Nope. Not over the phone. See you in fifteen?"

"Okay."

Michael ended the call and leaned back in his chair, scrubbing his hands over his face. He had to stop by Nick's office on his way out and give him the short and dirty summary.

Nick waved him in and finished his telephone call. After he hung up the receiver, he turned his attention to Michael.

"You look like a man who just saw a ghost," Nick said.

Michael gave him a quick summary of what the ME had found.

"I guess you better check to see if Mickey really was out with the truck that night. If he was and he has an alibi for the night, we're left with no suspect except for Craig."

"Craig claims he was out at a shoot, a crash, and then came home where he stayed the rest of the evening, upset that Rachel and Sadie had gone on vacation so abruptly," Michael replied. "He has no one to back up his claim, so he has no alibi."

"So, am I right in thinking it's either Craig or Mickey who killed those men?" Nick asked, his hands behind his head.

"That's what I'm thinking, and given Mickey's past, I think it's more likely it was him."

"I guess we need to follow up on Mickey's alibi witnesses. See if their story holds."

"Will do."

Michael got up and left, eager to get to the bar and have a drink with Tess. He knew she'd be blown away by what he was going to tell her.

CHAPTER THIRTY-THREE

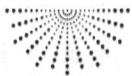

TESS SAT with her mouth open, a suitably surprised expression on her face.

"You must be kidding."

Michael shook his head. "Nope. I got the news directly from the ME herself." He leaned back when the waitress came by to drop off their drinks and appetizers.

Tess sat for a moment in silence, trying to process the information.

"So that means Rachel was pregnant with her father's child when she came to Seattle. Rachel's sister was buried up in the mountains near Mt. Baker. She was likely murdered, right?"

Michael nodded. "That or she died accidentally, and the parents didn't want anyone to know, but how would you explain the disappearance of an eight-year-old?"

"Rachel said she was home-schooled. Maybe no one knew the girl went missing."

"Could be," Michael said. He picked up a tequila shot and a bite of lime and held it up. "To the investigation. Let's hope we find whoever killed those men. Let's hope that both Rachel and Sadie are safe."

Tess picked up her own shot of tequila and followed suit, licking the salt, downing the shot and then sucking on the lime wedge. She shuddered as the alcohol went down her throat, but in truth, it felt good.

It helped to chase away the sickening feeling she had after what Michael told her. Being a bit numb would be a welcome reprieve.

"I hope they're alive," Tess said and reached for a hot wing. "Do you suppose Mickey killed the two men and then helped her escape?"

"Could be. Or Craig did. Could be either of them. I have to check out Mickey's alibi. If it holds up, Craig's our man."

Tess ate in silence for a few moments and she knew that they were both weighing the possibility that both Rachel and Sadie were also dead, but that didn't seem as likely now that they knew Mickey left the bar with Rachel.

"Mickey's involved in some way. I bet he's protecting her. Helping her run away."

"My thoughts exactly," Michael replied. "I guess we're going to ask him to come in again and answer some more questions in the morning. If Nick isn't happy with his answers, they'll consider taking him into custody. One way or another, I think he was there at the scene. The ME said that there were prints from two other men at the scene, tracking blood around. One was for a size ten Doc Marten boot. I seem to recall that Mickey wears Doc Martens..."

"So, he was there," Tess said and took in a deep breath. "Maybe Rachel's dad abducted Sadie, and that's what she meant by her past catching up with her. Rachel asked Mickey for help getting her back. Mickey goes to the cabin and kills both of the men when they find them abusing Sadie. Mickey and Rachel try to clean up the scene, and then Rachel and Sadie take off. She goes back to Seattle and asks Craig to come with her, but he refuses. She leaves and who knows where she is."

"Sounds like a good summary of what might have happened. Now, all we have to do is get Mickey to confess and it's case closed."

Tess glanced up at Michael to see if he was joking. He laughed.

"Simple, right?" He smiled at her and picked up another hot wing. "I must say that I'm really loving my job with the DA's Office. All the goodness of a detective and a Special Agent combined. None of the having to shoot bad guys if necessary."

"I'm glad you're enjoying it," Tess said and smiled. "And I'm glad you're my boyfriend. I get all the juicy details."

Michael reached out and took Tess's hand. "So, I'm your boyfriend, am I? That sounds so high school."

She grinned. "You're my main squeeze. My significant other."

"How about fiancée?" he asked, his face becoming serious. "The divorce will be finalized in a few months. We could set a date once it goes through."

"You're serious?" she said, squeezing his hand.

"Never been more serious. I think we're perfect together."

"If that was a proposal, I accept," she said, smiling widely.

"I should get down on my knees and offer you an engagement ring, but I was too busy investigating a double murder and missing persons case to pick one up."

"I don't need a ring," she replied.

At that, Michael stood up and leaned over the table, kissing her warmly. It was at that moment that his cell rang, bringing them back to the present. He grinned and sat back down, taking out his cell and checking the call display.

"It's Nick. I better get this."

He answered and listened while Nick talked.

"Oh, that's interesting."

He glanced over at Tess and raised his eyebrows.

"He's usually out on Friday nights with the truck. He told me he took the truck out as usual."

Michael listened some more, and Tess leaned forward, curious about what they were talking about. Obviously, the police were questioning Mickey's alibi for the night Rachel left town -- or went missing. Tess still wasn't sure which it was. Try as she might, she couldn't imagine Mickey killing Rachel and Sadie as well as the two men at the cabin, but she supposed it could be true. He had served time in prison for serious felonies. It would be key to check his alibi and make sure he didn't have the opportunity.

"Okay, it should be interesting. I can go after I'm finished with my meal and talk to some of Mickey's assistants with the charity. I'll pop into the office and update you."

He ended the call and looked at Tess. "So much for getting drunk tonight. When we're done, I have to go and question Mickey's people to check his alibi."

"Such is the life of a Special Investigator, I guess," Tess said with a smile. "In contrast, I can go home and fall asleep."

"Yeah, I may be pretty late if I'm going to find the truck and speak with whoever is working tonight."

They left the bar and Michael walked Tess to her car. They kissed and he drove off.

Tess sat in her vehicle for a moment, and checked her messages, expecting to see one from her mother about the coming Easter holiday and why Tess had been too busy to visit. Before she started her car, she glanced up and saw a vehicle parked down the street, the lights off but the engine running. A single dark figure sat in the driver's seat.

She pulled out of her spot and drove north, planning on taking a shortcut to the apartment. When she saw the vehicle turn on its lights and pull out when she was about a block away, she frowned.

Was the vehicle following her?

She kept diving north for a few blocks, watching to see if the car turned off or kept following. Then, she decided to pull a U-turn in the middle of the intersection. She had to time it just right and hope that no police were in the vicinity. She watched the vehicle as she passed it, and felt the driver turn to watch her, but that could have been simply because she'd pulled a U-turn illegally. She kept driving, watching in her rear-view mirror, but the car apparently kept driving north so she exhaled and kept driving.

It must just be because she was on edge after the recent revelations about Rachel and her ties to the murdered man at the cabin.

CHAPTER THIRTY-FOUR

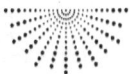

THE FIRST THING Rachel did was check on Sadie, who was breathing and quiet, but still drugged. She'd thrown up again and the men threw a blanket over it, not letting it get in the way of their perversion.

Rachel pulled a clean blanket over her and then sat on the coffee table across from her, watching her, hoping she hadn't been given too much of whatever it was they used to drug her -- most likely ketamine.

Now that both men were dead, and the threat was over, Rachel cried. Her hands shook, and she struggled to catch her breath, but she let it all out. She wept for every moment of fear and self-hatred she'd felt at his hands over the years. She wept because of what he'd done to her and what he made her do to him and all the other men. She wept for Sadie, her sister -- her beautiful identical twin sister -- who her monster of a father killed while he raped her. She wept for her mother, who was too young herself, and too weak to protect them and who also died at his hands.

At that moment, she wept for Sadie, her own daughter, the product of incest and rape, who was completely innocent of everything and who had also been defiled, although, luckily, she was too drugged to remember any of it-- *hopefully*.

Once Rachel was finished mourning everything and everyone, the next thing she did was remove her clothes and set to work cleaning herself up. Her shirt and jeans were soaked in blood and blood covered her from head to foot. Although it was night, she went outside to the external shower and rinsed off. A light shone down on her, and she watched while the bloody water washed down through the slats in the shower stall, soaking into the dirt below. She examined every inch of her body in the light but saw no wounds other than chafing marks on her wrists and ankles where she'd been zip-tied. She didn't want any of her own blood mixed with that of Bill or her father.

Satisfied, she went to the house for a change of clothes, finding something to wear in her father's suitcase. It disgusted her to wear his clothes, but she didn't want to leave naked, so she pulled on a t-shirt and some of her father's underwear and a pair of his jeans. She needed his belt to keep the jeans up because they were too big, but they'd do. Overtop, she pulled on a sweater, which hung down almost to her knees, but it would keep her warm. She even wore a pair of his socks, and took care to wear his boots, so no one would see her smaller footprints in the blood.

When she was dressed, she stuffed her bloody clothes in the fire pit with some dry kindling. She poured lighter fluid over the whole mess and lit them up. The kindling cracked and popped in the heat, the clothes burning up -- hopefully into ashes, indistinguishable from the other junk her father burned there.

She checked on Sadie once more, but the girl was still unconscious. It was good -- Sadie would remember little of the events of the night. Besides, Rachel had more to do before they could leave. She found a pair of rubber gloves under the sink and put them on, so she didn't leave any prints. She removed the memory chips from each camera, wanting to ensure that whatever images and film they had of Sadie were destroyed. She threw the chips in the fire as well and watched them burn, melt and disappear into the embers. She kept the memory card from a camera in the large duffel bag belonging to her father. It would contain evidence of his crimes, which she might just mail in one day when she and Sadie were safe somewhere far from Silver Lake.

She dressed Sadie and carried her into the car, lying her on her side in the back seat, fastening one of the lap belts around her and tucking a blanket from the cabin around her to keep her warm. She'd likely sleep for hours, based on the amount of ketamine in her system.

Then, Rachel went back and did her best to remove every bit of evidence that she and Sadie had ever been there. She'd watched dozens of episodes of crime shows that talked about crime scene investigations and knew there would be traces of her and Sadie in the cabin. Besides fingerprints, there would be hair and fiber evidence. Wearing the rubber gloves, she wiped down every single surface she remembered touching. She found a small vacuum and cleaned up all the carpets and the sofa where Sadie had lain, hoping there were no stray hairs that would be used to identify either of them. She washed the vomit out of the cushions but was afraid that some of the liquid seeped into the foam. Over top, she poured bleach, hoping that destroyed any of Sadie's DNA.

She considered burning the place down, to remove any trace evidence she failed to clean up, but she didn't want to call attention to the place. Let it sit undetected for a while. No one was supposed to be at the cabins during spring, so she hoped it was a while before anyone found her father and Bill.

Once she was satisfied that she'd done everything possible to erase evidence of her and Sadie having been at the cabin, she hopped in her vehicle and drove back to Seattle. She'd stop by Mickey's and ask him for help. He'd know what to do. Besides, he had promised her if she ever needed anything -- anything -- he was there for her.

She would pick up Sadie's Ventolin, in case she had an asthma attack. She'd pick up her laptop and some clothes from the apartment, as well as a few of their personal belongings. Then, she and Sadie would leave Seattle for good.

She hoped Craig came with her, but given he really loved his job, she would understand if he didn't.

She would be a fugitive from the law, but it wasn't the first time she'd run away.

When she got back in town, Sadie started to wake up and was confused.

"Where are we, Mommy?" Sadie asked, rubbing her eyes. "I don't feel very good."

"I know," Rachel said and glanced back at the girl, who was still lying on the back seat. "Just stay where you are. We're almost home."

"Where were we?"

"We went for a drive to the mountains," Rachel said, wondering if the girl would remember meeting her "Grandpa" or whether it would be lost due to the amnesiac effects of the ketamine. Heavy doses could prevent long-term memory formation, she'd read. "You got sick."

"I don't remember," Sadie said, sitting up fully, glancing around. "I'm so sleepy."

"We'll be home soon, and then we're going away for a vacation."

"Where?" Sadie asked, her little brow furrowed. "I have school."

"Somewhere warm," Rachel replied. "It's okay. I've already cleared it with your teachers."

That seemed to satisfy Sadie, who yawned and said nothing more as she watched the streets.

Rachel parked in the lot outside their apartment building and took Sadie's hand, walking up the back stairs, hoping no one saw them. It was nine and she didn't expect Craig to be back yet. She used her key to open the door to the apartment and was surprised to see that he was home. He was supposed to be working late at a shoot.

"You're home," she said when she saw him. Sadie went inside and flopped down on the sofa, still semi-drugged with Ketamine. "We're here to pack our bags."

"I thought you'd already gone," Craig said and came over to Rachel, frowning. "You said you were going away for the weekend." Then he looked at her more closely. "What are you wearing? Those aren't your clothes. There's blood on them!"

She glanced down, seeing that some blood had spattered on her when she was moving Sadie.

"It's a long story," she said and took his hand. "Come in here for a moment."

She led Craig into the bedroom and closed the door.

"Look, I don't have time to explain, but we need to leave. Tonight. We need to pack our bags, and leave. I have to get out of Washington State. I was thinking of going to California. Maybe northern Cal, near the redwood forests. I could get a job as a waitress. You could freelance."

"What?" Craig said and laughed. "We can't just up and leave. I have a job. We have this apartment. Why is there blood on your clothes?"

"Because. I'm in trouble and I have to leave. *Tonight*," Rachel said firmly. She went to her closet and got a change of clothes, removing her father's t-shirt and jeans and putting on fresh clothes of her own.

"Why?" Craig asked, his expression one of confusion and disbelief as he watched her quickly remove her clothes from the dresser. "Why do you have to leave tonight? Did something happen at work? Was it Mickey?"

She shook her head, knowing Craig didn't trust Mickey completely. "No, it wasn't Mickey. Look, it's complicated. I need you to trust me. We just need to go. Now."

"I can't leave," Craig said. "Not like this. I have a job with the *Sentinel*. I'm working on a big collection that will be on exhibit at The Beanery."

She shook her head, tamping down her emotions. She couldn't afford to get all upset. She had a feeling Craig wouldn't want to just up and leave. That was okay. She had a plan.

THE GIRL WHO RAN AWAY

"If you can't come with me now, you have to help me leave. Can you run to the gas station and get some cash out for me? I know we were saving it for a holiday, but I have to leave tonight. After I go, you have to burn my clothes, okay? Go out to the dump and burn them."

"Rachel, what are you talking about? Why do you have to leave? Why tonight? I can't just do what you ask without you telling me why."

"Just help me, okay? I need help, and I have to leave Seattle. Tonight."

Craig just stood there with his mouth open.

Rachel turned away in frustration. She'd have to do everything herself and would make sure to stop at the gas station on her way out of town to take out her share of the vacation money.

"Just burn the clothes, okay? If you do nothing else, make sure you burn them. Better yet, I'll take them and burn them myself."

She went to the closet, pulling out her suitcase. She plopped it on the bed and began stuffing clothes in it that she didn't use. She grabbed her backpack and filled it with her usual clothes. For her plan to work, she needed two suitcases.

Craig stood watching, uncomprehending. She wanted to explain everything but if he wasn't coming with her, perhaps it was better if he didn't know -- that way, police couldn't grill him and find out where she was.

She went to Sadie's room and packed two bags for her as well, one with old clothes and the backpack with clothes she did like and use. Then, she filled one duffel bag with a few toys as well as personal items like shampoo and her brushes and toothbrush.

Craig followed her around the apartment as she collected up whatever she needed. On her part, Sadie sat on the sofa and watched Frozen on the DVD player.

When Rachel was ready, she stood at the door, Craig at her side.

"I'm taking the car," she said. "You'll still have the truck. I have to leave now."

"Rachel, why?" Craig asked. "What's going on? At least tell me so I understand."

Rachel shook her head. "It's better you don't know if you're not coming." She dragged the suitcases into the hallway and went back to the apartment. Finally, she stood in the entry to the apartment and glanced around at the place. She'd miss it. She'd been happy there for a long time. She could cry, if she let herself, but she wasn't going to. She needed to be strong, if she and Sadie were going to get through this.

Craig came to her in the hallway outside the apartment and took hold of her shoulders. "Tell me."

"I can't."

He shook her roughly. "Tell me what happened. I can't let you just walk away."

"Come with me," she whispered, hoping against hope that he'd change his mind. "Just trust me."

He shook his head. "Don't leave me."

She pulled away from him and took two backpacks, grabbing Sadie's hand and they left the apartment. "Can you at least carry the suitcases and bag out to the car?" she whispered, seeing light blocked off in the doorway to the apartment next to theirs. The woman living there was probably listening to their conversation.

Craig followed with clear reluctance, grabbing the two suitcases and the trash bag with the bloody clothes before following them to the rear entrance.

"Where are you going?" he asked, stopping her at the doorway. "You have to tell me something."

"We're going north. I have something to take care of. I can't tell you anything."

"Are you going to see your father or something? Is it because I went to Bellingham?"

"Yes, *Craig*," she said, her voice breaking. "It *is* because you went to Bellingham. Now, I have no choice but to leave."

He followed her out of the building to her car.

Sadie squeezed her hand. "Where are we going, Mommy? Why isn't Craig coming with us?"

"Shush," Rachel said. "I'll explain later. Now, get in the car. You need to lie down in the back and go to sleep, okay sweetie? I have to make a stop somewhere and then we're going on a vacation. We'll be driving all night."

"Okay," Sadie said and didn't argue, getting inside and lying down as she had before, the middle seat belt around her for safety. Rachel pulled the blanket up and covered her.

She turned back to Craig and stood on her tiptoes to kiss him, but he didn't kiss her back at first. Then, when she was ready to pull away, he pulled her into his arms.

"I'm so sorry," he said, his voice emotional. "I just can't come like this. Not right now when I have nothing to go to and so much going on here. Give me time. When I have things figured out here, I'll come."

"Okay," she said, but she knew he never would. He wasn't the kind of guy to go on the run.

She kissed him one more time, and then she got in the driver's seat and started the car. Craig stood in the parking lot and watched as they drove off.

Tears filled Rachel's eyes, but she couldn't stay in Seattle and he couldn't leave.

Rachel drove north to Aurora Avenue and Mickey's bar, so she could run in and talk to him. He'd be able to help her.

When she arrived, she parked out back, and left Sadie in the locked car. Mickey was in his office, adding up dinner receipts. The bar stayed open late on Friday and so the night had just begun.

"What's up?" he asked when she slipped inside and closed the door. "You look like you've been through the wringer."

"I need license plates to get out of the country into Mexico."

He frowned. "Uh oh," he said and put down the document in his hand. "I don't like the sound of that. What happened?"

"My past finally caught up with me."

She told him that she was going to go south, to Mexico. She needed to change license plates so the police wouldn't be able to trace her movements.

"Can I ask why? What happened that you need to leave the US?" He glanced at her wrists and must have seen the abrasions on them. "Did someone hurt you?"

"You can come and help me," she replied, her eyes filling with tears at the thought of what had happened. "I have a mess to clean up and I need to leave town -- fast."

"Okay," Mickey said and stood up, grabbing his leather

jacket from a coat rack in the corner. "Let's go. You'll have to drive with me to my place. I have extra plates in the garage. Then, we can clean up whatever mess you've made."

"We have to go up north," she said. "We'll be gone for a while."

"Okay. I'll have to skip the food truck tonight. Whatever you need."

The two of them left the bar through the rear entrance, not seeing anyone in the process. Rachel hopped back in the car and followed Mickey to his place at the edge of town. Once there, he rummaged through his garage while Rachel kept the car running, her hands still shaking despite the time that had passed.

He emerged from the garage and had two license plates in his hand and a tool she could use to remove old ones and put new ones on.

"Follow me up to the mountains. It's a place east of Deming. You'll understand once we get there."

"Of course," he said. "Whatever you need."

Rachel drove off, heading to the cabin. She hoped that Sadie would have no memory of the events of the night. From the time Sadie was born, Rachel had promised that the girl would never suffer the kind of abuse and neglect that she had suffered, and she intended to ensure that didn't happen.

She stopped at a Chevron station on the edge of town for gas, noticing Mickey's truck driving behind her. She grabbed some drinks from the store and a couple of sandwiches from the display case.

Then, they left town, heading north on Highway 9 instead of the interstate.

On her part, Sadie had closed her eyes, and had her Winnie the Pooh toy stuffed under her arm. She was still quite drowsy from the Ketamine and Rachel hoped she would actually sleep most of the night away.

It would be better that way.

CHAPTER THIRTY-FIVE

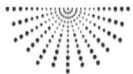

MICHAEL ARRIVED at the building where the charity Mickey ran kept its truck in time to see the volunteers finish setting it up for the night. There were four volunteers in all, and they watched him with interest as he approached after parking his Jeep.

He glanced around the lot. The food truck was like any other, with an awning and several propane burners where the food was kept hot. That was the truck Mickey was supposed to be working the night Rachel and Sadie went missing -- or left town.

On the property was a semi-truck with a container, including shower stalls so that street kids and homeless people could have a shower and wash clothes.

He went to one of the women, an older lady with short steel-gray hair and dark rimmed glasses. "I'm Michael Carter, an investigator with the DA's office. I'm looking into the disappearance of Rachel Martin and her daughter Sadie."

The woman glanced at Michael's ID and shrugged. "Don't know either of 'em. Can't help you. Sorry."

She seemed intent on avoiding talking to him.

"I wanted to ask about the night she went missing. Were you working on Friday, two weeks ago?"

"I work every Friday."

Michael nodded. "Good. Who was working with you that night?"

She gave him the once-over. "I don't have to talk with you. You're not police."

"No, I'm not but it sure would help our case if you would."

"Sorry," she said. "I know my rights. Talk to someone else."

Then she went on with loading up food into the back of the truck.

"I'm trying to clear Mickey's name," Michael called to her.

"He doesn't need his name to be cleared," she called back, clearly hostile to all authorities. She carried another armload of food from the building to the truck. "He's a saint. If you don't realize that, there's something wrong with you."

Michael shrugged. He went up to one of the men who was also filling up the food truck. "Can I speak with you for a moment?" He held out his ID.

"If Lila doesn't want to talk to you, neither do I."

Michael exhaled in frustration. "I'm only trying to corroborate Mickey's alibi for the night two men were murdered up north. All I need is for you to confirm that he was working on the truck that night."

"Mickey works every Friday night on the truck."

"But this particular Friday night is what I need you to confirm.

"If Mickey said he was working, he was working."

Michael turned to another of the younger men working with him. "How about you?"

"I'm with him," the young man said and shrugged.

Michael clenched and unclenched his fists, frustrated that no one wanted to speak with him.

"Okay," Michael said. "I can ask the police to come by and take you in for questioning, if that's necessary."

"Knock yourself out," the older man said and lifted a tray of bottled water into the back of the truck. "We got work to do to help people. You know, important work. Not harassing local heroes, unlike you."

Michael shook his head and turned away, giving up. He could see that people were loyal to Mickey and wouldn't volunteer any information without being forced.

He arrived at his Jeep and opened the driver's side door, preparing to get in when a younger woman who looked in her twenties arrived at his side. She had longer dark hair in a knot on top of her head and was thin, dark circles under her eyes.

"Excuse me," she said, her voice soft. "I didn't want to talk to you in front of the guys," she said and glanced back towards the trucks, "because they seem really angry, but I was working the food truck that night."

"Thank you," Michael said and remained standing, the driver's side door open. "What's your name?"

"Hanna. Hanna McDonald."

"Thanks, Hannah. Can you tell me if Mickey was working that night as usual?"

"He showed up, but not until really late."

"How late? Do you remember what time?"

"Just before we were shutting down for the night. It was, like, almost three. James said he called in earlier and said he had an errand to run and would be late. We thought he'd only be an hour, but he was gone for five at least."

"Are you sure about that?" Michael asked, a surge in his gut at the prospect that Mickey was their man.

She nodded. "I remember because I liked working with him. I looked forward to it."

"What was he like when he showed up? What was his demeanor?"

"His demeanor?" she asked, confused.

"I mean, did he seem relaxed or upset?"

She made a face. "I don't know. He apologized for being so late. We didn't think he'd make it before we closed up for the night. He's a really nice man, so whatever you think he did, I'm sure you're wrong."

"I don't think he did anything," Michael replied. "Just making sure we've checked out his alibi."

"He's like a father to a lot of us," she said, standing with her hands on her hips. "That's why no one wanted to talk to you or police. We're afraid they'll try to pin something on him. I've read some of those cases where police plant evidence and force people to confess. The police don't like him because of his past. They're always hoping to catch him doing something illegal so they can put him away, but he's so good. He's repented and is living a good Christian life now."

"That's good to hear," Michael said and smiled at her. "He has a strong defender in you."

"He does. In all of us."

"Thanks for coming forward, Hannah," Michael said and

glanced around at the work being done to get the trucks ready for another night out. "You're doing good work here."

"You're welcome. We are."

He gave her his business card and then, she left Michael and went back to the main staging area, taking a route around the building to where the other volunteers were busy working. No one noticed that she had been speaking to him, and he figured that was good. She didn't need to be harassed by the other volunteers, who might not like the idea she was helping police.

Michael got in his Jeep and sat for a moment, deciding to call in to the police station before he went home to relay this tidbit of very significant news to the detective in charge of the case.

Chambers was off for the night and so Michael left a message on his cell.

"Hey, just wanted to let you know I spoke with the volunteers who work on the charity's truck that goes out on Friday nights about Mickey. No one wanted to speak with me at first, but one of the volunteers came up when I was leaving and admitted that Mickey was late getting to the truck that night, arriving after midnight. He called in and said he'd be late. Call me if you want to talk about it. Otherwise, I'll be in tomorrow for a while in the morning."

Michael ended the call and then drove to the office to update Nick.

When he was done, he drove to his apartment. Where was Mickey for the five hours? That was more than long enough to get up to Silver Lake and back again, with time to spare.

It was a development that did not bode well for Mickey.

Not at all.

. . .

When he arrived home, before he'd even had the chance to get out of the car, Chambers called him back.

"Nick just called me. I think we're going to bring in Mickey tomorrow for questioning," Chambers said, his voice sounding pleased.

"I thought you might like that bit of news," Michael replied. "It seems Mickey had the opportunity to drive up to the cabin, take care of business, and then drive back."

"My thoughts exactly. I'll speak with the prosecutor in the morning and we'll bring Mickey in for a few questions."

"I'll be there, bright and early. My only question is where are Rachel and Sadie?"

"Hopefully, on vacation like she said. We'll see what Mickey has to say for himself. Our missing persons might end up at a Holiday Inn down in San Diego after all."

"Hope so," Michael replied and ended the call.

He had a good feeling that they were finally going to move forward with the case. If things worked out for the best, Rachel and Sadie would be able to return to Seattle, and maybe the case would be solved, if not closed.

It wouldn't be for a while, depending on what Mickey had to say.

Back at the apartment, Tess was asleep on the sofa, the television turned to a news station. She had the warm fuzzy blanket she liked wrapped around her and her hand tucked under her cheek against the pillow.

He sat on the sofa beside her. "Hey, sleepyhead," he whispered, not wanting to startle her awake. "Time for bed."

She blinked awake and smiled, stretching her hands over

her head.

"How late is it?" she asked and glanced at her Fitbit. "It's not late at all. I guess the tequila made me sleepy. What did you find out?"

"Something very interesting," he said and rested his arm on the back of the sofa when she sat up beside him.

"Do tell."

He exhaled. "Mickey called in that night and said he had an errand to run and would be late getting to the truck. He didn't get back until almost three in the morning."

"Oh, God," Tess said, disappointed. "That's not good at all."

"You're right. It gives him more than enough time to get up to the lake and back."

"And kill two men, try to clean it up. Do you suppose he was involved in the porn ring in some way?"

"He wasn't involved in porn from what I recall of his record. Just drugs and armed robbery. Can't rule it out though. He had opportunity. He was one of the last people to see Rachel before she left -- or went missing. He was gone for five hours."

Tess shook her head. "Would he have killed Rachel and Sadie?"

"Without bodies, or any sign that either of them were killed, it's only speculation. He may have killed the two men in the cabin. Maybe to protect Rachel and Sadie? The ME found Sadie's vomit on the sofa. She'd been drugged. Maybe Mickey went crazy and killed both men. Maybe he rescued Rachel and Sadie and they're hiding somewhere."

"If so, why wouldn't they just come home?"

"Your guess is as good as mine."

Michael leaned back on the sofa, his hands behind his head.

It was going to be very interesting to hear Mickey respond to questions when they brought him in...

CHAPTER THIRTY-SIX

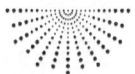

Tess spent the next morning on the sofa, catching up on episodes of *The Walking Dead* while Michael went in to the police station. She would kill to be a fly on the wall in that interrogation room when they brought Mickey in for questioning, but she'd have to wait until Michael called to fill her in on how the morning went.

When she got too bored, she checked her phone and saw that Kirsten had called and left a voicemail. Tess entered Kirsten's number and waited for her to answer.

Kirsten had been horrified when Michael sat her down and informed her that Eugene was the killer and had been killing young girls for two decades.

It was understandable.

"Hey," Tess said when Kirsten answered. "How are you?"

"I'm all right," she said. "Thank God for Phil, or I'd be a mess. We're moving away from Paradise Hill, and I just wanted you to know."

"No way," Tess said and chewed her fingernail. "What will your mother do?"

"She's thinking of coming. With everything that happened, both of us want to leave. Phil doesn't think we'll ever sell our house, but he doesn't care. We're moving to Yakima. Phil will be closer to the office. Mom will get a place near us so she can help look after little Lou."

"I'm so glad," Tess said. "It'll be a new start for you guys. Put the past behind you."

"I hope so. The boys, well, they're being bullied at school. I took them out and we've got them registered to start as soon as the holiday is over. We're changing their names to Carter. They don't need their father's crimes to haunt them the rest of their lives."

"That's good," Tess said, feeling bad for Kirsten and Mrs. Carter. She'd be so torn, fighting her feelings of family loyalty and her need to protect Kirsten and her grandchildren.

They talked for a while, and Tess told her about the current cases she was covering for the *Sentinel*.

"When are you two going to get married?" Kirsten asked, her voice teasing.

"Michael asked me," she said.

"No way!" Kirsten exclaimed. She laughed and Tess was glad she had something positive to tell Kirsten. "I knew you two would get together in the end."

They spoke for a while longer and then Tess promised to come and visit them in Yakima once she had some time off later in the year.

Tess ended the call and remembered back to the first weeks after the arrest and charging of Eugene for the murder of so many girls in Washington State. Kirsten had wept, feeling partly guilty for never pushing Eugene when he went out late at night and spent the night out of town.

"I didn't want to fight with him," she told Tess one night when they sat around Mrs. Carter's dining room table to discuss the case. "I wanted us to have a happy life, but he was so cold to me most of the time when we were alone. He was sweet to the boys, and he was always a perfect husband in front of other people, but when it was just us alone? If I entered a room he was in, he'd leave me and go to another room, like he was avoiding me."

"I'm so sorry," Tess had said, feeling sick for Kirsten. "He had us all fooled."

"He almost killed Michael," Kirsten said. "He would have killed you. I wouldn't have ever forgiven myself if anything happened to either of you. I just didn't want anyone to think there was anything wrong between us. I was so proud of being married back then that I tried to ignore how strange he was in private."

"We're fine," Tess said, but of course, Eugene had cost Michael his job with the FBI as a field agent. Tess had recurring nightmares and still had the creeps now and then when she was alone at night or when she was somewhere alone in the city.

Her therapist said it might take months or even a year or two for Tess to fully get over the trauma of that night.

She hoped it was less than that. She really wanted to join the FBI and work for them tracking killers and bringing them to justice. She hoped she was strong enough mentally for the work and that the PTSD that affected her since her abduction would diminish. If not, she would keep working at the paper.

At least she and Michael would be together...

. . .

When she went out later that morning to pick up some groceries, Tess stopped at the gas station to fill up her tank. While she was waiting, her mind occupied watching the clouds go by on a decently sunny April day, she glanced down the street and saw a vehicle that seemed familiar. She stared at it more closely and a shock went through her -- it was the same vehicle that she thought was following her the previous day.

She turned away, not wanting the person in the driver's seat to know she'd 'made' him, as it was called in surveillance. After filling up her tank, Tess got into her car and drove off, taking care not to look on the street in the direction of the vehicle. She took a different route home, one that swung by the police department. She wanted to see if whoever was following her -- if someone *was* following her -- kept it up when they saw where she was going.

She glanced in the rear-view mirror and saw the car behind her -- it was truly following her. There could be no doubt about it.

Finally, she arrived at the police station, and parked in front. She texted Michael to let him know she was outside.

TESS: I'm outside your building and I think someone has been following me.

In a moment, she saw the little dots that indicated he was typing a response.

MICHAEL: Wait there. I'll be right out. We're taking a break in the interrogation, so I have a moment.

She looked in her rear-view mirror and saw that the vehicle was driving up the street. It passed right beside her vehicle and kept driving, turning right at the next intersection.

She tried not to look at the car directly, keeping it in her line of sighed in the corner of her vision.

In a few moments, Michael came out of the building and walked over to her car, coming to the passenger's side and leaning in the open window.

"Which car is it?" he asked, his voice low.

"It drove up and turned right at the next block," she said. "What should I do?"

"I'll get in. We can take a drive and see if it's still there. If someone's following you, they may park and watch what you're doing."

Tess nodded and after Michael got in her car, she drove off, turning the same corner that the car turned on. Sure enough, the brown sedan was parked about half a block from the corner.

"It's there," she said, keeping her eyes forward.

"Stop here," Michael said and Tess did.

"What are you going to do?"

But Michael didn't say anything. Instead, he jumped out of the car and strode over to the parked sedan. He knocked on the window and from where she had parked, she could see that Michael was quite animated.

Finally, he walked back to the car and got inside.

"What happened? Who is it?"

Michael shook his head. "Guy said his name was Dick Johnson. Reporter for *US News Daily*," Michael said and rolled his eyes. The *Daily* was a rag that specialized in salacious stories about people in the news. "They're doing an article on Kincaid's murders."

"Did he show you his credentials?"

Michael shook his head, smiling a bit. "No, but he had that

look. Besides, there were about a dozen copies of the *Daily* on the seat beside him and a laptop. I got his license plate and will check it out later."

"Why didn't he just call and ask to talk to me?"

"I don't know," he said. "The *Daily* isn't the most reputable paper. Stories about alien babies and celebrity facelifts. Maybe they were hoping to find some dirt on you for their article. I told the guy you weren't interested in talking to him."

Tess exhaled and leaned back, closing her eyes. "I'm glad it was just a reporter." She gave Michael a faint smile. "For a moment there, I was afraid it was some serial killer hoping to pick me off or something. When you told me that you were curious about the person who called in the murder scene, I started thinking maybe it was someone who was at the crime scene but escaped or something."

"It could be but why would he have waited a week to call it in?" He squeezed her hand. "Can you take me back to the office? I have to finish up some work before I can leave."

"Sure," she said and sighed. "I'm sorry I interrupted your afternoon."

"Don't apologize. After what happened in Paradise Hill, you have every right to be extra cautious. Besides, we were on a lunch break. Mickey is not cooperating, as you can imagine."

"He isn't?" she said, frowning. "I was hoping that he'd tell you that he went there with Rachel to rescue Sadie and killed the men in self-defense."

"I was, too, but we've given him every opportunity to say as much. He's not giving us anything new."

"Well, he'll talk soon enough," she said. "See you when you get home."

She stopped at the police station, and Michael leaned over and gave her a kiss.

"See you later," he said. "But it may be much later, depending on how the afternoon goes."

"Good luck," she said, watching as he walked back inside.

Tess drove off, relieved that the man following her was just a journalist, if you could call someone who worked for the *Daily* a journalist. She had really been afraid for a while that someone dangerous was following her. The very last thing Tess wanted at that moment was some creep targeting her because the case in Paradise Hill had hit the national news.

CHAPTER THIRTY-SEVEN

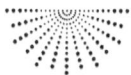

THEY ARRIVED at the first destination over two hours later.

Rachel remembered the site from before, when she was a girl. It seemed a lifetime ago, because so much of her life since then had changed, but once she was back again, she remembered.

She remembered it so vividly that her hands shook.

"What's the matter?" Mickey asked, when he got out of the truck and stood beside her at the edge of the forest. He put his hand on her arm. "Tell me. Why are we here?"

She shook her head, unable to speak.

This was where he took her. *Sadie.*

In the forest, not far from the road.

Rachel stepped gingerly into the woods, her flashlight shining through the darkness. She remembered the spot because he had taken her there many times during the five years between Sadie's murder and when Rachel finally ran away.

There was a special tree, a huge redwood, that had fallen

over, its trunk rotted away, moss creeping up the side. He used that tree as a landmark. Just beyond it, was Sadie's grave.

Rachel stepped carefully over the roots and branches that had fallen to the forest floor, the soft crunch of the wood beneath her feet the only sound so late at night.

Mickey followed her, and she heard his own footsteps in the crackle of the branches.

"Where are we going?"

She stopped at the grave marker. No one but her and her father would know that's what it was. To them, it would be a simple rock, but Rachel knew different. He'd used it to mark the spot so he could come back and gloat. He'd used it to threaten her into silence.

She could picture him standing there, hands on his hips, admiring the grave he'd dug, Sadie's body beside it, waiting to be buried. She was so tiny, just like Rachel, her face pale, a thin cotton nightgown covering her skinny body, bruises on her arms and legs. She looked like a broken angel, her fair hair spread out on the ground beneath her head, her neck at a strange angle.

"That's what happens to little girls who disobey," her father said as he dug a hole in the soft earth. He turned to her and narrowed his eyes. "That's what'll happen to you if you ever say a single word about this to anyone. No one. If you tell your mother, I'll kill her in front of you and then I'll have you all to myself."

On her part, Rachel was too terrified to say anything in response. She cried silently because he didn't like it when she made a sound. Tears ran down her cheeks as she watched him lay Sadie on her side, her knees bent, hands folded in prayer in front of her face, a rosary cross on a long chain woven between her fingers.

"If she'd been more obedient, she'd still be alive, but she was bad. She disobeyed me," her father said, justifying his murderous ways. "She was punished. Like you'll be, if you disobey me."

He grabbed Rachel by the neck and forced her over to show her Sadie before he covered her up with the dirt.

"See? Look at her. She was a very bad girl. She disobeyed me. I'm the head of the household. I make the rules and I enforce them. If you disobey me, you'll be there beside her. I can kill all of you because you don't exist. Do you understand that? You don't even *exist*. There's no record of you or her. No birth certificates. No proof that you ever were born. That means I can kill you and no one will ever know."

He shoved her down on her knees in front of him and began to unzip his pants. She knew what to expect but she was too upset to comply, covering her face with her hands.

When she resisted, he slapped her across the face. "Do you want to join her right now?"

At that point, Rachel cried out loud. "No, please Daddy. I don't."

She didn't fight him.

She never fought him again because she knew what he'd do.

Now, as she stood looking down at the grave, Rachel fought back tears. She'd been able to manage five more years with him after that day. Even after he killed her mother, she stayed, because she was just too afraid. Finally, when he started to use the knife, it had all become too much, and she had to run away.

The stab wounds had been too much to bear.

He'd used a knife on her, exploring how much he could do without actually killing her. He'd stab her and then he'd sew her up. At first, the wounds were small. He seemed to enjoy seeing her blood flow. Then, they got deeper.

She knew he'd kill her one day if she stayed.

So, she ran away.

She handed the flashlight to Mickey. "Shine it on the ground here," she said and bent down to the grave. She began digging, using her hands to remove the wet earth and twigs that had fallen over top the grave. When she reached something hard, she thought it might be a rock, but it was a bone. A small bone, like that in a child's hand. She removed more of the dirt where she thought the hands would be and there it was, after all the years.

The rosary.

"What's that?" Mickey said and bent down. When his flashlight shone on Sadie's skull, he gasped out loud. "Rachel..."

"It's my sister," she said softly. "My twin. My father killed her. He buried her here. He used to come up here with me and visit her grave to gloat. He'd make me do things to him while he stood here. He thought he was smarter than everyone."

"You never told me anything about your family," Mickey said, his voice filled with horror. "I had no idea."

"I never told Craig either. If I had, he might never have gone looking for my family. My father was a monster, Mickey. He prostituted me when I was only eight years old. It went on for five years, and then he started playing torture games, using a knife on me. That's when I ran."

"Oh, *sweeetheart*," Mickey sighed, holding the flashlight on the skeletal remains. "I'm so sorry. I figured maybe you had a dark past, and that's why you were doing drugs and were a street kid. I didn't know it was your father you were running from."

Rachel removed the rosary from the dirt, digging a bit deeper to expose more of Sadie's skeleton. She was able to pull the rosary through the neck because the vertebrae had disarticulated. She shook the dirt off it and wiped the crucifix clean.

"That's what I came for," Rachel said and admired the cross. "It was her rosary. It belonged to my mother, but Sadie always wore it. She thought it would protect her, but nothing could. He was too evil."

Rachel stood up and slipped the rosary in her pocket. She stared down at Sadie's grave, at the bones she'd exposed, and then turned to Mickey.

"I want you to take me and Sadie somewhere," she said, her voice breaking. "We're going to leave the car here."

"Why?" Mickey asked, his voice still haunted. "Why leave the car?"

"Because I want them to find my sister. They'll finally know what he did. If we don't leave the car, no one will find it. No one found it for thirteen years."

"Why don't you just tell them?" Mickey said in protest. "I know some people in the police department from my years working with the charity. I can take you. You can report him and what he did."

Rachel shook her head. "It's too late for that now. All I can do is run away. Sadie and I will go. We'll go to Mexico. I can get work at one of the resorts. Then maybe, we'll go farther south. If we can find a permanent place to live, maybe Sadie can even go to school."

"Don't leave," Mickey protested. "Tell the police everything. They'll arrest your father. He needs to be put in jail."

But Rachel only shook her head. "It's too late for that. I need you to take me somewhere. It's not too far from here."

She grabbed the two backpacks and the duffle bag that she'd packed for her and Sadie out of the trunk and put them into Mickey's truck bed. She also removed the bag of bloody clothes, intending on dumping them somewhere much farther south where no one would find them. Then she carried Sadie from the back seat of her car and laid her onto the rear bench seat in Mickey's truck.

"Where are we going?" Mickey asked, too shocked to protest.

"To Silver Lake. We have one more stop, but we have to hurry. I want to be there before it's too late."

She gave Mickey directions and they drove off.

CHAPTER THIRTY-EIGHT

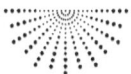

MICHAEL SAT in the viewing room and watched Mickey's interrogation. He got a text while he waited from one of the admins, who had the results of the plate check he'd requested.

According to her text, the plate came back to a James Robinson of Bellingham. No records of note except a couple of speeding and parking tickets.

Certainly not Dick Johnson from the *Daily*.

That unsettled Michael. He made a note to call the *Daily* and see if there was a James Robinson from Bellingham on the payroll. If not, he'd have to go and ask Mr. Robinson aka Dick Johnson to clear up a few things -- primarily why he had been following Tess.

He sent a text to Tess, while he listened to police question Mickey.

MICHAEL: *Maybe don't go anywhere alone today. The plate of that newspaper reporter came back to someone with an entirely different name from Bellingham. Until I know he's legit with the paper, you shouldn't go anywhere alone.*

TESS: *Okay. How's it going?*

MICHAEL: *Mickey's a pretty cool cucumber. He's very chill despite being here for so long.*

TESS: *I just can't believe he killed those men but if Rachel came in to see him and they left together...*

MICHAEL: *Many of us are capable of violence if the situation demands.*

TESS: *Don't I know it. See you later.*

MICHAEL: *Later.*

Michael watched Mickey. He'd just finished a sandwich one of the detectives had bought for him from the cafeteria and was drinking down a fresh cup of coffee. He looked calm, like he was unfazed by being brought in for questioning.

No matter what they did, Mickey didn't seem that he was going to crack.

He spoke with Detective Chambers during their lunch break.

"What can you do to rattle him? He's far too cool under pressure."

Chambers shrugged. "We only have opportunity," he said and rubbed his head. "We don't have any actual evidence that he was ever at the crime scene."

"What about the footprint? Could you match it to him?"

"We're getting a warrant now to search his apartment and the garage he rents for the mission, see if we find anything but the boots that he's currently wearing are not similar to the print we found at the crime scene."

Michael nodded. "That might turn up something."

"You're welcome to come along when we go in, check it

out. I think I'll let Mickey cool his heels in the interrogation room while we search his place."

"Good idea," Michael replied. "If you find anything, you can present it to him, see if that puts a crack in that cool facade of his."

"My thoughts exactly."

When the judge had approved the search warrant, Michael joined Chambers and the other officers who were going to Mickey's apartment and then the garage to do a search for any evidence that might link him to the crime scene.

They arrived at Mickey's place mid-afternoon and as before, got the building manager to open the door to the apartment so they didn't have to break in. Once inside, the detectives and evidence techs spread out, each taking a room and conducting a search for evidence. They were most interested in Mickey's boots and shoes, to see if they could match a pair to the print at the crime scene, but after two hours of searching and taking samples, they came up empty. They did collect Mickey's computer and boxes of video tapes, just in case Mickey was involved in the crime and was a member of the child porn ring that Michael and Chambers suspected existed in the Pacific Northwest.

They next went to the garage where Mickey kept the semi and food truck. The place was closed up and there was no building manager to be found. Chambers had to use his lock-picking kit to open the front entrance. Once inside, they split up and each took an area of the building to conduct their search. For an hour, they checked every nook and cranny in the large garage space.

Michael was responsible for the workbench, and was busy opening and closing drawers, only to find tools and other items necessary to service an engine when he heard a shout from the other side of the garage.

"Got something," one of the detectives called out.

They all converged on the corner of the garage and there stood Detective Pierce, Chambers' partner. He had a boot in his gloved hand, holding it up from inside a barrel of trash.

"He didn't think very far ahead," Pierce said with a shake of his head. "Must have figured his alibi would hold and so he didn't have to get rid of these. There's a dark stain on the sole and it's the right kind and size to match the print at the crime scene. I'm pretty sure we'll find blood when forensics gets this."

One of the forensic techs went over and bagged the boot, and Michael felt relief that perhaps they had Mickey -- finally. He'd stonewalled all day, but now he'd have to come up with some story to explain his bloody boot that matched the one at the crime scene. Michael could only hope that the story Mickey told also solved the question of where Rachel and Sadie were and that they were safe and sound.

They took the boot back to the main headquarters and turned the evidence over to the forensic unit techs. They would be able to confirm the presence of human blood right away but getting a profile off the blood would take longer.

Michael returned to the observation room and saw that Mickey was sitting quietly, looking a little more frazzled as he waited for someone to come in and continue questioning him.

"What's your approach?" Michael asked Chambers, who sat watching Mickey through the two-way mirror.

"I'll confront him with the boot and blood stain," he said. "See what he says. He won't be able to deny he was there when we tell him we matched it to a print at the scene. The only question is whose blood it is and what happened to Rachel and Sadie."

"Hopefully, he'll spill once he realizes we have him at the scene," Michael said. "Get a confession. He hasn't asked for his lawyer yet, so hopefully, we can get him talking."

"My thoughts exactly," Chambers said. "Wish me luck. I'm going back in. I'm taking a few photos of the bloody footprint and one of his boots with the trace blood on the sole. Hopefully, that will knock some sense into him that he better come clean."

"Good luck," Michael said. "I'll be watching with breathless anticipation."

Chambers laughed and left the room.

Michael watched through the two-way mirror, and soon enough, Chambers entered the interrogation room and sat down in his chair once more.

"Look, Mickey," he said in a soft voice. "We've been at this all day. I'm sure you're getting tired and we're all tired. Why don't we wrap this up? No more stalling. We know you did it. We have evidence you were at the crime scene."

"What crime scene?" Mickey asked, his voice sounding flippant. "I'm all ears."

"The one up at Silver Lake," Chambers said, opening the file and placing one of the two photos on the table in front of Mickey. Michael could just make out that it was the bloody boot print with the characteristic tread pattern on the sole.

"This is curious," Chambers said. "It's not a common boot. Has this specific sole. Really characteristic. No other boot has that particular design so we knew it would be a matter of finding someone connected to the case who owned that kind of work boot."

"And?" Mickey said, his voice much less firm now.

"And, we got a search warrant and went to your apartment and the garage where you keep the food truck and the semi container."

Chambers removed the second photo -- one of the boots removed from the garage trash can.

"We found this in the garage trash bin, underneath some garbage." Chambers folded his hands and looked directly at Mickey. "They match. And we've confirmed that it's human blood on the sole. That boot made that print at the crime scene. We have a statement from one of your volunteers who works Friday night on the food truck that you weren't working that Friday night. This volunteer reports that you were gone for five whole hours and didn't return until just before they were supposed to lock up for the night. Five whole hours, Mickey. That would give you time to drive up to Silver Lake, kill those men, and drive back."

Mickey visibly shrank into himself at that.

He leaned back and ran his hands over his head, clasping them together and staring at the ceiling.

"Okay," he said, his voice low. "I'll tell you what happened."

"I'm all ears."

Then, Mickey confessed. Michael almost held his breath while he listened.

"I did it," Mickey said, his voice sounding tired. "I killed those two men. Rachel came to the bar and told me she needed help. This was about nine thirty or so. She said that her father found her, and he'd abducted Sadie and had her up at Silver

Lake. She wanted me to follow her up there and help her get Sadie back. I agreed. We drove up in separate cars, and when we went inside the cabin, both men were naked and in the middle of abusing Sadie while they videotaped it. I had my knife and just flipped out. I stabbed the one man who was on top of Sadie maybe a dozen times in the back and neck when I saw what he was doing to her. Then, I slashed Rachel's father in the gut, and he ran outside. I followed him to the outhouse and stabbed him maybe a dozen times in total. After that, I threw him into the pit because that's where he belonged -- in a pit of shit and piss. He was a monster. He deserved to die."

Mickey folded his arms and leaned back.

"You're willing to swear to that in a formal confession of guilt?"

"I am," Mickey said. "I did it and I don't regret it. Neither of those two monsters deserved to take another breath for what they've both done."

Chambers leaned back and returned the photos back into the file, closing it up.

"Okay," he said. "I'll ask you to write your confession down in your own hand and we'll transcribe it, and have you sign it. I'll be back in a moment with the documents."

"I'm not going anywhere," Mickey said in a voice filled with resignation.

While Michael watched, Chambers left the room. On the screen, Mickey covered his face with his hands.

Chambers came into the observation room and raised his hand up to Michael for a high-five. Then, they fist bumped.

"This is a good day," Chambers said. "I'm so glad we went to the garage and found that damn boot or we would have had to let him go. Now, I'm going to speak with the prosecutor in charge of the case, and we'll decide what to charge him with. We'll have to wait and see what he says happened with Rachel and Sadie. If they're both still alive, and he can prove it, we'll see what he's charged with. But we got him for the double murder, at least."

Michael nodded. It was a relief whenever a suspect confessed, but there was still the question of where Rachel and Sadie were.

Until that question was answered, it was still possible that Rachel and Sadie were dead. If that was the case, the matter was far from over.

Something nagged at the edges of Michael's mind, despite the initial pleasure he got at the confession. He couldn't quite nail down what it was, but it was there in the back of his consciousness, like a dark cloud ruining an otherwise sunny day.

CHAPTER THIRTY-NINE

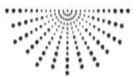

THEY ARRIVED at the cabin north of Silver Lake in ten minutes. The sky was brightening quickly, so she didn't have much time. When they pulled into the driveway, she saw that no one had been by and found the bodies. She relaxed a bit. Her father had said that no one used the cabins at that time of the year because it was still too wet and cold. She might have some time before anyone found the bodies, and so she and Sadie could escape.

"What's going on, Rachel?" Mickey asked, getting out of the truck after she did. "Tell me."

"The less you know, the better," she replied, shaking her head. "Just know I have to leave. I'm taking this van. I'm going to California. Then, maybe Mexico."

"I have some contacts down in Cabo if you want to work."

"Thanks," she said.

She had the keys and opened the back of the van to expose the interior. Her father had made it into a bit of a camper, with a bed in the back and a place for an electric cooler and other camping equipment. She and Sadie would be able to live in it for a while. At least, until they found his body and started to look for his van. Then, she'd have to find another vehicle. But she had some cash saved and ID for her and Sadie and could start over again somewhere new. She'd done it before. She had faith that she could do it again. She would have liked Craig to come with her, but he deserved more than living on the run as a fugitive.

In her mind, the police would find her father and Bill. Then, they'd know she killed them both and would be searching for her. If they found her, they'd take Sadie away and put her in foster care. They'd put Rachel in jail for the rest of her life.

She couldn't let that happen.

She and Sadie would go to Mexico and get lost in the sea of people at one of the resorts. Rachel could be a bartender. Or a cocktail waitress. She would even clean hotel rooms, if it came to that. Mickey would give her names of a few places she could go and get work under the table. People he knew down in Cabo San Lucas.

She hoped it took a week or more for the bodies to be found. That would give her time to drive down into Mexico. She had fake ID from Mickey for them both.

Hell, she'd walk across the border if she had to.

Once she was in Mexico, she figured she'd be safe. No one would be looking for her there. After she knew she was safe, she'd let Craig know. He could come for a visit if he wanted.

She loved him, and she wished things were different, but they weren't.

"Whose van is this?" Mickey asked. "How do you have the keys?"

"It's my father's."

Mickey went to the cabin and was going to open the door, but Rachel called out. "No. Don't go in. It's better you know nothing."

"Rachel, you're scaring me..."

He went inside anyway, and she sighed, but she had work to do. She moved Sadie onto the bed in the back of her father's van and then turned the van on, checking to see how much gas it had. She'd have to fill up soon, but on what was left, she might be able to make it to the border. She planned on driving all day and night, stopping only to sleep. She had to get Sadie to safety as soon as possible.

If they found her, they'd take Sadie away and no one was going to take her from Rachel.

Not ever.

"Oh my God," she heard Mickey say from inside the cabin. He came out and actually stumbled out the door in shock. "There's a dead guy in there."

"That's Bill," she said, her tone flat. "I don't know his last name, but he's my father's partner."

"He's dead!"

"I know," she said plainly. "I killed him. I stabbed him until he was dead."

"*What?*"

Mickey stood there with his mouth opened in shock. "There's blood everywhere."

"I told you not to go in. I killed them both. They kidnapped Sadie and forced me to come out here. He was going to kill me because he was afraid that I was trying to find him. Because Craig went up to Bird Camera in Bellingham and asked about us."

Mickey didn't say anything for a moment. Instead, he watched her working. "You killed them both? Where's your father?"

"They were sexually assaulting Sadie and filming it. I was knocked out, tied up, and when I woke up, I got free, I used my knife and I killed them both. My father is in the outhouse. I killed him, too."

Mickey went to the outhouse, his flashlight beam bouncing around in the darkness.

"Oh, *God*," he said in horror. He came back over to where she was. "Rachel, we have to call the police."

"No, we don't, and we aren't going to," she said firmly, tucking a blanket around Sadie, who was sleeping. "If they know I did it, I'll go to jail for the rest of my life and they'll put Sadie in a foster home. Who knows what will happen to her, then?"

"They won't, Rachel," he said. "You did it in self-defense."

"They'll put me in jail and put Sadie in foster care. I read this article about a girl who killed her abuser. She's in jail now for thirty years."

She leaned inside the van and arranged their possessions on the floor behind the seats. Then she went inside and took some of her father's food and some jugs of water for the trip south.

He followed her. "Rachel, you can't just run away."

She shook her head. "I can, and I will. I'm not going to jail. By all rights, he deserved to suffer more for all the things he did. He killed my sister. He killed my mother. He raped me and made me have sex with other men, for years. I was only eight years old when he started. Eight!"

Mickey didn't speak. He only shook his head.

"I'm not staying. Help me load up the van."

Mickey stood there in silence for a moment as if he was deciding whether to help her or call the police.

"They'll come looking for you when they find the bodies."

"No, they won't," she replied. "No one even knows my real name. My birth was never registered. My father was never married to my mother and he delivered Sadie and me when we were born. You have to realize that he was one of those preppers. He considered himself a sovereign citizen, who didn't believe in the government. He didn't pay taxes, and he didn't register our births. For all intents and purposes, I was never born. The government doesn't even know I exist. I never went to school. I never saw a doctor. That's why no one ever looked for my sister or my mother."

Mickey was still deciding what to do, still shocked by it all. Then, he sighed. "Okay. I'll do whatever you want me to. If you want to go south, I have people who will help you. No questions asked."

"Thank you," she said and put her hands on his arm. "You've always been there when I needed someone. You got me the fake birth certificate and social security number. You helped me get clean and sober. You got the fake ID for me and Sadie. You got me the license plates. I'm going to leave now, and I'm never coming back."

Then, she did feel tears biting the corners of her eyes.

"Goodbye," she said. "You were like a real father to me. You were the only man besides Craig who was ever nice to me."

"Does Craig know?"

She shook her head. "I didn't tell him. I asked him to come and help me, but he couldn't. Don't report me missing, okay? Not for a week at least. That will give me time to get out of

Washington and find a new place to stay. If they ask you, tell them the last time you saw me was my shift today at lunch. Tell them that I said I was taking Sadie away for a holiday. That I was turning off all my social media and was going to take a break from everything."

"They'll think Craig killed you," he said softly.

"He didn't," she said plainly. "If they ask you, just tell them I left the bar at lunch and never came back. They'll find the car in the mountains and think my father killed me or something. They'll find the skeleton and they'll know he murdered Sadie. They'll figure it all out eventually. They'll know it was me and they'll come looking for me, not Craig. But I'll be in Mexico or maybe I'll go somewhere that there's no extradition treaty with the US. I heard Montenegro has no extradition treaty. I may go there. There's a lot of ex-pats living there."

He shook his head. "They'll think Craig killed you. Innocent men have gone to jail before for murders they didn't commit."

"He didn't kill anyone, did he? They'll know. They'll find evidence."

Mickey sighed and watched as she got in the van and turned on the engine.

"Goodbye," she said. "I'll let you know things are okay once I'm somewhere safe."

He audibly sighed. "I'm sorry all this happened to you," he said.

She shrugged, no longer caring. "So am I. But it's my fault. It's all my fault."

Then, she drove off.

. . .

She drove for eighteen hours and found a place to camp in the parking lot of a Costco outside Carlsbad, California. They stopped only once for Rachel to take a nap and to let Sadie go to the bathroom at a truck stop outside of Redding, California. They ate a quick supper of sandwiches she bought at the store, and then they were off once more, driving for another eight hours straight until dawn.

Sadie slept all night, tucked away in the back, and Rachel watched the road, listening to a radio station playing old gold hits of the 70's and 80's. Mickey's music. She'd left her cell phone in the car near Mt. Baker and bought a burner at a 7-Eleven. It would have to do until she started her new life with her new identity.

While they drove, Sadie asked Rachel about what happened. She had very little memory of anything, so Rachel just told her a story of how Sadie had gotten a fever and was so sick, she fell asleep. When she realized that she couldn't stay at the cabin, Rachel decided that they should take a vacation and drive down to California for a while. Maybe, they'd move there for good if they liked it.

"What about Craig? Is he coming to live with us?"

"Not right away," Rachel said softly. "He has lots of work to finish first. Maybe he'll come down when he's finished with his work, but you and I can have some fun, right? It'll be an adventure. Like Frodo and Sam when they left the Shire."

Sadie frowned. "They went to Mordor."

"We're going to California. It's not like Mordor."

"California?" Sadie said with wide eyes. "Can we go see the ocean? And Disneyland?"

"Yes," Rachel said. "We can. We can go surfing. Would you like that?"

Sadie smiled widely at that. "Yes. Can we see dolphins? And whales?"

"We'll see whatever there is to see, how's that?"

Sadie nodded and watched out the window, seemingly unharmed from her ordeal. Luckily, she didn't remember what had happened to her and that was perhaps the only blessing from everything.

Ketamine was useful for something.

CHAPTER FORTY

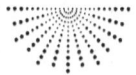

THE NEXT MORNING, after spending a late evening at the police department reading over Mickey's detailed confession, Michael drove up to the cabin at Silver Lake, intent on looking over the crime scene for something -- anything -- that might help him to understand the crime scene better so he could get a mental picture of what happened and satisfy himself that the smidgen of doubt he'd been harboring was nothing.

In all likelihood, the unease he felt was indigestion and nothing more.

He'd read the police report and gone over the forensic evidence. It was clear the two men were stabbed and then whoever did the murders tried to clean up to remove evidence of their presence. That matched up with what Mickey claimed in his confession.

He spent an hour walking around the perimeter of the cabin, checking inside, and trying to imagine how the murder took place. Where was Rachel during this? There was no clear evidence she was there but there was evidence that her daughter, Sadie was, from the vomit stain on the sofa.

He went out to the yard and glanced around. A fire pit sat at the edge of the property. It was a wet mess since it had been raining heavily over the past two weeks. There was nothing to be found but burnt embers from whatever fires had been lit previously. The ashes had been turned to a dark blackish-gray muck. After a cursory examination, he took a stick and poked around the ashes, trying to see if there was anything the forensic team missed in their initial investigation. In one corner of the pit underneath some rain-soaked wood that never burned, was what looked like blackened cloth. He used the stick to pry it out from under the wood and soon, he had extracted the whole item.

It was the burned remains of a cable knit sweater. From the looks of it, the sweater was for a woman with a small build. The material had been almost completely consumed by the fire except for one shoulder and sleeve and part of the neck and material on one side. There were dark stains on the sleeve and neck that Michael suspected were blood.

Whatever fire had been lit to burn the clothing had been extinguished before the entire item of clothing was consumed. Beneath that, a small metal and plastic memory card from a camera.

Michael removed a plastic bag from his pocket and placed the intact memory card inside. He hoped they would be able to retrieve the data on the card. It might provide more evidence for the investigation. If nothing else, it would confirm if the men were indeed filming child pornography, and whether Sadie had been used as a victim.

While he was packing up the sweater in a larger bag from the hatch of his Jeep, a dark sedan drove up, and parked behind his, effectively blocking his way. It was the reporter from the *Daily* -- or at least, James Robinson from Bellingham, who may or may not have been a reporter with the paper. Michael was angry that the man had followed him up to the crime scene. He ignored the yellow tape, stepping under it and coming over to where Michael stood at the back of his Jeep.

Michael put his hand on his hip, where he had his sidearm.

"Hey," Michael said when Robinson walked up, his hands in his pockets. "You're not supposed to cross police lines without permission."

"I know," he said. "I spoke to the owner of the place. He said I could come by, take a look at the place for my article. Just wondering when police will be finished."

Michael turned around to place the evidence bag into the back of the Jeep.

He was going to confront the man about using a fake name, but before he had a chance, a blow to his head knocked him out and he fell to the ground.

When he awoke, his head hurt like a bastard and his vision was slightly blurred at first.

Damn...

Whoever it was, the man was obviously not from the *Daily*. He must have been involved in the pornography ring. It was at that moment that Michael knew what the man had come to retrieve.

He climbed up to his hands and knees and felt the back of

his head -- it was wet from the dirt -- or blood. He checked his fingers and sure enough, dark blood was thick on his fingers.

"Crap," he said out loud to no one. "Damn it all to hell."

He stood finally and checked the back of his Jeep.

One of the evidence bags was gone -- the one with the intact memory chip. Whoever Michael's attacker was, he didn't care that police had the bloody sweater. The man who attacked him was more interested in the memory chip -- most likely because it could implicate him.

Michael checked his vehicle and luckily, the man hadn't taken his keys, so Michael would be able to drive back to Seattle. He sat inside his vehicle and considered what to do next. He needed to call the police and report the assault, get them out to the site to check for any evidence.

There would be fresh tire tracks from the Ford the man was driving but there were so many, it would be difficult to detect, especially since the rain was just starting. By the time police arrived, the tracks would be partially washed out.

He called Nick.

"Hey," he said and pressed a tissue against the wound on the back of his head. "I was out at the crime scene on Silver Lake and found some evidence. I was packaging it up when a guy claiming to be a reporter for the *Daily* arrived in a dark brown sedan, late model, Ford Focus. He claimed the owner gave him permission to come to the cabin and look around for his article, but when I turned away to put some evidence into my Jeep, he attacked me and knocked me out. I just woke up to find he left with the evidence. I'll call Bellingham PD and get them out here to take my statement. Do you want to send someone from Seattle?"

"I'll call Palmer in Bellingham. He'll come out and take

your report, since the assault occurred on his turf. I'll send Chambers out to check the place out, see if we can find anything else."

"Okay," Michael said. "I'll wait."

"If you need to get medical attention, I can have them send an ambulance."

"Nah, I think the cut's pretty shallow. I have a first aid kit in my Jeep and will patch myself up. I'll check in at the ER on my way back home if I think I need a stitch or three."

"I'll leave that up to you."

"Thanks, Nick."

Nick cleared his throat. "I guess you should have taken someone with you when you went to the crime scene."

Michael exhaled. "I guess I should have but it was on a whim. I've just been feeling dissatisfied with the case and wanted to spend some time at the scene myself. You know, check it out again in case we missed something."

"Which we obviously did," Nick said in a low voice. "What did you find?"

"A burned and bloody woman's sweater and an intact memory card. They were both in the fire pit. It looks like the techs checked the fire pit out but missed one corner where some unburned wood was. The remains of a sweater and the memory card were located beneath the wood. It was hard to see unless you moved everything around."

"Which the techs are trained to do," Nick said, a note of frustration in his voice. "Let me guess. The guy who attacked you took the memory chip."

"Bingo," Michael said. "He didn't take the sweater, interestingly enough."

"Tell me about the sweater."

"It's a woman's sweater, on the small size. Blood on the sleeve and body."

"That doesn't sound good for our missing persons cases. Do you expect it was Rachel's? Was it a girl's sweater or a woman's sweater?"

"Woman's, I think," Michael said, having come to the same conclusion.

It suggested that Rachel -- and maybe Sadie -- were both dead.

"We should be able to get some good forensics off it, see whose blood it is."

"Hope to hell it's not either of theirs," Michael said. "I've been thinking that they escaped and left Seattle and are currently hiding out somewhere but maybe I'll have to reassess that. Has Mickey said anything more?"

"No, he's quiet as a mouse now that he's confessed. Hasn't said anything about Rachel and Sadie except that they're both alive and safe."

"Damn," Michael said. "I guess we'll have to wait to see who that blood belongs to."

"I guess so," Nick replied. "This is good, Michael. I knew you were a good hire. Just be more careful in the future not to go to crime scenes by yourself on a whim, okay?"

"I learned my lesson, boss," Michael replied with a laugh. "The hard way."

Nick laughed. "I'll call Palmer and get someone out there right away. Take care, Michael."

"Okay," Michael said. "Thanks, Nick."

"Don't mention it."

With that, Nick ended the call and Michael leaned back, a

bandage pressed against his head, waiting for police from Bellingham to come and take his statement. He decided not to tell Tess what happened -- no need for her to worry.

Plus, whoever attacked him was still at large...

CHAPTER FORTY-ONE

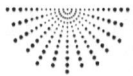

When Michael arrived home much later that evening, he had a pressure bandage wrapped around his head.

"My God, Michael. What happened?"

Michael removed his coat and hung it up in the closet. "I got clocked from behind while I was at the Silver Lake crime scene. I took a trip to the ER for some stitches on my way home."

"What? What do you mean, you got clocked from behind?"

"Someone hit me when my back was turned. I was knocked out for a bit but I'm fine."

"Michael, you should have called me," Tess said and went to him, her hands on his chest. "I could have come and picked you up at the ER."

"I'm really fine," he said and pulled her into his arms. "No ill effects. All my fingers and toes work and my eyesight's back to normal. The doc in the ER said I might have a headache but there's nothing permanent."

"You should have let me come and meet you there," she

said and hugged him. "I thought this job with the DA's office as an investigator would be safer than as a field agent with the FBI."

"I was stupid," he said. "If I'd taken someone with me, I would have been fine. Or at least, the guy might not have approached us. Or," he said and laughed sardonically. "We might have had a gunfight, if he wanted that evidence so badly."

"What evidence? Who attacked you?"

"The guy who claimed to be the reporter for the *Daily*." Michael had a guilty expression on his face.

"I *knew* it," Tess said and they went over to the sofa and sat beside each other, Michael's arm around Tess. "He was no reporter. He was someone involved in the case, right? Someone who was there the night it happened?"

"Could be. I poked around looking for something we might have missed. Found a memory card. Looks like it might be readable. He took it after he knocked me out."

"Do you suppose he knew it was there and was coming to get it?"

"I have no idea. He might have just lucked into me finding it and wanted to take it to make sure he wasn't on it. He didn't seem interested in the other evidence."

"What other evidence?"

Then, Michael hesitated as if he didn't want to tell her.

"What?" she said and pushed his shoulder. "Tell me."

He made a face of pain, his eyes squinting. "A bloody woman's sweater which was partially burned in the fire pit."

"Oh, *God*," Tess said and a jolt of adrenalin went through her. "Not Rachel's?"

THE GIRL WHO RAN AWAY

"Can't say yet but the forensic unit has it and will run tests to see if they can get a profile and match it to someone."

Tess leaned her head against Michael's shoulder, a sense of dread filling her at the prospect that Rachel was also dead. Had Mickey killed everyone?

"Do you think Mickey killed Rachel and Sadie, too?"

"I have no idea. We're going to present the evidence to him and see what he says. He's already confessed to killing the two men, but now, we have evidence of a woman's bloody sweater and an attempt to get rid of the evidence. Who knows what they did manage to burn? We'll see whose blood it is and go on from there."

Tess covered her eyes. "Oh, I hope it's not Rachel's or Sadie's. What will Craig do? He'll be sick to learn that Rachel and Sadie were at the crime scene where two men were murdered."

"Yeah. Craig has no alibi either but there's no evidence that puts him at the crime scene. As far as we're concerned, he's no longer a suspect."

They sat for the rest of the evening, talking about the case, not really feeling like doing anything else.

The next day, Michael went into work, despite the knock on his head. He had a mild headache, but nothing more and when Tess pressed him to stay home, he refused.

"I have to go in and find out what's developed since I was in yesterday. The Chief is holding a press conference to update the public on Mickey's arrest."

"Okay, but if you start feeling unwell, make sure to go right to the hospital."

"I don't have a concussion," he insisted. "The ER Doc said I was lucky. I just got knocked out. No lasting damage besides the hair that had to be shaved around the injury. And my pride, of course."

Tess shook her head in disapproval but gave him a kiss and watched him leave.

She spent the day working on her article covering the double murder at the Silver Lake cabin and the ties to the disappearance of Rachel and Sadie. The connections weren't yet clear, but the police chief was holding a news conference on Monday to update the press and public about recent developments.

She turned on the television before supper after Michael called to tell her that Mickey was being processed and would be taken to a cell to await trial. Following his transfer, the Police Chief would hold a brief press conference.

The camera focused on the door to the police station, which showed the back of the building and a waiting van that would take Mickey to the King County Jail where he would await a preliminary hearing. Mickey walked with his head up and his back straight. He held his hands out in front of his body, and they were obviously cuffed. A jacket had been thrown over them, but he didn't appear to be at all ashamed of being led away from the police station. Reporters yelled questions at him, but he didn't even look at the cameras. Instead, he quietly walked to the awaiting van and was helped inside by one of the officers.

The van drove off and the reporter described the scene, saying that Mickey seemed very composed.

She waited for the press conference to begin, wondering what the police would say about the case. The Chief came out and stood before the cameras. Behind him stood Detective Chambers and another official. The Chief gave an update on the case, and on the arrest of Mickey Howell for the double homicide. He noted that there was still no identification of the second John Doe, but he gave them assurances that police were working on identifying him. They would be turning to the ancestry database to see if they could locate a relative and learn his identity that way. The police chief did mention that there was an apparent blood relationship between the John Doe and the missing woman and her daughter, but didn't go into any further detail, despite repeated questions from the reporters gathered at the press conference. He did confirm that police believed that Rachel and Sadie were alive and in hiding but that they had to do more investigation of the matter before they could conclude either way, but he was hopeful.

Then, it was over, and the discussion turned to local news. Tess turned off the television and sat back, wondering what happened to Rachel and Sadie. She hoped the two were somewhere safe and hadn't met the same fate as Rachel's twin sister, buried in a shallow grave somewhere in the middle of the forest.

She called Craig.

His cell rang three times before he answered. As usual, his voice sounded subdued.

"Hey," she said, trying to sound hopeful. "How are you? Did you hear the news? They arrested Mickey and charged him with second degree murder. Michael thinks that Mickey's lawyer will accept a plea for manslaughter, considering the circumstances. And they think Rachel and Sadie are both alive and hiding out down south. Maybe Mexico."

"If she had told me why she wanted to leave, I would have

gone, Tess," Craig said, his voice sounding dejected. "She wouldn't tell me. She just asked me to pick up everything and leave. I couldn't. Not without knowing why."

"Has she contacted you?" Tess asked.

"No," Craig said. "Not yet. I sent her messages through Facebook but there's been nothing so far. I thought she loved me. I thought she'd let me know she was okay, if she was. This not knowing is so hard."

"I know, I'm sorry, but Mickey said she was afraid that if anyone knew where she was, her life and Sadie's life would be in danger."

"But she could call me and tell me where she was. I'd leave as soon as I could. I keep sending that message to her but nothing. Maybe she doesn't have internet service very often or something."

"Maybe," Tess said, trying to be sympathetic.

She said goodbye and promised to have lunch with Craig in the coming week, to talk about the case. She ended the call and sat in silence for a moment. Maybe Rachel didn't care enough about Craig to let him know she was okay and invite him to join them. It was possible, although everyone thought the two were really happy together. They had been through such a traumatic event together, perhaps she was just trying to stay alive.

Hopefully, things would work out for Craig. Tess couldn't help but feel sad for him, all alone in the apartment that used to be shared with Rachel and Sadie.

Now he was all alone.

CHAPTER FORTY-TWO

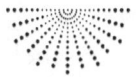

AFTER A FULL DAY OFF, during which time Michael spent doing as little as possible, he went back to work, hoping to get an update on the case.

"Call me if you get any news that you can tell me," Tess said when he left the apartment.

"I will," he said and kissed her goodbye.

At the office, he sat down with Nick to talk about the developments in the case.

"We matched the blood on the sweater to the victims," Nick said, and Michael sat back, relieved to learn that at least it wasn't Rachel's or Sadie's blood.

"That's hopeful," he said. "I heard the press conference and the chief of police stating that he thought they might both be alive, but in hiding."

Nick nodded. "According to Mickey, they're both alive and well and living down south somewhere. He said he helped them leave the state and that he'd never reveal their location because there are still people out there who worked with her father and Sutton who would want to harm her and Sadie. We told him that unless he could provide evidence that proved both were alive, they could charge him. We displayed the burned sweater and Mickey was totally unconcerned by it."

"What did he say when you showed him the sweater? How did he seem?"

"He was fine. He said Rachel got blood on her in the mayhem, and after she picked up Sadie from the sofa and carried her into the van. Mickey tried to burn the clothes and memory cards so that no one could ever use the images."

Michael shrugged. It sounded reasonable enough.

"Can he prove that Rachel and Sadie are both alive?"

Nick removed a sheet from the file on his desk. "He told us to check his Facebook private messages. This turned up."

On the sheet of paper was an image of a white sand beach, with the footprints of an adult and a child, a wave almost washing the prints away. The water was very clear and quite turquoise. Beneath the image was a message.

It's beautiful here. Thank you for everything.

The message was from Rachel, who was one of Mickey's Facebook friends. There was no location information attached to the image.

"Have you contacted Facebook to find out where the image was posted?"

"We put in a request," Nick said. "If it turns out that it's legit, we may be able to at least close those missing persons cases."

Michael nodded and examined the image. The water was clear and quite blue-green, and the beach was very white, which suggested it wasn't taken at a beach farther north along the Washington or Oregon coast. Beaches farther south were lighter in color.

"Could they be in Mexico?" Michael asked. "That beach is pretty white. Or Florida. There are some really white beaches in the Pensacola area. That water is quite clear and a distinctive color."

"Could be. We'll see what Facebook provides as to location. Whatever the case, it doesn't mean they're still where that picture was taken."

"No, but it would be a start. And depending on when that was posted, it would give us some information to use to try to track them. We know they took her father's van and used the license plates Mickey gave them. We could check with CCTV along the highways to see if we could find the vehicle."

Nick rubbed his chin. "If she posted from her Facebook page recently, I think that she and Sadie are both alive. If so, we'll do what we can to find her. It sounds like a case you might like to take on, am I right?"

"You mean I'd have to travel to California and then Mexico, track down video of the vehicle, maybe talk to local hotel owners, that kind of thing?" Michael said with a grin. "Sounds like a tough assignment."

Nick laughed. "It's a dirty job but someone has to do it."

Michael nodded, glad that Nick had assigned him the case. He wondered how Craig would take it, having Rachel and Sadie leave on him like that. Michael had experienced a similar abandonment the day that Julia took the boys and left their home. It was one of the most difficult times of his life.

"Hopefully, if we don't find her, she'll feel safe enough to return some day," Michael said.

"That sand looks pretty inviting. Don't know if I'd come

back if I were her. Especially not if she believes there are people who might be looking for her who would harm her and her daughter."

"I suppose you're right. I'm surprised Craig didn't go with them."

"He wasn't up to it, I imagine. Doesn't strike me as the adventurous type."

Michael nodded. "Craig seems like quite a reserved person. Not the type to live on the lam, I guess. Whatever the case, I'll feel a lot better about things if we can confirm that they're both alive."

"You and me both."

Michael picked up the file and left Nick's office, wanting to make copies of the most recent evidence for his own file. After he returned the file to Nick, he went to his desk, but he couldn't really focus. His wound ached so he took some Tylenol and then, when he checked the kitchen to see whether there was any decent coffee and found the carafe was empty except for some burned coffee at the bottom, he decided he'd done enough work for the weekend.

"That's it for me," he said, poking his head into Nick's office.

"Go home, young man. Stay home for two whole days, okay?"

"If you insist," Michael said with a grin.

He grabbed his briefcase, pulled on his jacket and left, eager to fill Tess in on the newest developments.

He arrived home just before four o'clock, two cups of coffee in hand that he'd picked up from his favorite coffee shop. Tess met him at the door and took the cups from him.

"You come bearing gifts, I see," she said. "Good news?"

"Just talked to Nick about Rachel and Sadie," he said and followed Tess into the living room. He flopped down on the sofa beside her and accepted the coffee cup from her. They clicked their cups together and took a sip. Tess leaned back beside him and rested her head on his shoulder as Michael filled her in on the latest details.

"I'm glad that it looks like they're both alive," she said. "Hopefully, Mickey will get a light sentence or even a suspended sentence."

"We'll have to wait and see what the prosecutor says but I think he might. It would have been better if he came forward with this information right away and the fact he hid the truth from police for so long is not in his favor, but I understand he was trying to protect Rachel and Sadie while they escaped. Now, all we have to do is find out who her father really is, and who the man is who attacked me," Michael said and leaned back, slipping his good arm around her shoulders. "And of course, find her, make sure she's really okay."

"Poor Craig," Tess said. "I called him to see how he was doing. He sounds pretty broken by it all. Even knowing that she's probably alive, I expect he feels abandoned."

"I know," Michael said. "I was thinking about him when I saw the picture she sent Mickey. She should really let Craig know she and Sadie are okay, if they are."

Tess sighed and shook her head. "Maybe she will. She's probably just trying to survive in a whole new place and really hasn't been focused on anyone else."

"She's a survivor," Michael said and thought of the pictures he'd seen of her and Sadie.

Rachel was a survivor. She'd run away from an abusive family and made a new life in Seattle. Then, when her old life caught up with her, as she'd said herself, she ran away again. He hoped that she'd eventually be able to stop running.

If there was any justice in the world, one day, she would.

EPILOGUE

THE RESORT in Cabo San Lucas was on the cheap side and didn't provide all the extras the really expensive hotels provided, but they hired Rachel on the spot, attracted to her skill as a bartender and cocktail waitress and her facility with the English language. The recommendation from Mickey didn't hurt.

She would work shifts in the evening, from eight until closing. They could only offer her a few shifts a week doing that, but they also offered her some cleaning shifts, if she was willing to fill in when the regular girls were sick.

"I'll do anything."

In return, they let her stay in one of the small rooms with a king-sized bed and a roll-away for Sadie. The bathroom needed to be renovated but they didn't have the funds so Rachel and Sadie, now known as Rose and Elsa, occupied the room. Mickey had really pulled through with the fake IDs, and Sadie was completely entranced that her new name was Elsa, having fallen in love with the movie character who had white-blonde hair like hers. Rachel just wanted a name close enough to her own that it was easy to remember and Rose made her think of her friend who was murdered and turned up in the dumpster.

Rose fit the bill.

So, within a week of 'the event,' as Rachel thought of it, she and Sadie were at the tip of the Baja California peninsula in Mexico, sitting on the beach, looking out at the Pacific Ocean.

She was honestly too shell-shocked from the trip down the coast, the change in scenery and the new routine in their lives, to think about what happened.

She signed into her Facebook profile using the hotel's internet and a VPN she registered for free, then posted a private message to Mickey to let him know she and Sadie were all right. Until she knew what happened back home with the murders of her father and Bill, she couldn't risk contacting him more directly.

Maybe once that was settled, she'd contact Craig and he could come for a vacation, if he didn't want to come and live with her and Sadie.

Rachel knew that she could probably never go back to the USA.

If she could, she'd eventually make it down to Montenegro and live there. It would be hard for Sadie to keep on the move, but Rachel was not going to let them take her and put her in foster care. Rachel would survive all right in prison -- she was sure of it -- but it was Sadie she thought of. Sadie would never be in foster care if Rachel could help it.

Montenegro sounded perfect. They wouldn't extradite her

back to the US in case they ever discovered she was alive and had killed her father and Bill.

Rachel had started to relax, glad that there had been no news about the murders. She hoped it took a while to discover the identities of the two dead men. That would give her and Sadie time to recover from their ordeal.

Sadie seemed no worse for the wear. All she remembered was talking to her 'grandpa' and then getting sick. Rachel told the girl she developed a bad case of the stomach flu, which gave her a high fever so she couldn't really remember what happened to her.

"Be glad you don't remember," Rachel said in a joking manner. "All you did was sleep and throw up and all I did was look after you and clean up the mess."

Sadie seemed satisfied with that response and didn't push. If her body remembered what the two perverts did to her, her conscious mind didn't. Rachel hoped that it stayed that way and that the girl never had to get counseling. She was afraid the abuse would resurface later in Sadie's life and require therapy, but they'd cross that bridge when they came to it. Otherwise, Sadie seemed happy to be in Mexico, staying with Rachel in the hotel, doing her school work and when Rachel was finished with her shifts, going to the beach, learning to boogie board and eating the fantastic Mexican food at the resort. She didn't ask too many questions about why they left Washington behind. She seemed willing to accept Rachel's explanation that she wanted to travel and see the world. The only questions were about why Craig hadn't joined them.

"He'll come and join us when he's done with his work. He has several big projects he's working on, but he will soon. He loves us both."

"I know," Sadie said and continued to do her work at the tiny table in their room. "I miss him."

"I do, too," Rachel said.

For the first full week they were at the hotel, Rachel really thought they might be able to stay for a good long time, but she was wrong.

News about the murders turned bad when Rachel opened up her browser and read the *Seattle Sentinel*.

Craig was now the main suspect in Rachel and Sadie's disappearance.

It had taken five full days of travel to get there, and two days to recover and get settled in the hotel. Then, she assumed Mickey or Craig reported her missing. There was no news report about them that day, the Friday, a week after the murders. There was no news report until the following Monday. Then, there was just a small photo taken by Craig of her and Sadie standing in the park together. The accompanying article said that they had gone for a short trip to Oregon for a mother-daughter getaway and had not come back or been in contact with Craig.

Then, the vehicle had been found and that changed everything.

Rachel figured that when they found the car, they would find her sister's skeleton and would eventually discover that the victim was her twin sister. She had watched years of episodes of Law and Order and read books on forensic science. They would eventually connect her to their father, who would also be identified through DNA.

In Rachel's mind, they would realize that her father was a murderer. They'd go looking for her mother and the focus would be on that, and not on whoever killed her father.

She knew they'd suspect Craig of murdering her but figured that they had no evidence and couldn't convict him.

She never expected that the police would suspect Mickey and that they would charge him with the murders, and he would confess...

Now, they'd realize she took her father's van and they'd track her south through California, where she sold the van and used the clean license plates Mickey had given her for her escape. There, she bought an old VW camper van, in case she and Sadie needed a place to live if times got tough. It was cute if old, with a tiny sink and mini-fridge, and a hot plate. All they had to do was find a camping ground and they could plug in and even cook food if they needed.

Either way, they'd know she and Sadie were alive.

Because of one footprint in blood that had not yet dried and Mickey's penchant for unique boots, they suspected him, and he confessed, taking the fall for her...

It wasn't right, but hopefully, there would be some evidence to prove he didn't kill them.

No one thought that she, Rachel, had done it. Mickey's footprint made it look as if he did. He was a man, after all. Men, not women, were violent enough to kill two men much larger than her.

For a few days, she debated what to do. Should she turn herself in?

If she did, she knew what would happen -- what had happened to other women who killed their abusers. She'd be put away for life. Sadie would go to a foster home, and who knew what kind of people she would end up with?

They could be like her father -- a murderous pedophile who got away with bad things for too long.

No, she would never abandon Sadie to abuse and neglect the way she had been abused and neglected as a child.

Over the next week, Rachel earned enough money for the next leg of the journey south. The shifts cleaning the rooms was grueling and she agreed to take on a double shift twice, to make extra money. She needed every extra cent she could get, in order to get as far as she could each day of travel.

Once she was in Montenegro, she'd be safe.

Even if they did figure out that she had killed her father and Bill, not Mickey, the government of Montenegro would be unwilling to extradite her back to the USA.

She and Sadie would begin a new life in the ex-pat community there. She trusted her gut that it was the right thing to do. Mickey would be cleared eventually -- he didn't kill anyone.

As she stood on the beach outside the resort on her break, while Sadie played in the sand, she thought about Craig and what he was going through. She felt bad but couldn't worry about that now. She had one focus and that was keeping Sadie out of the foster care system. She would fight until the bitter end to prevent that.

One day, maybe she could let Craig know where she was, if she could trust him to keep silent.

Maybe one day, they could all be together again, but until that day, Rachel knew she was on her own.

Just like she had been all her life.

. . .

THE END

THE NEXT GIRL, Book Two in the Girl Who Ran trilogy, will be released in the Summer of 2019!

ABOUT THE AUTHOR

Susan Lund is an emerging author of crime thrillers and romantic suspense. She lives in a forest near the ocean with her family of humans and animals.